MEAGAN PRINGLE

Vicariously

Copyright © 2022 by Meagan Pringle

All rights reserved. No part of this publication may be reproduced, stored or transmitted in any form or by any means, electronic, mechanical, photocopying, recording, scanning, or otherwise without written permission from the publisher. It is illegal to copy this book, post it to a website, or distribute it by any other means without permission.

First edition

This book was professionally typeset on Reedsy. Find out more at reedsy.com

*To the readers that live vicariously through the lives of their
favorite fictional characters*

Acknowledgement

Thank you for the amazing support I have received. It truly means the world to me!
Thank you so much to @_lalistories on *Instagram* for designing the amazing cover. Your talent is remarkable!

* * *

To the aspiring authors out there:
Always stay true to yourself and your story. We all have our unique voices. Never change who you are as a writer to please others because not everyone will like your work - it doesn't mean you should stop writing. No story is a disaster, because it's *yours*. Tell your story the way you want and the right people will find you.

* * *

Author's social media:
Instagram: meagz_the_writer

TikTok: meagz_the_writer

Prologue

I'd never observed a hockey match or any sport. I'd always been more fascinated by the words of *Agatha Christie or F. Scott Fitzgerald.* Viewing a bunch of sweaty guys on the ice, bodies slamming each other against tempered glass, never fascinated me - but I could never say no to my best friend.

Before coming to the game, I'd read up on the terminology. I always enjoy preparing for new experiences and having to know everything beforehand.

I won't be watching much.

We paddle along a river of spectators to arrive at our seats. I see only joyful faces as everyone expects what is supposed to be a *game-changer.*

Whatever that means.

"Isn't this exciting?" Nevaeh says as she raises her hands along with the crowd.

I wince as my eardrum rings.

"I can't imagine a better place." She rolls her eyes at my

typical sarcasm.

"At least pretend to have fun." She pleads as she joins the crowd in the overenthusiastic cheers.

The players glide onto the ice as they wave at the adoring crowd. I roll my eyes at how idolized they are for something I find simplistic.

As the game begins, I feign as much interest as possible - but it's difficult to enjoy something you have a basic understanding of. I winced as the puck got tossed back and forth across the rink, wondering how it didn't fly over the glass and hit an unsuspecting spectator in the face.

There's so much happening that I lost sight of the puck. One player pounded his stick into the ice as the puck soared mid-air before slamming into the net.

The crowd around me jumps out of their seats as they raise their hands in celebration.

It's too much team spirit for my liking.

I reach for my copy of *Crooked House* before opening it up on the bookmarked page.

Everyone in the book is a suspect. That's the best part.

I was so enchanted by the talented words of *Agatha Christie* that I hadn't noticed the first period had ended.

"Are you reading?" Nevaeh exclaimed, as she yanked the book out of my grip. "Who reads during a hockey game?"

"People that don't enjoy hockey but love reading," I argue as I grab it back.

She scoffs as I return my attention to the engaging plot, fading out everything else around me again.

I wasn't sure how long I'd been reading, but Nevaeh broke me out of my spell by nudging her elbow into my ribs.

"Ow!" I exclaim as I rub the injured spot.

Prologue

"You missed the entire game!" She exclaims.

My eyes widened as I gazed at the group of players embracing each other in cheerful celebration. I purse my lips, not upset about missing the game.

"It's okay, H." She grins as she wraps her arm around my shoulder. "We'll be back soon and I will drag you to every game."

If I didn't dread college before, I sure do now.

I glance towards the ice as the players skate around in celebration, waving at the adoring fans. One takes off his helmet, eliciting a riot of cheers. Even from the distance, I noticed his dashing smile, making my insides churn.

I watch as he skates off.

"That's Campbell Atwood." Nevaeh whispers into my ear with a mischievous smirk. "The newest and hottest on campus."

I repeat his name in my head as if attempting to keep it in my head where it can never disappear. I watch in adoration as he waves at a group of people wearing jerseys with his name on before skating off the ice to follow the rest of his team.

My eyes linger on that spot before I'm nudged out of my thoughts by Nevaeh. With flushed cheeks, I gather my belongings and follow her out of the stadium. However, I'm left wishing that I could see him again.

Chapter One

The second I'd settled in on campus, I headed straight for the bookstore. It's always been my happy place. My element is when I'm near literature and the different stories. Being in a bookstore is like having an infinite lifeline. Every novel becomes immortalized between the pages. The thoughts and feelings all have different meanings to each. Nobody interprets anything the same.

It's our escape from reality. We get to live fantasies too unrealistic for reality.

It's thrilling.

I always loved books that strayed from the norm. That broke all the rules. The more utterly ridiculous, the better. I don't believe books should be realistic because what would we be escaping from?

I took my time scoping my surroundings and getting comfortable with the place I will call home for the next four years. The silence is gratifying. Besides the elderly lady behind

Chapter One

the counter, I'm the only other person in the store.

Just how I like it.

My eyes pirouette through the infinite choices. Each is as delectable as the next.

I admire, as well as envy, the creative visions of the authors. They'd succeeded in something I could only dream about. Their words are bound to be indulged by book lovers everywhere.

I'd always dreamed of seeing my books on the shelves. To have someone find the inspiration behind my words, as I have done with countless creative visionaries.

I reach for a tattered copy of Wuthering Heights.

"That's my mom's favorite book." The unexpected voice surprised me, and I dropped the aging book. "I'm sorry."

Wholesome laughter flitters into my ears as the mysterious figure reaches for the book. The moment they stand upright, I glimpse at their face, and my breath hitches. Cerulean eyes gaze into mine as they dazzle with wonder over a glimmering smile. His smile is so bright it's blinding. My tongue feels heavy as I grasp the book from him and hold it against my chest. He combs a fallen lock of hair back with his fingers, but it falls right above his eyes. His smile never fades despite my lack of communication.

It's him.

"I'm Campbell."

I wanted to speak, to tell him my name, but it was as if an anchor was weighing down on my tongue. His smile fades. My lack of communication skills can be insufferable at the most inconvenient of times.

How many chances will there be to find an attractive guy? Especially in a bookstore. Something as incredible as this may never happen again.

The silence is suffocating.

"I'm Hazel," I introduce myself, as my brain functions again. "Hazel Ellis."

His Cheshire grin makes a comeback.

"Pleasure meeting you, Hazel Ellis."

The apples on my cheeks burn as I bite my lip. I could only imagine how red-faced I must be. I dropped my head before he could notice.

"So, do you attend this school, or are you visiting?"

I didn't know what to say.

It's the longest a guy has ever spoken to me. Back in my hometown, I repelled every guy that approached me, yet the first guy I met here made an honest effort. I couldn't wrap my brain around why a guy resembling a literal *Greek Adonis* was attempting to make conversation with me.

"I'm a freshman." I keep my gaze on the ground.

His stare is too intense. As if my life is the most enthralling conversation he could have. *How tragic.*

"I was hoping you weren't just visiting." I risk a glance.

He smiles, showcasing how deep his dimples are. A smile any wider will crack his face in half.

"Why's that?"

"Because." He rubs the back of his neck. "It means we'll see more of each other."

Some may describe his words as arrogance, but the confidence was as welcoming a breath of fresh air. Everything about this exchange is foreign to me.

"You seem certain."

"That's because I am." He tucks his hands into his sweatshirt pocket. "If you want something, you make it happen."

Chapter One

His dazzling eyes glisten in the light. As if he'd drained the entire ocean and placed it in his eyes. With a look, you're drowning in them.

"What is it you want?" I implore as I'm captivated by his hypnotic gaze.

He tilts his head to the side as he considers my words.

"Not sure," He confesses. "I will let you know about that."

My mind was blank, as I wanted a witty response.

"Campbell!" A bulky guy knocks on the store window and motions for Campbell to approach.

Guess it's goodbye.

He turns to me with a suave grin.

"Hope to do this again soon, Hazel Ellis."

He brushes past me, allowing me to inhale the faintest scent of Rosewood.

"I lied." He breaks me from his spell before I twirl to face him. "My mom hates reading. I just wanted an excuse to talk to you."

My face burns as if it were scorching in boiling oil. I walk out of the store and into the cold outdoors. The promise of fall is approaching. I close my eyes as the gentle breeze tickles my pores.

The trek to the dorm is relaxing, as if my thoughts have stopped.

The dorms are chaotic as a horde of girls flitter about to load their stacks of luggage into their rooms. I dodge suitcases and families. My bags occupy one bed where I tossed them before leaving - the other was empty before my departure, but it seems my new roommate has arrived. I enter with caution, unsure of the protocol.

I've never shared a room with someone.

Vicariously

"Hi!" The chirpy voice greets me the second I enter. "You must be my new roommate."

"I'm Hazel." My tone is aloof.

I've always preferred to keep to myself. Making friends isn't my priority.

"Maisie." She doesn't look put off by my lack of interest, or she hasn't taken notice. "So, any plans for the day?"

"I'm supposed to be meeting a friend soon."

My best friend since the second grade, Nevaeh St. James, and I made a pack years ago that we'd attend the same college together. *Best friends forever.* We were ecstatic to find out we'd both gotten accepted. Unfortunately, our dream of being roommates together crashed and burned.

I could get over the minor inconvenience. At least I will have one friend to get through the next four years.

Maisie looked upset by my reply. Something pleaded for me not to invite her. I don't do well with new people, but the pang of guilt in my chest overruled those pleas.

"Want to join us?" It's as if my question ignited life back in her body.

Her grin sprouts.

"I'd love that."

* * *

I'd always loved the smell of ground coffee beans. The succulent, bitter fragrance welcomes me as I open the door to the local cafe. The scent surrounds me, but it's not overpowering. I take another deep inhale through my nose. Embarrassed by the thought that I am standing in a crowded

Chapter One

cafe sniffing the air makes my face appear hot.

"Hazel!" a boisterous voice calls my name.

Nevaeh.

Heads turn in the direction she's waving. I keep my head low and cover my burning face with my hair. She embraces me in the warmest of hugs as I reach the booth in the furthest corner. We pull apart before she glances over my shoulder.

I forgot about Maisie.

"This is Maisie, my new roommate." I introduce. "This is my best friend, Nevaeh."

Maisie offers a friendly smile, but Nevaeh doesn't acknowledge her as she slides into the booth.

"Can you believe we're here? I've been waiting for this the entire summer!"

Nevaeh and I are complete opposites. I'm a solitary person, and she's the life of the party. She was always popular and had boys fawning over her at every opportunity.

Which is why I don't expect college to be any different.

"I heard the frat guys host a party every year. They say it's welcoming the newbies, but I believe it's just an excuse to party." Nevaeh pipes.

She wriggles in her seat.

"Count me out."

I quiver at her fiery gaze. She'd mastered the look in the third grade.

"Hazel, we agreed college is the time you risk things and let yourself out of your shell."

"It's only the first day!" I argue.

I slump into the booth with folded arms and a distinct pout. I couldn't care less that I'm acting like a scolded child.

There have been countless horror stories about the dangerous scenarios at fraternity parties. I agree I need to step out of my comfort zone, but attending a frat party is like jumping into a swimming pool without testing the water first. I'm not ready for extremities.

The bell chimed as someone new entered. I didn't care, but Nevaeh looked entranced.

"Who is *that?*" Maisie and I turn.

Campbell.

I wanted to tell her of our meeting in the bookstore, but I recognized her signature smirk.

She has her sights set on her next target.

Opting to stay mute, we gaze as he approaches a table occupied by a rowdy group. They welcome him with handshakes and fist bumps before he approaches the counter.

"I'm going to talk to him." Nevaeh leaps out of the booth and speeds toward him.

We can only watch as if it were a soap opera. I roll my eyes as she bumps into him - pretending it was an accident. I'd observed her flirtation cues so many times I have them memorized. From the jutting of her hip to the twirling of her ash blonde curls. Typical Nevaeh.

"I wish I had her confidence." Maisie chimes from behind me.

You're not the only one.

I'd been so occupied with my scorching envy - that I did not notice she was approaching with Campbell shadowing her.

"Ladies, meet Campbell." Her voice is higher pitched than usual.

"Hello, Hazel Ellis." I had to bite my lip to prevent a smirk from escaping the moment Nevaeh's jaw went slack.

"Hi, Campbell." My voice becomes restrained as Nevaeh's

Chapter One

icy gaze directs at me.

"You know each other?" She questions.

"We're old friends." Campbell grins.

"We met at the bookstore this morning," I explained. I don't want to give the wrong idea. "That's it."

"Ouch," He places his palm on his chest. "I was just telling everyone about my new best friend."

I roll my eyes. He is not amusing.

"Are you attending the party tonight?" He questions. "My frat is hosting."

Of course, he's in a frat.

"I am," Nevaeh pipes. "Hazel isn't one for parties."

He glances at me with a raised brow.

"I promise we don't bite."

"I'm not one for crowds." I shrug. "Or people."

I cower under his gaze. I'm not used to having so much attention on myself, especially around Nevaeh.

"Well, I hope you change your mind." He speaks before returning to the rowdy table.

"Do you know who that is?" Nevaeh gasps. "I cannot believe I didn't recognize him!"

I shrug.

"That's Campbell Atwood, *the* guy on campus."

"What makes him special?" I mutter.

"Are you serious?" She gasps. "Last year Campbell scored the winning goal in his debut match, becoming an instant hockey legend. Never achieved by a freshman."

I didn't understand the fuss. Someone could be a legend in their debut match?

Beginner's luck.

Maybe I'm bitter. Or, it's the unpleasant taste in my mouth

from the unwanted interactions of the day. I don't care.

"I'll go." Our heads turn towards Maisie. "I've never been to a party unless you count my cousin's twelfth birthday."

Nevaeh's smug grin reels Maisie in. It's only a matter of time before she breaks me. With a relentless sigh, my shoulders sink in defeat.

"I'll go too, but don't expect me to enjoy it."

* * *

I broke into a sweat the moment we arrived. My outfit is far too restricting. I attempted to swallow as my heart lodged in my throat. Someone trashed the front entrance of the frat house with beer cans and glasses. A trio of girls ran past us as they assisted their friend in heaving her contents into a nearby bush. I wince at the sound.

People have been taking advantage of the endless free drinks.

I avoid the littered mess. The closer we get, the rowdier everything appears. Appalling music booms in my eardrums. I grind my teeth.

There is a cluster of people invading every inch of the home. I resist the urge to gag as we brush past a couple making out against the wall.

Nevaeh leads the way as if she owns the place. She makes a beeline for the kitchen and scopes out the assortment of drink choices lathered along the counter. I bite my lip as I reach for a can of *Red Bull.*

"Hazel Ellis, you came!" Campbell greets, beaming as he approaches the counter.

"We had to beg her, but I wouldn't miss the party," Nevaeh

Chapter One

says.

She twirls the ends of her hair. I sigh.

Her target locks. Campbell Atwood does not know what's about to strike.

"And I thought we had a moment in the bookstore," He feigns a pout. "Guess we'll just have to reenact it."

Nevaeh gets upset. I could sense her gaze on me before looking at her. The second our eyes lock, her head drops to the side.

Typical playbook behavior.

"Hey, Maisie, let's have a look around."

"I am more than happy to show you around," Campbell says, but I hardly listen to him as I'm too distracted by my best friend shaking her head.

"That's okay," I assure with a plastic smile. "We'll find our way."

I grip Maisie's arm and usher her out of the room.

"Why are we leaving?" Her visible confusion is amusing.

"It's a code Nevaeh has when she likes a guy and wants to be alone."

"Campbell likes you, though." Her candid reply makes me scoff.

"Don't be ridiculous. Nevaeh has always been the one to grab the attention."

"There's a first for everything." She shrugs but continues to walk.

She must have sensed I didn't want to talk about it further.

I groan as I feel sticky from the constant close contact. Many of the partiers are too drunk to comprehend personal space. It doesn't help that I'm a natural klutz.

Needing to escape to a dark and isolated corner, I bump

Vicariously

into the back of someone.

"I am so sorry," I apologize as I cup my hands around my mouth. "I didn't mean it."

The slender guy is hovering over me, but his smiling expression eases my fear.

"It's no problem," He grins. "Why complain about a pretty girl falling for me?"

If I didn't vomit earlier, I sure will now.

I don't know why his comment rubbed me the wrong way, but I pushed it aside and apologized again before escaping through a crowd. I didn't get far before he was gripping my arm.

"Did I say something to upset you?" He questions.

"Yes," I reply and yank my arm out of his hold. "Now, if you'll excuse me."

"What's your problem?" He stands in my way.

"Right now, it's you." My voice is bitter.

Our confrontation gathered a crowd.

"Do you have any idea who I am?" He questions with a scoff.

"The royal douchebag?" I replied.

He reaches for my arm again, but someone steps in and blocks him. My eyes widen as Campbell grips his arm and his knuckles turn white. The veins in his neck protrude. I fear they might burst any second.

"Grab her arm once more. I dare you. I'll yank yours out of its socket." He seethes. "Do I make myself clear?"

The guy's bottom lip trembles as he nods. Campbell tosses his arm with such force the guy does a complete 360.

"Get out of here." He barks.

He rushes off as the crowd observes the brutal exchange.

"Are you okay?" His change of tone could give you whiplash.

Chapter One

How did he go from hateful to gentle, like a flipped switch?

"Thank you." My mouth feels as dry as a desert.

He notices the crowd.

"There's nothing to see here." He instructs as if he were a drill sergeant ordering his troops to rush into the firing range.

Everyone follows his command.

"Let me walk you to your dorm."

Do I look as frightened as I think?

"I'll be okay," I fail at keeping my voice stable. "It's not far."

"Then it shouldn't be a problem if I walk with you - there's no way I'm letting you go out there alone after what just transpired." I open my mouth to argue, but he places his finger in front of my lips. "There's no room for arguing, Hazel Ellis."

I sigh as he places his hand on the bottom of my back. He steers me through the crowd, stopping to open a closet at the front door. He offers me a gray sweatshirt.

"It's freezing like the Arctic out there, and you're underdressed for the weather."

I glance at my outfit. He's correct. Nevaeh chose something that required the least amount of fabric to make. I didn't realize how cold I was until I wore the sweatshirt. A familiar scent of Rosewood infiltrates my senses.

I could cut the air with a butter knife. A gentle breeze and tattering leaves are the only sounds to be heard.

"So, you're a freshman." He makes conversation.

Even though we'd covered this, I indulged him.

"I am. What about you?"

"Sophomore." He places his hands in his coat pocket.

He kicks a stray pebble in an impressive distance before glancing at me.

"So, Hazel Ellis, what do you want to be when you grow

up?"

I scoffed at his generic question.

"A writer." It might be my first genuine smile since arriving. "For as long as I can remember."

"I should have realized when I met you in the bookstore." He quips. "You couldn't take your eyes off the books."

I blush. I get sucked into a fantasy realm whenever I'm near a book.

"So, what have you written?"

"Just a few short stories. I've been short of ideas."

The dreaded writer's block cursed me. All inspiration for new material has evaporated from my mind.

"What about you?" I try to steer the conversation away from my inability to write. "What do you love?"

He inhales the crisp air as the wheels in his head turn.

"Hockey," He states. "At first, I only played it to make my dad happy, but the first time I stepped onto the ice, it was as if an unknown force was telling me it's what I'm supposed to do."

I smile at his words. I had the same experience when I wrote my first short story.

I'd been hooked ever since.

"It doesn't hurt that I'm damn good at it, too."

His ego ruined the moment.

Despite his arrogance, I couldn't help but smile. His confidence in himself has me envious. I'd never been in control of myself or my abilities. There was always a cloud of doubt over me waiting for the perfect moment to storm.

Most days include more rain than sunshine in my head.

"You should watch me play sometime." His voice pierces the peacefulness.

Chapter One

"Thanks, but I'm not a fan of hockey."

"What if I can convince you to change your mind?" He suggests. "The real action only starts in a few months, but you can watch me practicing."

After a drawn-out walk, we reached the dorm buildings. I turn to Campbell.

"I'll think about it."

His corner lip twitches.

"Take your time. I know where to find you." He spoke and gestured to the building. "And if you're not there. I'll follow the books."

I smile.

"I'll be seeing you, Hazel Ellis." He winks.

I watch his retreating figure until he's enveloped in the night, before striding up the stairs. I bolt towards my laptop, situating myself on my bed before typing. It's as if my fingers were as eager as my brain to jot my thoughts on paper.

I've once again found inspiration.

Chapter Two

I wrap my coat tighter around myself as the harsh breeze attacks. The molten-red leaves get yanked back and forth before losing their grip on the branches and dropping to the bottom.

Classes have begun. Judging by my schedule, I'll be in for a strenuous semester. I scoured the campus for the particular building.

Why didn't I bring a map?

My inability to comprehend direction has inflicted its miserable curse on me. I must look insane standing in the middle of the quad. I glanced around the area as if a giant sign was going to appear, pointing me in the right direction.

"Good morning, Hazel Ellis." I sigh at the familiar voice.

"Please stop calling me that." I am not in the mood for idle chit chat.

"Okay, *Ellie*." I whip around with furrowed brows. "It's the shortened version of your last name." He explains, as if I'm a

Chapter Two

child learning a new concept.

"What do you want, Campbell?" As I tense up, I sigh.

I'm going to be late on my first day.

"I just want to help you get to class." He shrugs. "You seem lost."

"I am." I confess with a groan and pass my schedule.

His eyes skim the paper. He gazes at me with a smirk.

"What?" My impatience is a curse.

"It's right behind you." He points over my shoulder.

I spare a glance at the sizable stack of bricks. My cheeks burn. I avoid his gaze and take my schedule before tucking it into my pocket.

"You don't like me, do you?" He grins.

"Just because I don't fawn over you like everyone else at this school doesn't mean I don't like you."

"So, you do like me?" I might die of heatstroke as my cheeks scorch.

My tongue feels as if I am trapped in the desert.

"I have to get to class." I blubber before speed-walking into the building.

I became intimidated by the size of the lecture hall alongside the horde of students in the class. I made myself comfortable in an isolated row, but I couldn't help but feel as if someone was staring at me. I shake it off.

I'm just being paranoid.

As I wait for the lecture to begin, the burning gaze reignites as I tap my feet. My eyes lock with someone below me as I glance around the hall. An unfamiliar bottle blond faces my direction. She's not attempting to hide her hateful gaze. She mutters something to her friends. They turn in sync to glare at me. I slouch lower in my seat, but they continue to stare.

It's getting weird.

My saving grace comes as my professor walks in and eyes dart to him. I breathe a sigh of relief as he introduces himself. The stalker-ish girl would glance at me over her shoulder, but it would only be a momentary thing. I focus on taking notes on what is crucial for this class.

"Nice penmanship." Someone whispers in my ear.

I whip around with round eyes.

"What are you doing here?" I whisper-yell.

Campbell leans forward. His head is wedged between my seat and another.

"I happen to be in this class." He glances at the professor. "I wish I wasn't."

I roll my eyes.

"You're distracting me." I directed my attention to my notes.

He was supposed to get the memo and leave.

"I'm bored."

I wouldn't be so lucky.

"Go bother someone else." I snap. "I'm sure there are tons of people on this campus dying to hang out with you."

"That takes the fun out of it." He whines like a spoiled child. "It's fun annoying you. You're adorable when you're mad."

I scoff and focus on the paper on my lap.

"It's only the first day." He glances down at my notes. "He's not going to make you take the final now."

I grit my teeth.

"So, I was thinking." He speaks as if I haven't been ignoring him. "You should come to watch my practice tonight. You told me you'd think about it."

"I'm busy." I declare. "I made plans with my friends."

"Bring them with you." He grins. "We can have a date

Chapter Two

another time."

I dropped my pen at his unexpected statement, but the voice in my mind kept whispering haunting words.

He's just kidding. He doesn't mean that. He just wants a reason to see Nevaeh.

I wanted to deny him. To say no because I couldn't be less interested - but Nevaeh likes him. What friend wouldn't support their own when an opportunity like this arises?

Do it for Nevaeh.

"Okay," I pipe. "We'll be there."

* * *

The cold infiltrates my body. My natural warmth is defenseless against it. I rub my reddening nose with the sleeve of my cardigan with the odd sniffle as we descend the stairs of the rink. I wrap my arms around myself and rub them as if I'm making a campfire.

I don't do well in freezing conditions.

A few players are on the ice doing warm-ups. I wish I could join them. Desperate to get my blood pumping and my temperature up. Nevaeh struts down the steps like a runway model. We dawdle behind her like penguins.

More players step out onto the ice. The name *Atwood* on the back catches my eye. Nevaeh doesn't miss it. Her smile stretches. I'm seated with Maisie as Nevaeh moves closer to the ice.

"Is she always like this?" Maisie whispers into my ear.

"Only when she likes someone." I shrug.

I glance at my best friend as she stands watching the players,

Vicariously

exuding confidence. She captures the attention of a few of them as they skate along. She doesn't notice them. Her eyes locked on one guy.

"Hey, Atwood." She calls as he skates nearby.

He skids to a halt and glances over his shoulder. Even from my seat, I could see her signature flirty grin as she twirled the end of her curls. He skates closer and takes off his helmet. He runs a hand through his locks, but a few strands fall just above his eyes. "Hey," He greets before glancing at us over her shoulder. "You came."

His eyes lock on me as I shiver.

"I told you." I chime.

Nevaeh glances at me over her shoulder with a frown. I sigh and lean back in my seat with my arms folded.

"You're amazing." She bites her lip as her sultry gaze returns to him.

"Thanks, I know." I roll my eyes at his arrogant reply.

How modest of him.

"Do you have any plans after practice?" She continues to make conversation, but his attention drifts to his hockey stick as he twirls it around.

"We were thinking of grabbing something to eat at the diner after practice." He shrugs before glancing at me with a smirk. "You're more than welcome to join us."

"We'd love to!" Nevaeh exclaims.

"Great, I better get back to practice." He places his helmet back on before gliding along the ice.

"He is so gorgeous. It hurts." Nevaeh sighs as she collapses in the seat next to us.

I sneak a peek at Maisie. She's been quiet.

"You okay?" I question her.

Chapter Two

"I'm fine, just tired." She sighs. "I think I'm going to skip the hangout."

"You both are." Nevaeh shoots out of her seat.

I jumped at her outburst.

"What?" Maisie questions.

"I need you to do this for me." She glances at me. "How am I supposed to hook up with him if I can't get a moment alone with him?"

"But he invited Hazel too." Maisie offers.

"I know, but I'll tell him she's got the flu or something." She brushes Maisie's comment away.

She pouts her lip.

"Please do this for me?" She begs.

I glance at the players as Campbell messes around with his teammates. A wild grin etched on his face. I cannot deny that he's one of the most charming guys I have ever encountered.

I'd never have a chance.

I analyze my best friend. She's a *Goddess.*

I could never compete with that.

Guys like Campbell Atwood don't date awkward and nerdy girls like me. Someone as alluring as him deserves to be with someone pleasing.

Like Nevaeh.

I stand up and offer her a plastic smile.

"Of course, *Nev,* anything for my best friend."

* * *

I gaze out my dorm window in the deep night. The moon is drenched in a pool of stars as they pirouette around it -

Vicariously

only adding to its naturalistic beauty. I'd always admired the darkened allure of the night, how it never demanded attention. I always related more to the darkness - existing but unnoticeable. It never makes an impact. It's everything around it that gets the attention.

I will forever be in the darkness behind the stars.

Maisie is sleeping, but my mind is spinning like a roller coaster. I couldn't help but think about what Nevaeh is doing at this moment. I know she will effortlessly win Campbell over.

No guy has ever rejected her.

For our entire friendship, she'd always been charismatic. She always knew the right thing to say and do. It surprised me when she approached me one day and declared me her best friend. Out of all the potential candidates, she chose *me*.

I jump as there's a gentle knock on the door. I glance at the clock on my bedside table.

It's past midnight. Who would knock on my door at such a time?

I don't know who I expected, but it would have been anyone but Campbell Atwood.

"Campbell, what are you doing here?" My voice becomes strained.

"Nevaeh told me you were feeling sick." He raised a brown paper bag. "I brought you soup."

It feels like a golf ball getting stuck halfway down my trachea.

He brought me soup?

"Thank you," I replied in a daze. "You didn't have to."

"There's some for Maisie too." He shrugs.

"That was very thoughtful of you."

Chapter Two

I don't know what to say. From moments I've had with Campbell, I'd always thought of him as narcissistic, yet he's bringing me soup at midnight. He scratches the back of his neck as he rocks back and forth on his heels.

"Well, I hope you feel better. I guess I'll see you around?"

I clear my throat and nod my head. He offers a tight-lipped smile. I'm about to close the door when he reappears. I glance at him.

"I wish you were at the diner tonight."

As he leaves, my mind kicks into overdrive once again.

Guess I won't be sleeping tonight.

* * *

I'd battled with my eyelids the entire morning to keep them from closing. The dark patches and swelling are noticeable - no amount of makeup would cover it. I bury my face in my hands. The pounding in my head feels like a rock band is having a concert near my brain. The thumping is unbearable.

It doesn't help that Nevaeh has spent the entire morning raving about Campbell and their moment last night.

"He's so perfect." She sighs as she stares into the distance.

I roll my eyes and glance at Maisie. She looks as exhausted by the conversation as I do.

"He kept asking about you." My ears perk at her words.

"Really?"

"Yeah, I guess he wants to get to know you since we're best friends."

"I'm sure that's the reason." Maisie replies, but Nevaeh doesn't pick up on her sarcasm.

Vicariously

"He invited us to his practice tonight." Maisie and I groan.

"I've had enough social interaction for the next few months." I mutter as I stab my fork into my scrambled eggs.

"What happened to *making the most of your college experience?*" She questions.

"I got to college and realized how miserable it is." I mutter with a pout.

I could sometimes be overdramatic.

"H, you need to get out more."

I groan and unlock my phone. I have a class in twenty minutes.

"I'll think about it."

* * *

I clutch my copy of *To the Lighthouse* outside the lecture hall. I couldn't wipe the smile off my face. I still cannot believe I've spent countless classes discussing books.

I'm startled by a gentle tap on my shoulder.

"Sorry," A deepened voice apologizes before lifting a pen in front of me. "You dropped this."

"Thank you." My cheeks turn crimson.

His pearly white teeth unveil themselves in a dashing smile. I can't help but swoon.

"I'm Trent." He introduces.

"Hazel."

"Beautiful name." He grins. "I'm happy I chased you down to give you the pen."

My forehead feels hot. My entire face heats.

"It's my favorite pen." I cringe at my words.

Chapter Two

I am the worst at making conversation.

"Hey, why don't we get together and study sometime?" He questions. "I could use the help."

"Sure!" I replied a bit too enthusiastically.

"Great!" He smiles. "I have hockey practice tonight, but maybe afterward?"

My smile drops.

"You play hockey?"

"Just made the team." He beams.

"Congratulations."

"Thanks," He chirps. "Why don't you come to see me practice tonight? Then we can study afterward."

I wanted to avoid confrontation with Campbell, but I knew that was not possible. It doesn't hurt that Trent is super attractive.

"I'd love to."

His eyes widened, as if he hadn't expected me to agree.

"Awesome!" His smile is infectious. "I'll see you tonight."

* * *

I don't know what to expect or what to do. The nerves struck me with an iron hammer the second we entered the rink. As usual, Maisie and I are trailing behind a confident Nevaeh. Maisie chews on the inside of her cheek. She didn't want to join but when I told her about my encounter with Trent, curiosity got to her.

I scope the skaters on the team, only to realize I'd never gotten Trent's last name. They're too far away for me to see their faces, but I spotted the name *Atwood* on the back of

Campbell's jersey.

I approached the barrier, hoping Trent notices me, but my unfortunate luck struck again. Campbell skates in my direction, and Nevaeh stands next to me.

"You came after all." Campbell grins as he slides the helmet off his head and shakes his mop of hair with his fingers.

"Of course." Nevaeh eagerly replies.

I attempt to avoid his gaze, but I can feel it piercing the side of my head.

"Hazel." The familiar, scruffy voice captures my attention.

I grin as Trent appears next to Campbell.

He takes off his helmet but pays no attention to his shorter hair. He offers me a grin before glancing at Nevaeh.

"Hey, Trent." I greet and gesture to her. "This is my best friend Nevaeh."

"Hey." He directs his dazzling smile at her before looking back at me. "I'm ecstatic you came."

Campbell tensed next to him. I ignore him.

"Glad to be here."

I bite my lip and glance down to hide my blush. Campbell clears his throat.

"Enough talking. Let's get back to practice." His voice is hoarse.

I lock eyes with Trent.

"See you later at our study date." He winks before putting his helmet on and skates toward his teammates.

I glance at Campbell. His jaw clenched as he casts a hostile glare at Trent's retreating figure. He doesn't say a word as he straps his helmet onto his head and glides to join the rest of the team.

I observe in curiosity as they divide into two teams. Trent

Chapter Two

and Campbell are on opposing sides. Trent's teammate grabs the puck first and passes it to him. He handles the puck down the ice. Until a body collides with him, shoving him into the tempered glass. He loses control of the puck and falls onto the ice with a harsh thud.

Campbell takes control of the puck and scores. As if it were as easy as first-grade math.

"Atwood!" Their coach bellows. "This is only practice, not so rough!"

"Sorry, coach." He calls with no attempt at feigning apathy.

He skates past me with a devilish grin. I roll my eyes before rushing to Trent as he steps off the ice. He's clutching his ribs as he sits down.

"Are you okay?" I kneel in front of him.

My forehead crinkles.

"I'm fine," He gasped, followed by a groan. "Think I just got the wind knocked out of me."

My eyebrows pull together as I observe him attempting to take deep breaths.

"Sorry about that, Keller." My jaw clenches at the voice behind me. "I must have slipped or something."

I roll my eyes at his idiotic and insincere apology.

"It's okay," Trent musters with a smile. "It happens."

I glimpse over my shoulder as Campbell leans against the tempered glass with a sickening smirk. He glances at me and drops his left eye in a subtle wink before skating off.

Chapter Three

To say I was frustrated by Campbell's immature behavior is an understatement. He purposefully targeted Trent for no logical reason. It's as if he took sadistic pleasure in making the new members suffer.

What sportsmanship.

I angrily jot down notes for my essay due in a week. I planned on relaxing in the quad underneath a large *Bur Oak* tree. The leaves flutter carelessly with the breeze and puddle around me, embracing me in scarlet. I pick up my copy of *To The Lighthouse* and continue reading the next chapter.

A shadow looms over me. I glance over the pages as Campbell smugly stands with his hands tucked in his front pockets.

"It's a Saturday and you're reading." He teases before bending down to glimpse the cover. *"To the Lighthouse.* Never heard of it."

"Shocker." I mumble before continuing to read.

Chapter Three

"What's it about?" He questions, but I ignore him. "Come on. I'm trying to show an interest."

I still ignore him.

"There is an actual lighthouse, right?"

"Yes," I sigh and place my book down. "But that's not the point."

"Then what is?"

I groan.

"The lighthouse is a symbol of *the ultimate destination.* It symbolizes the characters finding true meaning in life."

He doesn't say a word, as if he's registering my words, but I think he just zoned out.

"Why are you hanging out with Trent?"

It's as if we're having different conversations in our minds. How did this happen?

"I'm not hanging out with him. I met him a few days ago."

His shoulders tense.

"Yet, he invited you to watch him practice."

"You've invited me to watch you practice," I note.

"It's not the same." He insists.

"Why is that?"

"It's just not."

I roll my eyes at his lack of response.

"He's a jerk." He continues. "The guy can't even take a little shove."

His words ignite fury in my body. I gather my material and stand up, locking my fiery eyes on his face.

"What you did was super uncalled for." I hissed. "What I do with my life is not your business."

I brush past him, shocked at my unusual outburst. I usually bottle everything inside, always too afraid to speak up.

Vicariously

However, Campbell has a way of bringing another side out of me. An unflattering side. With my tail tucked in between my legs, I scurry away from him, wishing to forget this dreaded conversation ever transpired.

* * *

The wind whistles into my pores as the leaves dance to the serenade. My feet glide through the piles of scarlet and gold. The fall breeze carries its fragrance of Earth, as well as a promise of rain to come. It tousles my hair into effervescent curls. Light escapes through the darkened clouds, generating enough warmth to make the bitter wind more bearable.

"Ellie!"

The voice calls, shattering my aura of serenity. I pretend I didn't hear him and continue my stroll through the campus.

"I know you can hear me, Ellie." He taunts.

I continue walking. The leaves crunch underneath his hasty steps until he's beside me.

"That was a little rude." He tucks his hands into his pockets.

"I thought you'd get the memo." I said.

"What's with the hostility, Ellie?"

I'm getting sick of that dreaded nickname.

"I just want to get something to eat and spend the rest of my weekend in my dorm."

He doesn't say a word as he strides alongside me.

"What do you want, Campbell?"

He grins.

"I'm glad you asked, because I need your help."

"With what?"

Chapter Three

He glides his fingers through his hair.

"Coach made me promise that this year I will try my best at keeping my GPA up." He bites his bottom lip. "I do not know what is going on in *English Lit*, so I thought I'd ask someone that does."

I pretend to consider helping him, but there is no way I want to spend any more time with him.

"No, thanks."

"Wait, what?"

"No. Thanks."

He strokes his chin with his hand.

"This isn't how I pictured the conversation to go."

I speed up my pace, but his long legs keep up.

"Please, I'm desperate." He whines. "I need help with Shakespeare. You can't get all your answers from *CliffsNotes*."

I snort. Why can I picture him copying and pasting straight from the source?

"Coach will bench me for the season if I don't get a better grade."

"Isn't there somebody else you could ask?"

He shrugs.

"Possibly, but you're the best choice."

He was trying to charm me and as much as I wanted to fight it, to show him I wouldn't fall for his charismatic tricks - I couldn't say no.

I don't want to.

"Fine." I sigh, as if the favor is the biggest inconvenience. "Let's go to the library."

"You're serious?" He glances at me doe-eyed.

"Let's go before I change my mind."

"I'll meet you there!" He yells as he takes off in a sprint.

Vicariously

I roll my eyes at his behavior and amble towards the library.

* * *

I venture inside the dimly lit building due to the daylight being unable to reach the room. My eyes flicker along the abundance of shelves as the indistinct conversations float over my head.
So much for silence.
I trail past a table of boys as they cackle like hyenas over something they found on their laptops. A large sign is stuck against the wall beside them with the words *shhh*.
Guess they didn't get the memo - or they don't care at all.
I drift toward the *classic literature* aisle only to halt in my tracks as Campbell is already standing on the other side of the row, analyzing the back cover of a book. He glances up and grins as he realizes it's me.
"Hey, study buddy." His gleaming smile twinkles. "Could you direct me to anything with pictures?"
"What are you looking for over here?" I groan.
"Preferably something by *Dr. Seuss*."
I resist the urge to strike him.
"You know that's not what I meant!" I holler.
"You have to admit, it was pretty funny." He giggles like a little kid saying a bad word for the first time.
He lifts the book in his hand and I squint to see the cover.
Romeo and Juliet.
"I believe we have some work to do."
Before I could even argue, he'd brushed past me and made himself comfortable at an isolated table. He daringly gazes at me as he pats the seat beside him. I hoist my bag higher on

Chapter Three

my shoulder before marching to the table and dropping into my seat with a pout.

"No need to sulk, grumpy." He teases. "I think we're going to make a great team."

He begins to take off his jacket when a familiar logo on his shirt piqued my curiosity.

"You like *Blink-182?*"

"They're my favorite band."

"Mine too!" I express with a surprising amount of eagerness.

His goggle-eyed expression is slightly humorous.

"I'm impressed, Ellie. I had no idea you had such great taste in music."

"I could say the same about you."

He snorts.

"That's a good one."

He stretches his arms before placing his hands on the back of his head. I flip through the pages of the book. He does the same with his own copy.

He gazes at the book in bewilderment, scratching the back of his head. His forehead scrunches.

"What's the problem now?" I ask.

"Is there an English version?" He asks. "I can't read whatever language this is."

"It's *Shakespearean English.*" I replied.

"No idea what that is, but it makes sense why I never bothered reading it." He tosses it on the table. "How about you give me a summary, some juicy details I won't find on the internet?"

I close my eyes and take a sharp intake of breath.

"That defeats the purpose. You need to give your own interpretation."

Vicariously

"How do I do that?"

"By reading the book." I furrow my brows.

"I know the gist of it, though."

I gnaw on my bottom lip.

"You need to have a decent understanding of it to give an analysis. You need to know the characters and the symbolism."

He curls his top lip.

"What are your thoughts on Romeo and Juliet?" He questions.

"I love it and hate it." I shrug. "I never understood how two people could fall in love so fast. I loved the idea, but it was a bit far-fetched."

He straightens his posture as he drums his fingers against the edge of the table. He pensively gazes in front of him.

"It may not have been love, but there is always something that draws us to a specific person, something inside you telling you to pursue them before it's too late." He rambles. "You might see someone in the crowd and they're doing something so unbelievable that you have no choice but to want to know their story."

I intently listen to his explanation.

"They acted thoughtlessly, but maybe they were both so afraid of losing their shot at being together. Maybe Romeo was being so forward because he knew if he didn't make a move immediately - someone else would and he'd lose his chance forever. Not everything has to be some pining slow-burn or a game to win their heart. If they kept waiting for *one day*, who knows if anything would have happened."

My jaw drops as I'm astonished by his unexpected analysis.

"You seem to be talking from experience." I note.

He clears his throat.

Chapter Three

"There was this girl." He begins with a gentle grin. "I saw her in a crowd during one of my games. I was foolish to let her slip through my fingers once, and I vowed if I ever saw her again. I wouldn't let the opportunity go to waste."

A wave of guilt hits me like a tidal wave. I'd practically forced him into a romance with Nevaeh, only for his mind to be on another girl.

"Did you find her?" I curiously wonder.

He mirthlessly grins.

"That is a story for another time, Ellie."

I suddenly see him in a different light. The different side of him is surprisingly intriguing. He's just a misunderstood boy in love with a girl. Some twisted love story intent on keeping them apart.

"You'll find her." I attempt to encourage him.

The corner of his lip quivers as we lock eyes.

"I know I will."

* * *

A calmative stroll eased my frustrations, enough for me to settle down in the local cafe with my work. I continued reading, becoming completely engrossed. I could barely notice anything around me - until a loud slam on my desk made me shriek. I blush as a few gazes turn in my direction.

I glance up at my attacker to find a familiar-looking face.

The girl that kept staring at me on the first day.

Her nostrils flare. I half expected the fire to escape from them. It seems the fire was in her eyes instead. I gently place my book to the side as she angrily glares at me, scrutinizing

Vicariously

me like an ant under a microscope.

"Leave Campbell alone." My jaw nearly hits the table.

"I'm sorry?" My brain could barely comprehend why she would be directing this warning toward me.

"You should be." She snaps. "Campbell is mine. Don't think I haven't seen the two of you hanging around."

I comb my fingers through my hair.

Does Campbell have a girlfriend?

It's none of my business if he does, but why would she threaten me? I'm not the one constantly flirting with him.

Not wanting to start any drama, I nod my head. She seems satisfied by my obedience and flips her platinum hair over her shoulder before strutting out of the diner. I lowered myself into my seat as the odd person sneaked a glance in my direction.

Everyone is so damn curious all the time.

The fear turns into a fit of rage as I think of how Campbell had deceived me. This entire time, he'd shared a heartbreaking story about how he'd been pining over some girl. Only to have a girlfriend all along.

I glance at my mug of hot chocolate and scrunch my nose. It doesn't seem as appetizing as it did before. This mysterious girl and Campbell have left a bad taste in my mouth.

"What was that about?" I jump once again.

Trent.

My face burns at the thought of him having heard the threats and thinking I'm obsessed with Campbell, but why would he ask if he already knew?

"Honestly, I have no idea." I brush the confrontation off as he slides into the seat across from me.

He chews his bottom lip as his eyes dance around the

Chapter Three

crowded diner. His entire body language is tense. I didn't want to question him, so I remained silent until he was ready to talk. He drums his fingers against the edge of the table. I clear my throat.

His shoulders slump as he leans over the table.

"I wanted to ask you something." He finally speaks. "We're having a party at the frat house tonight. I was hoping you'd come - as my date."

I didn't know what shocked me more. An attractive male asking me on a date, or him being a frat boy.

Trent seemingly takes my lack of speech as a rejection.

"Never mind, I shouldn't have asked." He pushes himself from the booth.

"No!" I exclaim. "I would love to."

"Really?"

"Yes." His pearly white teeth sparkle.

"Great, I'll text you the details."

He winks before walking out of the cafe. I bite my lip to suppress a smile.

I cannot believe I have a date.

* * *

It's the second frat party I've attended in a month. That's more parties than I have ever been to in my lifetime. I spent high school drifting in the shadows, but it's as if college had other plans. I enter the frat house with my hands interlocked with Trent's. A few gazes are lured our way, but I push the insecure thoughts aside. It isn't the time for my doubts to rise to the surface. I let him lead me through the assemblage of partiers

Vicariously

and into the kitchen. It seems to be party protocol. You can't mingle without a drink in your hand.

A group of guys are gathered around a phone. Trent immediately joins them. I hover in the doorway, unsure of what to do next. I jolt in fear as an arm is placed around my shoulder.

"Ellie, so glad you could make it." The tiresome voice infiltrates my eardrums.

I push Campbell's arm off me.

"Hey, H!" Nevaeh exclaimed, "I didn't know you were coming."

"Last-minute thing." I mutter.

Trent joins us. He places his arm around my waist. I bite back a smirk as Campbell's jaw tightens. It's as if he's trying to fry Trent's hand away.

"You came with Trent." I couldn't place if it were pride or shock in Nevaeh's tone, but I pushed it aside and moved closer to him.

"I did."

An awkward silence follows.

"Do you want a drink?" Trent breaks the silence as he drops his head to talk into my ear.

I nod my head. He hurriedly approaches the counter. Nevaeh follows suit, leaving me alone with the last person I want to be around.

I'm not in the mood for his game of ultimate conquest.

"So, are you both on a date?" He leans against the wall.

"We are."

"He's a bit boring." He glances over my shoulder at him. "Not the best hockey player."

I roll my eyes as I scoff.

Chapter Three

"At least he's not an arrogant jerk." I seethe.

"Is that supposed to be directed at me?"

"Why else would I be looking at you when saying it?"

"I thought it was because you were getting lost in my eyes." He flirts.

I glance over my shoulder as Nevaeh converses with Trent. Why would Campbell attempt to flirt with me while on a date with my best friend?

He'd spewed some nonsense about some mystery girl in a lame attempt to make me empathize with him.

I should have seen through his lies.

"I am not about to stand here and watch you fail miserably at flirting when you're dating my best friend." I suddenly remembered the girl at the cafe. "Especially when you have a girlfriend!"

His brows furrowed in confusion.

"I don't have a girlfriend." He seems genuinely perplexed.

"Tell that to the girl that threatened me to stay away from you." I pout.

"I have no idea what you're talking about." He shrugs. "What did she look like?"

"Plastic blonde barbie." I spitefully mutter.

Realization washes over his face.

"Celeste," He groans. "She's not my girlfriend *anymore.*"

Anymore.

"Well, even if that were true. You came here with Nevaeh."

"Technically, I live here. I didn't come here with anyone. Nevaeh followed me here."

I wanted to bark more harsh words as my anger was reflected.

Our dates return with drinks. Trent places a red cup in

my hand, filled with unknown substances. I thank him and attempt not to cringe.

I can smell the abundance of alcohol.

He returns his arm around my waist.

"Want to walk around?" He whispers into my ear.

I eagerly nod. I want to get as far away from Campbell as possible. I offer Nevaeh a little grin and promise her to meet up later before brushing past them. He directs me to the same group of guys I saw in the kitchen. My heart rate starts to increase. They joke on their phones while we sit next to them. My head spins from their grating laughter. I cast a glance at my beverage. I have never been one for alcohol, but that cannot be said for Trent. I watch as he gulps it down as if he'd returned from the desert. He barely winces.

I glance around the room as he jokes around with his friends. I never knew you could feel so utterly alone in a group. I attempt to block out their hyena cackles as I gaze around.

My body starts to feel feverish.

I'm dripping with perspiration. My pharynx tightens.

"I'll be right back," I yell into Trent's ear over the disruptive music.

He barely nods before diving back into the conversation. I launch out of the seat before making a beeline for the exit. I lean against the porch railing, taking deep breaths. The crisp air is a welcomed contrast to the stuffiness inside.

I shouldn't have accepted Trent's offer. I'm not a dating expert, but if dating is always this complicated I would have been better off at my dorm and continued binge-watching *Gilmore Girls* for the umpteenth time.

The front door opens. I glance over my shoulder. I hoped it was Trent coming to check up on me. I scoff as Campbell

Chapter Three

approaches me with two bottles of ice-cold water. He sets them on the porch and reaches for the cup I'm holding.

I'd forgotten I was holding it.

He chucks the contents out onto the lawn and offers me one of the water bottles.

I quietly thanked him. I desperately needed a drink, but I wasn't prepared to drink what was in the cup.

"You don't drink?" I inquire as he takes a large gulp from his bottle.

"Not during hockey season." He replies.

I nod, gazing at the star-scattered sky, not wanting to acknowledge his presence.

"How's the writer's block?"

I turn my head to the right, but he's not looking at me.

"You told me you were short of ideas. Have you gotten any?"

It's as if he'd backhanded me.

He remembered.

I wish his change of mood would stop. I'm suffering from major whiplash.

"It's getting there." I trail off.

More awkward silence ensues.

"Shouldn't you be hanging out with your friends?" I question.

"Shouldn't you be with your date?" He fires back.

I should.

"You're right. I should go." I mutter, but he places his hand on my shoulder.

His signature smirk is back on his face.

"You can continue playing this little game of pretending to have a thing for Trent." He chuckles. "I'll play along because I know you're going to realize he's not the guy for you."

I frown.

"What makes you so sure about that?"

He chuckles and rolls his eyes as if I've just asked a stupid question.

"Because," His smirk grows wider. "We've had undeniable chemistry since our moment in the bookstore. You can't run away from that forever."

My heart skips a beat. I've never been more confused in my entire life. Everything about Campbell is contradictory and I don't know how much more of it I can take.

I immediately set off in search of Trent. I wanted to create as much distance between Campbell and myself as possible. His arrogant confession had sent me into a wave of doubt and paranoia.

I know why he said that. I know the kind of guy Campbell Atwood is.

Guys like him get a kick out of flirting with girls that have no interest in them. It's a means of inflating their already large ego. Trying to win me over is the ultimate conquest.

Guys always want what they can't have.

I am not about to let him have the satisfaction. There is a first time for everything. It's time someone knocks him off his pedestal of superiority. Since I arrived, I've hated this party, but I've begun to detest it even more.

The music is truly infuriating me.

I push through the intoxicated crowd, halting as two girls run ahead of me with beer-tainted dresses. They giggle and stumble into the restroom. I roll my eyes.

Trent hasn't moved. I'm surprised to find Nevaeh seated with them. She utters something before the group of frat boys explodes into fits of laughter.

Chapter Three

I tap Trent on the shoulder. He offers me a gentle smile.

"There you are." He pats the seat next to him.

I shake my head.

"I'm going to go home."

Trent follows me outside. Far away from the booming music.

"Is everything okay?" He questions.

"I'm just tired." I shrug.

He nods his head.

"Want me to walk you back to your dorm?" I shake my head.

"I don't mind walking."

"If you're sure." He states before leaning down to place a chaste kiss on my cheek. "Thank you for coming with me tonight."

"It was fun." I'm on a roll with these lies.

"Goodnight, Hazel." He squeezes my hand before walking back inside.

I decided to shrug it off.

All I need right now is my bed and a Gilmore Girls marathon.

Chapter Four

Fall arrived with regality, gracing us with its presence. The breeze is rich with the aroma of the Earth as the leaves dance from branch to ground. Cold weather has approached with purpose.

I am glad I dressed for the occasion. I've never been able to withstand low temperatures. The tip of my nose feels numb. I must look like a reindeer.

The school is buzzing, anticipating the first hockey game of the season. The team is the pride and joy of the campus. I don't understand the excitement. I have watched little hockey - but I am not impressed. Campbell Atwood is one of the reasons why. He'd completely ruined the experience for me. I didn't want to conform to the school's worship of their *Hockey God*.

He's nothing but a narcissistic jerk.

However, I want to support Trent.

We have spoken little since our date, but I know he has

Chapter Four

been training as hard as possible for his first game. It's not a shocker that Nevaeh has been buzzing along with the faculty - Campbell has been her only topic of discussion for months.

It's become unbearable.

I am thankful for Maisie. I was disinterested in making friends when we first met, but Maisie and I have a lot in common. It's refreshing to meet someone with a similar mindset. Our introverted nature has made living together enjoyable.

I scribble in my notebook as I jot down notes for ideas for a novel. I've always been forgetful. If I don't write it down, it never existed.

My pen escapes my hold as a loud bang on the door shakes me to the core.

Maisie groans and launches off her bed to answer it.

"Are you ready?" Nevaeh exclaims in excitement.

"No." Maisie and I mutter in unison.

"Stop being boring." Nevaeh scolds. "Let's get going. I want to talk to Campbell before the game."

Before reaching for her bag, I noticed that she rolled her eyes. I shut my notebook and stretch my arms above my head.

I take a deep, comforting breath.

My phone buzzes in my back pocket. I smile as I read Trent's text.

Meet me outside my locker room before the game. I need some good luck.

I hurriedly responded before rushing after Maisie and Nevaeh.

Eager students cramp the stadium. Everyone buzzed in anticipation for the start of what is expected to be a dramatic season. Their cheers incite a painful ringing in my ears and I place my hands over them to muffle the noise.

"I'm going to wish Trent good luck," I called out.

I've been eager to see him since I got the text and I don't want to wait a moment longer. Nevaeh rushed beside me. I glance at her curiously.

"I need to wish Campbell good luck." She states as if it's something I should have known already.

"What is going on between you two?" I question as we dawdle through the hallways in search of the locker room.

"He's playing hard to get." She smirks. "I'll win him over."

"You always do," I mumble under my breath. "Always."

A part of me was hoping that college would be different and that I wouldn't be the insecure person I always am when I'm around Nevaeh. I know it's wrong to be jealous of my best friend, but my mind is always deceiving me.

Once we are outside the locker room, I text Trent. As he approaches, I break out into a broad smile. He glances at a pouting Nevaeh after our quick hug.

"Hey, Nevaeh."

"Hey." She stares at the locker room door.

I roll my eyes.

"I was hoping you would wear this tonight." Trent questions as he extends a jersey toward me.

He bites his lip as I inspect the fabric in my hand.

His jersey.

My heart thumps against my chest as I bite back a face-cracking smile. No guy has ever asked me this before. The only question guys ever asked me was for homework answers.

"She doesn't want to wear your sweaty jersey." Campbell appears through the door.

He leans against the wall as he glances at us with a self-

Chapter Four

satisfied grin. I glare at him.

"Yes, I would love to wear it." I smile at Trent.

He seems pleased by my response. I slip the jersey over my head and admire how comfortable the material is.

A perfect fit.

Campbell scoffs and our eyes fall on him.

"Team meeting, let's go." He mutters before storming into the locker room.

"I guess I will see you both later." Trent replies before rushing after him.

I glance down at the jersey with a grin, but I don't enjoy it as much as I'd like. Nevaeh stares at the door in disbelief.

"He didn't notice me."

I frown and place a comforting hand on her shoulder.

"He's just nervous." I attempted to reassure her, but I don't think it was believable.

Campbell doesn't seem to be the kind to get nervous when it comes to hockey. Or anything.

She proceeds down the hallway back to the bleachers with folded arms. I scope the crowd in search of Maisie. She waves at us from the lowest level, so close she's nearly seated on the ice. I furrow my brows as we march down the steps.

"Looks like Trent wants you in the front row." She motions towards the seats with our names on.

Blushing, I take a seat next to Maisie followed by a sulking Nevaeh. I cheer as the players step out onto the ice. I clap louder once Trent steps on, but he's overshadowed by Campbell. The entire stadium roars as he waves. He's loving the attention. His smug grin says it all. He skates around the rink, delivering a subtle wink in our direction before rejoining his team. Nevaeh sits up straight as if his smile rejuvenated her.

"He winked at me." She grins.

The game begins and I find myself on the edge of my seat. I wince every time a player crashes into the wall. I glance at Trent sitting on the bench hoping to get his attention, but he seems entirely focused on his teammates.

The first period ends with neither team scoring. The players on the ice skate over to their coach. Trent waves at me with a grin. I wave back as my face burns. He walks off with his teammates, but Campbell stays behind smirking in our direction. I made eye contact with him and I could feel the smugness radiating off him even from a distance. I roll my eyes and sit down out of his view.

The second period is as uneventful as the first. I'm not sure if it's because of my lack of interest, or if the game was a snooze fest. Either way, I avoided looking in Campbell's direction the entire second and third periods. Things only got interesting during the final few minutes.

Campbell makes the game-winning shot to finish it. Jumping up from her chair, Nevaeh joins in the cheers. I continue to slouch, my arms crossed over my chest.

"I'm going back to the dorm." Maisie mumbles into my ear.

I think she was counting down the minutes until it ended. Trent skates toward me and I launch myself out of my seat to stand at the barrier.

"Hey." He utters.

He's smiling wide despite being short of breath.

"Hey." I greet as Nevaeh joins my side.

"Please tell me you're both coming to the victory party?" He pleads.

I pretend to mull it over before eagerly nodding.

Chapter Four

"We can celebrate my amazing goal." Campbell brags as he skates up to us.

He leans on the barrier next to me, and I move to the side.

"You were amazing." Nevaeh compliments.

"Thanks," He smirks. Our eyes lock. "What did you think, Ellie?"

"Well, hockey is a team sport. You couldn't have done it without the team."

He bites the corner of his lip and nods.

"You're right, Ellie. So modest of you." He glances at the seats behind me. "Did you like sitting in the front row? I pulled a few strings."

I gasp as if someone sucker punched me in the gut. *Campbell* arranged these seats? I thought this was Trent's doing.

"You were behind it?"

"Who else?" He seems smug. "I wanted you to witness my amazing talent as closely as possible."

I scoff. What a showoff.

The coach calls for Trent and Campbell.

"I'll see you both tonight." Trent grins as he skates off, but Campbell doesn't move.

He glances at my jersey with pursed lips.

"So, I'll see you tonight?" Nevaeh questions him as she leans further over the barrier.

"Sure." He speaks, but he's distracted by twirling his stick around in his hands.

The coach calls his name and shakes him out of his funk. He takes a deep breath and his signature grin returns.

"See you tonight."

* * *

Vicariously

The smell of cheap vodka makes my stomach feel queasy. Nevaeh ditched me the moment we arrived at the party. It seems in our short time she'd made a ton of new friends.

It's like high school all over again.

I've been searching for Trent, but the frat house is overcrowded. It would take a miracle to find him. A figure slams into my shoulder but they're gone before I could catch a glimpse. It's like being in a mosh pit. I rub my bruising shoulder and press myself against the wall wishing I could camouflage myself. I envy the ones that could effortlessly walk up to someone and start a conversation.

Simultaneous giggles vibrate over the music as I look to my left at a group of girls huddled around each other with their phones. I frown as they glance at me before whispering to each other. I self-consciously tuck a strand of hair behind my ear hoping they'd move away, but they continue to scrutinize. I cower under their intense gazes, especially when the familiar face joins them.

Celeste.

They don't bother to hide their pointing and stares. With a hateful glare, she stalks toward me. I press myself closer to the wall.

"It's Hazel, isn't it?" She questions in a sweet voice.

It doesn't take an expert to figure out she's fake.

I nod.

"I've noticed you're still hanging around Campbell." She sneers. "I hope you know he sees you as nothing more than a friend." Her eyes peer at me from head to toe. "You're not his type."

What is she implying?

"I'm not dating Campbell." My voice quivers.

Chapter Four

"I am glad we agree." She drops her head to the side.

Her friends surround me and I can feel my heart dropping to my stomach.

"There you are!" a voice exclaims.

Campbell brushes past the girls and wraps his arms around me in an unexpected hug. I'm too shocked to lift my arms. He pulls away.

"Let's go get a drink." He slides his hand into mine and drags me away from the wannabe *Mean Girls*.

"Thank you." I utter once we're in the safety of the kitchen.

"You look like you need an escape." He shrugs as if it's not a big deal. "Don't let Celeste intimidate you. She's nothing special."

I glance at the array of drinks to avoid his gaze. He says it like it's the easiest thing to do. I've always avoided confrontation, and I doubt I would change my mind.

Girls like Celeste were everywhere in high school. They're inescapable. I always believed I was cursed, as if I have a giant sign hanging above my head announcing that I'm the prime target for intimidation. A punching bag.

"So, where's your boyfriend?" He distracts himself by making a drink across the counter.

Is he referring to Trent?

"He's not my boyfriend." I bitterly replied.

We haven't even kissed. I wanted to believe it was because he was shy - but my mind keeps telling me it was because he wasn't as into me as I thought. As if he doesn't find me attractive. The back of my eyes burns with tears. I shake those daunting thoughts away.

"That's good," He smirks. "Then I can ask you out on a date."

I choke on my saliva.

Vicariously

"Excuse me?"

He strides around the counter until he's right next to me. He leans over it as he mischievously grins.

"Well, if Keller is too chicken to ask you on a date, I will."

I open and close my mouth like a fish out of water. Is he being serious?

"No." I simply replied.

His smile falters.

"No?"

"No."

He runs a hand through his unruly locks.

"I don't date guys that my friends are interested in." I figured I might as well give him an explanation.

I could never betray Nevaeh like that since he's just using me to get to her. Like every other guy I've met.

"So, what you're saying is the only reason you won't go on a date with me is because of Nevaeh?"

I roll my eyes.

"That's one of many reasons." I clarify.

"I don't like Nevaeh, though."

"Doesn't matter," I shrug. "Nevaeh likes you."

He chuckles humorlessly.

"She doesn't like me." He places his elbow on the table and supports his head with his hand. "She likes the idea of me."

I raise my brows.

"I don't follow."

He sighs.

"She wants the status that comes with dating me." He smirks. "I don't know if you noticed, Ellie, but I'm a pretty big deal around here."

Could he ever go a moment without being arrogant?

Chapter Four

"Must be pretty lonely." His smirk falters. "Not knowing if someone likes you for you."

He avoids eye contact with me.

"It's not as bad as it seems."

Someone clears their throat and our heads turn.

"I've been looking for you." Trent pipes up.

He doesn't move from under the doorway.

"Sorry, I should have just texted you." I apologize.

"Don't worry, Keller, I kept her entertained." Campbell straightens his posture as he delivers Trent a condescending wink.

Trent bites his lip. He ignores Campbell and locks eyes with me.

"Want to sit with the group?" He questions. "Nevaeh is there."

"Sure," I reply before glancing at Campbell from under my lashes. "See you around."

"Consider my offer, Ellie." He calls before I exit the room.

I halt for a second, not allowing the situation to mess with my mind. I grip Trent's hand and push through the swarm.

"Hey, you're back." A guy I've never seen before greets Trent. "We're about to play a game of *Truth or Dare*."

I hadn't realized Campbell was following us until he took a seat across from Trent and me.

"You don't have to play, Hazel." Nevaeh pipes up.

My cheeks burn as all eyes fall on me. My stomach flips. Why does it feel like they're judging me?

"Why wouldn't she play?" Campbell leans forward in his seat.

"She's always been too shy for this game."

I lower my head. They're all still staring.

Vicariously

"I think Ellie can speak for herself." Campbell comes to my defense.

I couldn't be more grateful.

"Fine," Nevaeh scoffs. "I'll start."

No one objects.

"Hazel," I close my eyes. *"Truth or dare?"*

I take a deep sigh and glance at her from the corner of my eye.

"Truth."

"Is it true you've never had a boyfriend?" She turns to the crowd. "She's always been so shy. Guys *never* noticed her."

I feel the back of my eyes prickle with tears. It's as if she's been dying to ask this question.

As if she doesn't already know the answer.

I stutter. The air thickens as eyes glance around the room. I dig my nails into my knees as a lone tear escapes the corner of my eye. It falls into my hand.

"This game is boring. Who suggested it?" Campbell pipes up.

"I did." Nevaeh replies.

"That explains the boring part." A chorus of laughter erupts.

I take that moment to flee back into the kitchen. The second I'm alone, my body is wracked with sobs. I clutch my hair in my hands as I lean against the counter. I sense a presence in the room but I couldn't muster the strength to look up. It's not even a big deal, but all the eyes on me were too much to handle.

"Chin up, Ellie." Campbell's voice soothes. "Are you going to let a knock-off *Regina George* tear you down?"

"She's my best friend."

He scoffs.

Chapter Four

"Some best friend."

I wipe my eyes with the back of my hand and sniffle. Shoes appear in my line of sight and I risk a glance. I jump at our proximity.

"No offense intended, but you picked a terrible best friend."

I mentally hit myself in my immediate reaction to defend her. Why would I want to after what she just did? My breath hitches as he tucks a fallen strand of hair behind my ear. He's so close I can feel his breath on my face. He lifts my chin with his finger. Our eyes lock.

"You didn't deserve what she did." He replies. "And any guy that rejected you was a complete idiot."

My tongue felt as though it had been severed. I couldn't utter a single word. I move closer. Our noses touch.

"Hazel." A voice calls.

We jump apart the moment Trent enters the room.

"There you are." He sighs.

He didn't see what transpired.

"Hi." I croak out.

"No need to cry." He states. "Nevaeh says she was just joking around."

Campbell scoffs.

"Wasn't funny to me." He offers.

Trent looks at him over his shoulder with a fiery gaze.

"I don't think this concerns you."

Campbell's fists clench.

"I was the one comforting your girl." He seethes. "What were you doing?"

"Please don't fight." I rub my aching temples.

My head feels as if it's inflated.

"Want me to walk you home?" Trent questions.

Vicariously

I shake my head.

"No," I shiver. "Please leave me alone."

I push him away from me and bolt out of the kitchen, dismissing their pleas for me to return, running until my legs feel numb and my chest is on fire. I ran to my dorm. I stop at the door and lean over placing my hands on my knees as I catch my breath.

Maisie is inside with a textbook in front of her at her desk. She whips around at the sound of the door. The moment our eyes lock, I burst into another fit of tears. She bolts out of her seat and embraces me in a hug which I happily return.

I just needed a friend right now.

She doesn't speak, allowing me to sob into her arms until I can't cry anymore. She leads me to my bed. I collapse on my pillow. She brushes my hair out of my face and my eyes feel burdened with sleep. I try to fight the exhaustion, but everything has physically and emotionally taken a toll on me. I win a few rounds, but sleep eventually lands the knockout punch.

Chapter Five

A storm of sadness hovers above me the moment I wake up. My head pounds as if my brain has a heartbeat. I clutch it with a groan. The sun shining in my bedroom blinds me until they adjust. I lick my desiccated lips in dire need of something to moisten them. I sit up and analyze my tattered outfit.

Maisie's bed is made. I rub my eyes with the palm of my hands until I see constellations. Every muscle in my body aches and it feels as if an anchor has been fastened around my chest. The entire night has weighed me down.

I push myself from my bed, avoiding the full-length mirror. If I'm as much of a mess externally as I am internally then it's best to avoid looking.

I don't know what possessed Nevaeh to act so out of character. She'd never done something like this before. She'd always have my back.

What's changed?

Vicariously

I shove the thoughts aside as I enter the library. It's less crowded than usual, but I prefer isolation. I dawdle through the aisles of books in search of Campbell. It's time for another tutoring session, but I cannot help but feel apprehensive.

I never know how to act around Campbell. His ambivalent nature is confusing.

One moment he's pleasant company and the next he's unbearable.

I cannot figure him out.

I find him hunched over a book in the same spot as our last tutoring session. He scattered the entire desk in papers, not noticing me until I'm next to him.

"Hey, Ellie!" He grins.

"What's all this?" There are piles of notes.

"I did some research last night and found out everything I could about *Romeo and Juliet, and* I thought I could use some of it for the essay."

I raise my eyebrows.

"You did all of this?"

He nods his head.

"I didn't want to look like I know nothing. I was hoping to impress you with my newfound vast knowledge of *Shakespeare.*"

I'm surprised by his uncharacteristic behavior. We'd only had a few tutoring sessions, but he had placed little effort into it. Not like now.

"I also got you this." He says as he reaches into a bag beside his chair.

He holds a mug out to me with the words *World's Best Tutor* printed on. I bite off a smile as I reach for it. I twirl it around in my hand.

Chapter Five

"You've saved my hockey career, Hazel Ellis." He chimes.

I take a seat and place my mug on the edge of the table.

"You just needed a bit more help." I shrug as if it wasn't a big idea.

"I appreciate it." He speaks. "I just wanted you to know."

I nod my head and glance at his thorough notes.

"Did you sleep at all last night?" I question in disbelief as I look at the stacks of paper.

"A few hours, but my mind was running."

He'd done everything. From character synopsis to analysis of themes. I am impressed.

"This is very impressive." I say, and he grins.

"Thank you, Ellie."

He rubs his eyes before raising his arms with a deep yawn. He slouches over the table.

"I think we should cancel the tutoring for today. You need rest." I suggest, and he shakes his head.

"I'm just starving. I missed breakfast." He says. "Why don't we go to the diner, get something to eat and we can talk *Shakespeare* there?"

I mull over his suggestion. It seems harmless enough.

It's for tutoring.

"Sure." We gather our things together and I place my mug in my backpack, safe from any potential harm.

The stroll is calming as we enjoy the fresh outdoors. Many people wave at him and greet him with beaming smiles. It's as if I'm traveling with a celebrity. I suppose he's seen as one in this school.

"It's impressive how much you know about books." He says.

"You know as much about hockey."

He tucks his hands in his pocket.

"You have a point." He notes. "Is there anything else you like besides writing?"

I bite my lip.

"I love music and binge-watching."

He grins at my words.

"Well, I already know you have great taste in music."

Hushed murmurs escape the restaurant as we enter. We take a seat at a table and I glance through the menu.

I've been craving a burger, and it seems Campbell had the same idea.

"So, what are you interested in?" I say, attempting to make conversation until our food arrives. "What do you like other than hockey?"

He drops his head to gaze at his interlocked hands.

"I was always good at geometry." He says. "I would always use it when I played hockey. It helped me play better."

"I'm impressed." I purse my lips. "That's something I never understood. It seems we're opposites."

We thank the waitress as she places the burgers in front of us.

"Opposites attract, Hazel Ellis."

I chuckle before opening my burger to remove the pickles. I've hated them for as long as I can remember. My hatred for them originated when my mom would put them on my sandwiches every day for school. I eventually grew tired of them.

"You don't like pickles?" He gasps.

"Hate them." I scrunch my nose.

He reaches over the table and grabs them to put on his burger. He chuckles as he shoves a fry in his mouth.

"Like I said, Hazel Ellis." He says. "Opposites attract."

Chapter Five

* * *

I stroll around the university, as I have no classes scheduled for the day.

I wrap my arms around myself and exhale the cold air. My teeth chatter as a torpedo of wind breezes past me.

"How could you do this to me?" A voice calls from behind me.

I whip around to find Nevaeh stomping toward me. I tuck my hands into my front pockets. Her face is bright red and I don't think it's from the cold.

"Campbell refuses to talk to me." She tosses her hands up. "I was joking last night, H, and now he thinks I'm some selfish jerk."

My chest tightens.

Is this my fault?

"I'm confused." I choke out.

"So am I!" she exclaims. "We joke around all the time, but the one time the guy I like sits near us, you decide to get upset."

She folds her arms across her chest.

"I don't understand what's going on, H." Her bottom lip quivers. "Is there something you're not telling me?"

"Like what?" I question.

"Maybe you like Campbell, so you're jealous."

Her words hit harder than a knockout punch from *George Foreman.*

"That's not true." I insist.

"Then why did you try to sabotage me?" She scoffs.

"I didn't." My hands begin to shake.

Confrontation gives me unbearable anxiety.

Vicariously

She exhales, pinching the bridge of her nose. Her eyes are closed as she takes soothing breaths.

"I'm sorry." She apologizes.

Her shoulders drop.

"I just need to get some rest." She mutters before bolting towards the dorm building.

I debated following her, but from experience, it was best to leave her alone until she settled down.

My legs feel as if they'd turn into gelatin. The entire situation has been blown out of proportion. I hate that this has upset Nevaeh. It's the last thing I ever wanted.

My legs drag my body before my mind can even register where I'm going, but I recognize the direction.

The frat house.

I stand at the door, raising my fist to knock, but I pull it back to my side before I could muster up the courage. I bite my lip as I hesitate a few times. I internally scold myself for being so awkward before pounding on the door. Footsteps approach and the momentary confidence evaporates from my body.

An unfamiliar older looking guy answers the door. He must be a senior.

"Can I help you?" I purse my lips at how strange I must look standing motionless and not speaking.

"Is Campbell here?" I squeak out like a scared child.

He moves the door wider, beckoning me inside. I step over the threshold with my hands behind my back. The home looks so much more spacious without the herd of partygoers.

"I'll get Campbell." The guy speaks before bolting up the stairs.

My shoulders slump the moment I'm left alone. I gaze at the array of framed pictures of past frat members littering the

Chapter Five

wall.

"Hazel." Trent's eyes are wide as he enters from another room. "What are you doing here?"

I debate whether to tell him the truth or fabricate a believable explanation.

"I was hoping to see you." He spoke before I could even think of a plausible explanation.

"You were?" I unconsciously smile.

"Yeah," He scratches the back of his neck. "I was wondering if you were busy tonight. I was thinking of grabbing something to eat at the diner."

Like a date? I wanted to question him, but delivering the line requires confidence that I don't have.

"Sounds like fun."

I attempt to contain my excitement.

"Great, then I'll see you tonight."

My head turns as someone clears their throat. Campbell is leaning against the railing with raised brows. I bite my lip and tuck a strand of hair behind my ear.

How long has he been standing there?

"You wanted to see me?" I mentally curse.

Why did he have to bring it up?

Trent glances at me with a raised brow. I avoid him and fold my arms across my chest.

"What did you say to Nevaeh?"

He tilts his head to the side.

"Nothing."

I scoff.

"You had to have said something. She was pretty upset this morning."

He shrugs.

"I haven't spoken to her since last night."
His detached tone infuriates me.
"Well, whatever you did. Fix it." I ordered.
My contorted face softens as I glance at Trent.
"See you tonight." I smile before rushing out the door.

***

The serene atmosphere welcomed me as soon as I entered through the translucent glass doors. My clammy hands, though, go against the aura. I slide them down my dress as I glance around for Trent. I'd spent hours with Maisie trying to find something suitable to wear. I've never had to dress for a date before. I fiddle with the hem of my outfit as I brush past the tables. My eyes land on the back of Trent's head. I hasten my footsteps with a nervous grin. My smile drops as I spot Nevaeh and Campbell sitting across from him.

Nevaeh is the first to spot me as she waves in my direction. I considered leaving right away, but I couldn't dare be rude.

"Hi." I greet them.

"Hey!" Nevaeh cheers. "Campbell thought it would be a good idea for us to double date."

I glance at the culprit. He's avoiding my gaze. The satisfied grin shows he knows I'm glaring at him. I slide into the booth next to Trent. He smiles softly. Nevaeh starts talking about the girl who sat in front of her in one of her classes, but I tune her out. Campbell puts his fist in front of his mouth to cover up his risky glimpse in my direction, but his smile is too big. I lean back in my seat and sulk.

Why would he ruin this for me?

Chapter Five

Placing his arms on the table, he leans forward. He delivers a subtle wink before returning his focus to Nevaeh. She endlessly drags on about her sociology professor.

"I'll be right back." I interrupt her to excuse myself.

I walk to the restroom, stomping my feet. I give myself a quick look in the mirror while running my hands through my hair. My cheeks are red from anger. The only thoughts running through my mind are a million ways I could murder Campbell Atwood. When I told him to make things right with her, I didn't mean to insert himself into my date with Trent.

Trent.

If this was a date, why did he allow Campbell and Nevaeh to join us? Had I read it all wrong? He never used the word *date*. I was getting too ahead of myself. I glance over my appearance before bursting through the doors. I collide with a figure standing outside.

"Whoa, Ellie, what's the rush?" I internally groan.

The rage that I've tried to keep dormant erupts.

"What is wrong with you?" I question with a scowl.

"You'll have to be more specific."

I bite my tongue.

"This was supposed to be a one-on-one date." I insist.

"I agree." He states with wide eyes. "Trent and Nevaeh should leave."

I place the palm of my hands against my forehead.

This conversation is going nowhere.

"Did you do this to ruin things between me and Trent?"

"No." He simply states.

I scoff. How unbelievable.

"How can I ruin something that doesn't exist?" My jaw drops.

Vicariously

"Excuse me?"

"Let's not pretend, Ellie." He smirks.

"Are you doing this right now when you're supposed to be on a date with my best friend?"

He raises his hands in surrender.

"I'm only doing what you told me to."

My head pounds from his insufferable egotism.

"Let's not keep our dates waiting any longer." He makes a show of brushing past me.

I follow him, frowning and mentally cursing. If only I could murder him, but there are too many witnesses.

"Are you okay?" Trent whispers in my ear.

I nod.

"I'm fine."

He doesn't question me. We sit in tense silence for a moment before Campbell pipes up.

"How's the book coming along, Ellie?"

"What book?" Trent questions with a look of bewilderment.

"Hazel has always wanted to be a writer." Nevaeh pipes. "She lets no one read it. I always told her she couldn't become a writer if she's too afraid to share her work."

My cheeks burn up.

"I love how different we are." I sometimes wonder if Nevaeh is obsessed with the sound of her voice. "In high school, I was the head cheerleader. She was a shy bookworm. We just clicked."

Campbell snorts.

"I should have known you were a cheerleader." She doesn't pick up on his condescending tone.

She beams with pride.

Trent places his arm behind my head on the top of the booth.

Chapter Five

I push my hair in front of my face to hide my blush. I couldn't tell if it was intentional or not.

"Ow!" He exclaims as he reaches with both hands to clutch his knee.

"Sorry," Campbell shrugs. "I had a muscle spasm."

The corner of his lip twitches. I scoff.

The rest of the double date is bearable, much to my chagrin. I breathe the cool air into my lungs the moment we step outside, enjoying the breeze until we're outside the dorms. I'm thankful the night is coming to an end. I'd had expectations for tonight, but Campbell made sure they crashed and burned.

"I hate to end the night here, but we have practice at the break of dawn." Trent replies as he ushers me away from the pair.

"I had fun."

The corners of his lips rise.

"I did too." He leans down to place a kiss on my cheek. I sigh. "I'll talk to you tomorrow."

"I had fun, Ellie." Campbell appears behind me. "We should do it again sometime."

Trent waves at us before turning around with his hands in his pockets.

"Just the two of us." Campbell whispers in my ear as he glides past.

He doesn't turn around as he catches up to Trent. I watch them fade away.

* * *

The wind whips through the trees as it creaks and groans

like a rocking chair. My cheeks feel as if I have rubbed them raw, and my chapped lips might crack any second. My boots crunch against the dying leaves.

I'm in desperate need of something to warm me up.

"Ellie!" The voice captures the attention of everyone in the area.

Campbell grinned as he bolted towards me with a face-cracking smile. He wraps his arms around me and spins me. My cheeks burn from the curious gazes.

"What was that for?" I ask the moment he sets me down.

He places a paper in my hand. *His essay.* I gasp at the prominent A written in red, followed by the words *amazing work.*

"You got an A!" I exclaim in delight.

"I've never seen one of them before." He beams. "At least, not on my papers."

I chuckle as I raise my hand for a high-five. I find it unbelievable how we can go from angry to cheerful in a matter of a day. I wanted to yell at him some more for ruining my date, but his beaming smile changes my mind. I find it unbelievable.

"This is amazing. You worked hard for it." I say.

"Couldn't have done it without your help, Ellie."

I shrug and hand the paper back to him.

"Where were you off to?" He asks.

"I'm freezing and craving hot chocolate." I replied.

"Mind if I join?" He asks. "It's on me, so I can thank my amazing tutor for helping me out."

"I can't say no to free hot chocolate."

We stroll through the campus, neither of us in a hurry to be anywhere.

"What did your coach say about your grade?" I ask, hoping

Chapter Five

to make conversation.

"I haven't told him yet." He tucks his hands in his jacket pockets. "I had to tell my tutor first."

I chuckle as we enter the cafe. The moment the warm mug of hot chocolate is placed in my hands, I inhale the sweet chocolate scent. The dark and rich texture envelops my taste buds. I sigh in delight.

"You must have wanted that chocolate." Campbell chuckles.

My eyes spring open as I'd forgotten my company.

"I needed some sugar." I blush. "Haven't been sleeping much."

"No need to apologize." He says with a grin. "I think it's cute."

I take another sip to mask my smile. My phone buzzes in my pocket and I glance at the *Caller ID*.

Trent.

I glanced at Campbell as he locked his scrutinizing gaze on my phone screen. His smile drops.

"I'll let you get to that." His entire demeanor changed in a second. "Have a lovely day, Hazel Ellis."

I watch in disbelief as he charges out the cafe. I wanted to chase after him and confront him about his weird behavior, but I doubt it's any of my business. It's for the best that I leave Campbell to dwell in his messy thoughts.

* * *

The school has been in high spirits coming off another win. Just in time for what is known as the party of the season. Nevaeh had been raving non-stop about how Campbell's

Vicariously

fraternity is party central and how their frat leader, Shaun, hosts the grandest party imaginable every year to celebrate his birthday. Since Shaun is a senior, he plans to celebrate it *one final time with the most epic party ever.*

The most shocking of it all is that Maisie agreed to attend the party with me.

I would have thought I'd have gotten used to the smell of cheap liquor by now, but it still makes my stomach churn. I lock arms with Maisie, afraid of losing her in this drunken pit.

Trent approaches us. It's as if an invisible force is pulling him from the side as he stumbles. He grips the wall to balance himself.

"You made it!" He slurs with half-lidded eyes.

As he gets nearer, I notice how bloodshot they are. His face was drenched in sweat. He's acting like a tightrope walker.

I glance at Maisie in embarrassment. It isn't how I planned on introducing her to Trent. We stare in horror as he regains his balance.

"Do you want something to drink?" He utters.

We shake our heads.

How did he get drunk so fast? Were we late to the party?

"Ellie," A cheerful greeting floods into my ears. "You came after all."

Campbell appears next to Trent.

"With a friend, I see." He sets his sights on Maisie, but she doesn't seem as impressed to see him as he hoped.

"This is Maisie," I said. "You know Campbell, Mase."

He tilts his head to the side with a smirk.

"Do you talk about me, Ellie?" He teases.

"No, Nevaeh." His smile drops.

His frown lowers further as Trent places a hand on his

Chapter Five

shoulder to keep himself upright. He glances at him with a sneer before stepping to the side. Trent stumbles and falls to the ground with a thump. Campbell suppresses a smile.

"Are you okay?" I question.

He groans.

"Don't worry, he's just drunk," Campbell argues. "He'll be worse tomorrow."

"You didn't have to do that!" I exclaim.

He chuckles in disbelief.

"Do what?" He raises his hands in the air. "He fell on his own."

I roll my eyes.

"At least help him up!" I shove Campbell.

He scoffs but helps Trent to his feet before tossing him on top of a nearby sofa.

"Happy?" He curls his lip.

"Ecstatic."

Looking across at Maisie. She has been observing the entire situation.

"Let's go back to the dorm." I told her.

Campbell gasps like you would during a dramatic climax in a movie.

"You just got here." He pouts.

"I'm tired," I fib. "Long day."

He snorts.

"Was I supposed to believe that?"

I glance at Trent. His eyes twitch before his head falls back with a groan.

"Let's hang out." Campbell suggests ignoring his frat brother.

I opened my mouth to protest, but Maisie is a step ahead.

"What do you have in mind?" I deliver an intense glare, but she mischievously winks.

Campbell smiles wide.

"Do you know how to skate?"

"A little." She shrugs.

"Well, I have the perfect plan."

Chapter Six

The frigid air attacked me as we entered through the glass door. The cold seeped through my thick layered hoodie. I shudder. The rink is even chillier without the abundance of spectators. I take in every angle of the building. The barren grandstands, the serene silence. The experience is already an upgrade.

"Welcome to my home away from home." Campbell extends his arms out.

A genuine smile stretches across his face.

"Who's up for a game of hockey?" He questions.

Maisie stands up and clutches her head with a groan. I rushed to her side.

"Are you okay, Mase?"

"I got the biggest migraine." She whines. "I think I need to get to my bed."

"I'll go with you." I pipe up.

"No!" She exclaims before clearing her throat. "I will not let

Vicariously

this ruin your night."

Campbell strides towards us with furrowed brows.

"Are you sure?" He questions.

"Positive." She assures.

She brushes past us before glancing over her shoulder. My eyes widen as she smiles wide and delivers a cheeky wink before rushing out of the stadium.

She did it on purpose.

"So," Campbell grins. "Think you can beat me?"

I snort.

"I've seen you play," I declare. "You're overrated."

He takes my words as a challenge and scoffs.

"You're on, Ellie." He winks. "Follow me so we can get set up."

Sitting on the bench, I glance at the skates. I can't lace them. I engage in a stare-down with them as if it would make them secure themselves.

"You talk a lot for someone that can't even tie their laces." Campbell mocks as he crouches in front of my outstretched legs.

I watch in awe as he secures my laces making it look elementary.

"I'm sorry," I retorted. "Guess it's been a while since I've played hockey."

"You've never played before, have you?" He denotes.

"I've barely skated." I sheepishly admit.

Once my boots are fastened, I extend my hands silently pleading with him to help me up. He grins. I grip his shoulder as he slowly coaxes me onto the ice. I feel like a fawn learning to walk right after birth. My legs wobble. I lost my footing and fell back, but Campbell's fast reflexes saved me before I

Chapter Six

could hit the ice.

"Thank you." I gasp through uneven breaths.

My heart pounds against my rib cage.

"You weren't kidding when you said you'd hardly skated."

"If you really want to know," I avoid his eyes. "I've never skated. Ever."

He analyzes my face for any trace of lies.

"Wow, I guess we'll have to attempt playing some other time." He grins. "It's time I taught you how to stay on the ice without breaking anything."

I admire Campbell's patience considering I've never been the most graceful. His encouragement never wavers despite my constant failures. Every fall he'd help me back up and start again.

After endless falling, I begin to get it, but my legs feel as if they've internally been set alight. My muscles stiffen. The experience has been fun, but the overexertion is killing me. I happily take off the skates.

"I need a break." I groan.

Collapsing on the bench, I exhale the pressure and massage my aching legs. Campbell takes a seat next to me, not even slightly out of breath.

"Believe it or not, I spend lots of alone time here." He speaks. "I enjoy playing without a huge crowd."

I scoff at his absurd statement.

"Please tell me you're kidding."

I'm not buying it. Campbell seems fueled by attention.

"I'm not saying I hate it." He grins and punches my shoulder. "I just like to take a break from the adoring crowd. Playing alone reminds me of how much I fell in love with hockey in the first place."

Vicariously

I mull his words over. I'd never seen it like that when it concerns my writing, having always dreamed of adoring fans obsessed with my work. I think you need to be successful to know what it's like to want to escape it, even for a moment.

"My dad used to play." I continue to let him vent. "He got injured in college and had to give it up. When I was born, I guess he saw it as an opportunity to live his dreams vicariously through me." He sniffs. "I didn't want to play at first because I feared never living up to his potential, but it's like the greatest rush. I can't get enough of it."

He folds his arms across his chest with a faraway gaze.

"I kept getting more confident every time I stepped on the ice. It's the only time in my life I'm certain I excel at something." He glances at me before inspecting his skates. "Is that how you feel about writing?"

I take a moment to fathom a response.

"I'd always been an outcast. Reading was my escape from my miserable life. I'd always been envious of how easy it was for others to fit in. One day, I decided if I can't live the life I want, I'd write about it."

"What life do you want to live?"

"I'm not sure." My answer is dishonest, but I am not prepared to share my thoughts and fears with someone I barely know.

I'm thankful he doesn't push it. We remain silent as the feeling returns to my legs. The ache slowly fades.

"You know, it's not a big deal that you've never had a boyfriend." My stomach sinks at his words.

Of all the topics he could have raised.

Unable to speak, I nod.

"I just don't know how it's possible that you don't have guys

Chapter Six

fighting over you."

"Guys never noticed me." I mumble.

"It seems to me the guys you know are complete idiots." I chuckle at his words.

The giggles die down as he doesn't laugh with me.

"Please, with Nevaeh as my best friend it's understandable why." I shrug.

"You are delusional, Ellie." I can't help but be offended by his words.

The shock is evident on my face. His gaze intensified.

"Have you not realized that I've been flirting with you since we met?" His eyes widened in disbelief. "I thought I'd made it obvious."

Freezing in place, my stomach itches. I curse my dreaded mind. Despite the confession, it's telling me to wait for the punchline.

"I'm not kidding." It's as if he could hear my thoughts.

"I don't understand," I utter. "Nevaeh likes you, so why would you be flirting with me?"

"Why wouldn't I?" He replies without hesitation.

"I'm nothing like Nevaeh." I couldn't look him in the eyes.

"Which is why I like you." He slides closer to me, tilting his body to gaze into my eyes. "I've dated girls like Nevaeh. They're all the same. They lack substance."

I take a large gulp.

"As much as you don't want to see it, you'll always be the better choice."

My brain couldn't fathom his words. I had to stop myself from looking over my shoulder wondering if he was talking to someone else this entire time. I'd never had a guy tell me I'm a better choice than Nevaeh or had a guy choose to spend

Vicariously

time with me instead of her.

It's always been her.

I didn't realize he was leaning closer until his hot breath brushed against my skin. I close my eyes and lean forward as if some magnetic force is pulling us together.

The shrill ringing of my phone breaks us apart. My heart lapses at the unexpectedness. I clutch my chest and reach for it.

"Hello?" I answer ignoring the *Caller ID.*

"Hazel," Nevaeh cries out, but the loud music muffles her voice. "Where are you? I've been looking everywhere for Campbell."

The severity of the situation presses down on me. Here I am with the guy my best friend likes, almost kissing him.

How could I betray her like that?

"I'll help you look for him," I speak before I can stop the words from brushing past my lips.

I hang up before she can say anything else. My screen turns black. I wince at my appearance, disgusted by my behavior.

"We need to go back to the party." My voice breaks as I hold back the tears.

"Why?" He questions.

His jaw clenches.

"Nevaeh is looking for you."

"I don't care." He hisses and reaches to grab my hand.

I yank it away as if electrocuted. I stand up and create a significant distance between us.

"This is wrong!" My words echo through the stadium. "My best friend likes you, and I am stealing you away."

"I'm not her property." He growls.

I clutch my hair in my hands.

Chapter Six

"That's not what I meant!" I insist. "What kind of friend am I for sneaking away with the guy she likes?"

"I invited you here, not the other way around."

His words don't stop the escaping tears of frustration.

"It doesn't matter." I clench my hands at my sides. "What matters is I need to be a good friend."

He scoffs.

"You mean the way she's a good friend to you?"

"What's that supposed to mean?" His accusatory tone offends me.

"Do you think she'd ever do the same for you?" He points out. "She'd choose herself every time."

"That's not true," I gasp. "Nevaeh has always been there for me."

His hair has fallen into his face. No matter how many times he brushes it with his fingers, it remains stubborn.

"Don't be naïve, Hazel, she'd betray you the moment she gets the chance."

"You know what, Campbell?" I yell. "Fuck you!"

I clutch my hair before dropping my hands to my sides.

"I can never decide where we are. One moment we're friends and the next you're doing this!"

He gazes intensely into my eyes as his skin reddens.

"Fuck you too, Hazel!" He bellows. "I am so sick of watching you be a doormat to Nevaeh! It's tragic."

I shake my head as my eyes brim with tears. My bottom lip quivers, but I refuse to let his words upset me.

"I think it's best to go back to my dorm."

He snorts.

"Fine, If you want me to leave you alone - then your wish is my command."

Vicariously

"Thank you."

I don't wait for a response. I bite my lip and hurriedly exit the stadium, wrapping my arms around myself as the fresh breeze glides past me. As much as I didn't want our night to be ruined - I knew it was for the best. I could never give up a lifetime of friendship for a guy I barely know.

No matter what I feel - I need to push those feelings aside. Campbell Atwood is off-limits.

Chapter Seven

I'm overburdened by the multitude of mingled conversations at the party. The pure mayhem ensuing before my eyes is unbelievable. A traffic jam of intoxicated freshmen blocks my path into the kitchen. The crowd has a life of its own and panic swelled in my chest as I brush past bodies. When the crowd moved, I did too, in fear of being trampled underfoot. Despite the frigid air, I can feel the warmth of bodies pressing in. They flowed like rivers, as if nothing could stop them.

My mind feels hazy from the pungent cigarette smoke exuding from the crowd standing around a keg. A couple a few feet away are engaged in a heated argument, followed by a distant shattering of glass.

The frat boys are gathered around their flat screen as they holler at the professional hockey players. Trent leaps off his seat along with the rest. Drinks get knocked off the table by their abrupt movement, but neither of them rushes to clean

Vicariously

the spill. I scrunch my nose at their horrible living habits.

"Hey!" Trent greets me as I dawdle toward them.

I muster a smile as their obnoxious laughter fries my brain. He doesn't seem to notice my displeasure as I take a seat next to him. I watch along with them. I battle to keep my eyes open until we're joined by more people.

Campbell and an unfamiliar brunette.

My jaw slackens as she seats herself on his lap. He wraps his arm around her waist with a conceited grin.

Where is Nevaeh?

He doesn't acknowledge anyone as he watches the game. The mystery girl is texting on her phone. The pair hardly converse except for a few odd words uttered. I flicked my eyes around the room in search of Nevaeh as my body tensed.

She wouldn't be hard to miss.

Mischief gleams in Campbell's eyes as they connect with mine, but I brush it off and settle on looking for Nevaeh. I ignore his fleeting gaze on the back of my head as I rush into the next room. I spot her with a group of unfamiliar girls taking shots. The girls cheer her on. By the time I'd reached her, she'd already knocked down five. She raises her hands in the air with a cheer. I tap her shoulder.

"Hey, H." she slurs as she leans against the table for support.

"Are you aware Campbell is hanging out with another girl?"

She chuckles through hooded eyes.

"I know the game he's playing." She utters. "He's trying to make me jealous."

Somehow I don't believe that to be true.

From what I'd witnessed, Campbell enjoyed the attention the beautiful model on his lap was giving him. However, I don't want to involve myself in their unnecessary drama. With

Chapter Seven

a final shrug, I exit the room intent on returning to hang out with Trent, but the moment I could hear the high-spirited roars of the group I turned for the exit.

The night air was savage as I walked along the frost-covered porch. I wrap my arms around myself as I look at the ashen night sky. The lack of stars reflects my inner morbidity.

I hate this night just like any other night. I'm stuck at a party.

The cold air forms like cigarette smoke with each exhale as I drone out the vexing noise inside.

"It's like I always know where to find you." Campbell muses as he hovers in the doorway. "The only person I know to show up to a party, only to stand outside alone."

I shrug.

"Not in the mood for people."

"When are you ever?" He chuckles before leaning against the porch railing beside me.

He's stood close and I move to the side to create a sizable distance between us, sniggering at my behavior, but remains silent as he follows my line of sight to the bland sky. I shift my weight from one foot to the other as I fiddle with the ends of my hair.

"Where's your date?" I question.

"Do you mean Paige?"

"If that's the model that was on your lap, then yes."

He snorts as he places his elbow against the porch railing.

"Nevaeh thinks you're doing all of this to make her jealous." I add.

"I think we've both clarified that I'm not into Nevaeh." He grins. "Or Paige - they're not my type."

I bite my lip and turn away from his intense gaze.

"You have a type?" He hums in response. "What would that

be?"

My stomach churns at his impish grin.

"Antisocial bookworms."

I'm flustered by his bold response - but it's no surprise. Campbell thrives on confidence. I fold my arms across my chest.

"I should see what Trent is up to."

I didn't care what Trent was up to; he was most likely glued to the television screen, along with his unsavory fraternity brothers. I just need to get away from Campbell and his sultry gaze.

"You can run away all you'd like, Hazel Ellis." He shrugs. "I'll just keep thinking of ways to make us bump into each other."

"What happened to you leaving me alone?"

"I got bored."

With a defeated sigh, I return inside until I'm back in the unwanted company.

"Are you okay?" Trent questions in my ear, but his gaze hasn't moved from the television.

"Perfect." I mumble and slouch in the seat, pouting like a kid that didn't get the Christmas present they wanted.

He only graced me with his full attention during the intermission, but I know he'd go back to ignoring me once the next period begins.

"Do you want something to drink?" I shake my head, groaning as he follows the group to the kitchen.

I could hear their grating laughter over all the noise.

"For the record, I would never ignore you." The menacing voice whispers in my ear.

I roll my eyes, not even bothering to turn, because I know who the voice belongs to.

Chapter Seven

"I wish you would." I grumble.

He doesn't take the hint as inserts himself into Trent's spot, drawing his arm behind my head on the back of the couch. He leans forward, trapping me in the corner.

"You don't need to be jealous about Paige." He whispers.

Our eye contact never falters. His sparkle with mischief as he leans even closer.

"You'll always be my number one girl, Hazel Ellis."

In the blink of an eye, he's gone and I'm left flustered. I glance around at the drunken partiers. They seem as if they don't have a care in the world.

Is it wrong for me to have one night without my deceiving thoughts? One night of losing my inhibitions. Before I can back out, I march towards the kitchen as Trent is standing around the counter with his friends.

"Hey." He greets me as I approach.

"I'll take that drink after all." He's pleased by my words as he concocts something with copious amounts of alcohol.

I smell it before it even touches my lips. As the rancid taste invades my taste buds, I feel a burning sensation in the back of my throat. I resist the urge to vomit and take another cautious sip.

One drink turned into two. Followed by another. And another.

It feels as if I'm on a boat being washed away by the angry current as I tumble from left to right. I lean against the nearest wall as my eyes seem to lag. I don't know who or what I'm looking for, but it's as if I am no longer in control of my mind. It's like an out-of-body experience, as if someone else is controlling me. As I clutch my head, I feel my arms around my waist. I lock eyes with unfamiliar hazel ones. I watch as their mouth moves, but everything is hazy. The figure looms over me before they disappear.

"Who do you think you are?" I could make sense of the muffled yelling. "Get away from her!"

My legs give out and I slither along the wall until I reach the freezing tiled floor. I lick my dry lips as my eyes flutter. I fight to witness the hazy scene before me, but I fade into unconsciousness.

Chapter Eight

The aching in my skull flows and ebbs like a high tide. It feels like I have inflated a balloon inside my cranium. The constant pressure is agonizing. I groan as my stomach flutters with nausea. I've never been hungover before, but it's like a crash after drinking too much caffeine. Only worse. Much worse. I wrap myself in the silky smooth duvet.

"Hey, sleepyhead." The mocking tone makes me wince. "I bet you're feeling awful."

I raised my eyelids halfway only for them to shut again, but I got a glimpse of my unwanted guest.

"What do you want, Campbell?" I groan.

"Well, this is my room." My brain stumbles to process his words. However, the moment I do, I haul myself out of his bed.

I regret my rash movement as I lose my balance, but Campbell's fast reflexes save me just in time.

"Always say no to alcohol, Hazel Ellis." He chews off a grin, but I am in no condition for jokes.

He fluffs the stack of pillows on his bed before assisting me. I sigh in delight as my aching back leans against them. Even with my eyes closed, I can feel his stare.

"What do you want?" I question.

"You're a funny drunk, Ellie."

I open my left eye.

"What's that supposed to mean?"

He shrugs, taking a seat on the edge of the bed.

"I did not know you found me that attractive." He chuckles. "You confessed your love to me last night."

If I weren't about to vomit before, I might just do it now.

"You better be kidding." I glare but wince at the stabbing pain in my head.

"Only a little," He shrugs. "You insisted I bring you to my bedroom, but I'm certain you implied nothing more than sleeping."

He chuckles at the memory.

"You fell asleep on the kitchen counter."

The embarrassment leaves a detestable taste in my mouth. My cheeks burn.

"We didn't, you know." I place my hands over my flushed cheeks. "Hook up?"

He huffs at my question.

"My idea of a good time doesn't entail taking advantage of a drunk girl."

The atmosphere becomes tense.

"Well, thank you." I clear my throat. "For taking care of me."

His entire demeanor changes as he launches himself off the bed.

"I'll get you something for your headache." He mumbles

Chapter Eight

before strolling out of the room.

I can hear some of his frat brothers outside the door. Their jarring voices reignite my migraine.

I'm thankful to see Campbell return with a large glass of water and migraine pills. I down it, chugging the entire glass of water. He's trying his best not to laugh at my behavior.

"Time to get up." He chimes. "I'm taking you to get the greasiest breakfast we can find. Your hangover will thank me."

I furrow my brows.

"How am I supposed to walk out of here without all of your frat brothers seeing me?" I question. "They'll think the worst of me."

"They already know you're here," he replies. "I told them we didn't hook up, so you don't have to worry about that."

"And they just believed you?"

"I have no reason to lie." He replies.

He furrows his brows and chews on his bottom lip.

"What about Trent?"

"What about him?"

"Does he know I'm here?"

"Don't know, don't care." He disregards the question before extending his hand in front of me. "Let's sober you up."

I avoid every mirror as I follow him downstairs. The house is quiet. I pushed Campbell out the door before anyone could enter the room and spot me leaving with him. I cannot deal with rumors. Especially rumors involving Campbell and me.

We don't speak on our way to the diner, because of my enlarged head. The painkillers haven't kicked in yet.

I insisted on being seated as far away from onlookers as possible and he didn't argue. I lean my head on the table as

Vicariously

I wait for my coffee. The pain has eased, but a piping mug of caffeine is the cure. I thank the waitress as she places it on the table. I take a sip, ignoring the burning on my tongue. Campbell's muffled laughter piques my interest.

"What?"

"Nothing," He smiles from behind his cup. "I just find it funny that this is our first date."

I choke on the beverage.

"Excuse me?"

"Don't worry, Ellie." He grins. "Our second will be much better."

"This isn't a date." I insist.

He looks at me as if I'd told him the sky is green.

"Then what else do you call two people that have undeniable sexual chemistry getting to know each other?"

My shoulders tense. He's trying to rile me up and I will not give him the satisfaction.

"I'm seeing Trent." I state.

"Trent's boring," He scoffs. "I don't know how much clearer I need to make it. Besides, why should I sit around waiting for the day he makes a move?"

The entire situation was making me uncomfortable. Not because I don't like Campbell, but because I couldn't betray Nevaeh in that way. I would be an awful friend if I'd been with the guy she likes. I have to put my friendship with her before any guy.

Easier said than done. Here I am, sitting across from the guy I swore I would avoid.

"Trent is a nice guy." I insist.

"If he was such a nice guy, then why wasn't he the one taking care of you last night?"

Chapter Eight

As much as I wanted to argue with him, I knew he was right. Where was Trent last night? I could remember the events of last night, but I'm too afraid to question what happened. As the pounding in my head eases, I take a few more sips of my coffee, sighing in relief.

"I didn't mean to upset you." He replies.

I shake my head.

"You didn't." I replied.

"I only said it because I want you to know you only deserve the best, Hazel Ellis." My breath hitches. "You deserve a guy that's going to love and respect every inch of you."

He takes a last sip of his coffee.

"I'll let you realize in your own time I'm that guy."

* * *

I hate people, crowds, and social interaction. If there was some way that I could attend college without having to converse with one person, I would be the happiest girl alive. However, the miserable reality of life is that we never get what we want.

I focus as best as I can on the lecture, but Celeste has returned to her favorite pastime of piercing daggers into my skull. It's distracting, but I don't have the guts to tell her off. I feign taking notes - anything to keep me from glancing in her direction.

Someone takes a seat next to me. I sat in this row to avoid anyone near me. There are hundreds of seats, so why would this latecomer sit next to me?

"Othello." His face is a little too close to mine. "Is it awful I've never read it?"

Vicariously

"I'd drop dead from shock if you did." I grumble.

"Wow, you're even grumpier than usual." He notes. "What's got you so upset?"

"Right now, this annoying guy just won't seem to leave me alone." I side-eye him before jotting down more notes.

"He has a handsome smile, though." I scoff at his lame attempt at charming me with his teasing banter.

"I've seen better."

He goes quiet and I think he'd left until his lips are by my ear once more.

"Want to have our second date after this?"

"To have a second date, we'd had to have had a first." I scribble my notes.

His endless babbling is too distracting. I'm falling behind.

"We did," He whispers. "Don't you remember our fun time in the diner? I think we connected."

If I grip my pen any tighter, it would snap in half. I take deep breaths to calm my bubbling anger.

"Go find someone else to annoy. You might find someone that likes it."

"If I did that, I wouldn't be able to see your cute, angry face." He slouches in his seat. "The way your nose scrunches up is the most adorable thing ever."

I refrain from reaching up to examine my nose.

"If you don't mind, I'm in the middle of class." It was the only response I could think of.

"I don't mind at all." He grins.

He tosses his head back and closes his eyes.

"I'll just take a nap."

I thought he'd attempted another tasteless joke, but the gentle rise and fall of his chest shows he had fallen asleep.

Chapter Eight

I scoff at his disregard for learning and keep my focus on my notes, but my eyes can't help but flicker toward his sleeping form.

Once we're all dismissed, animated chatter pierces the silent surface. Campbell doesn't wake up. With a grin, I place my hand over his nose and squeeze shut. He wakes up with a gasp. I snicker as he glances around the room wide-eyed, as if deciphering where he is.

"Good one, Ellie." He chuckles as he stretches.

I gulp as the hem of his shirt rises, unveiling the slightest bit of skin. I shake the thoughts away and clutch my notebook against my chest.

"Ready for that date?" He beams.

"I remember saying no."

"Your mouth said no, but your eyes said another." He exudes confidence. "I saw the way you were just looking at me."

My entire body becomes flushed.

"It's okay, Ellie." He examines me from head to toe. "I like what I see too."

In a desperate attempt at hiding my crimson cheeks, I exit the lecture hall.

"Should we hold hands?" Campbell extends his hand and I slap it away.

"Hazel!" our heads whip as Trent waves, with Nevaeh shadowing him.

Campbell curses under his breath, but I pretend I didn't hear it.

"Hey!" I exclaim.

"I didn't know you were in this class." Trent states as he inspects Campbell.

"I'm not." Campbell states.

Vicariously

Nevaeh's eyes set on me, but I cast my head down.

"Well, we bumped into each other on the way to the cafe," Trent explains. "Want to grab a coffee?"

"Sure!" I replied before Campbell could open his mouth.

The trek to the cafe is filled with strained conversation, especially when he approaches the nearest booth and Campbell slides in next to me. None of us question his decision. It's like déjà vu and PTSD all in one. Our awful double date has struck once more.

I trailed my hands over my jeans and glanced out the large window. I jolt as someone's hand covers mine on my lap. Campbell's impish smirk widens as I glance at him wide-eyed.

"So Nevaeh was telling me more about what you were like in high school." Trent attempts to make conversation.

My heart skids.

What could she have said?

"You know how shy you were." She pouts. "It was so adorable. She had a crush on this guy and she'd always stutter every time he was near."

She giggles.

"His name was Jason, and she asked him to the prom." She continues to explain, despite my discomfort. "I was so upset when he never picked her up."

A cloud of tension hovers above us.

"Jason sounds like a douche." Campbell scoffs.

"So, who did you go to prom with?" Trent wonders.

"She didn't," Nevaeh says on my behalf. "I told her she could have joined me and my date."

"So, you never went to prom?"

I shook my head as my eyes prickled with tears before exhaling.

Chapter Eight

Here I go again, allowing her words to affect me.

"I need some air." I launch over to the booth behind me and march out the doors.

As I clench my hair in a tight fist, I ignore the curious glances from passersby.

I hate I can be affected by words that hold no value, but it seems I only get that way around Nevaeh.

I bite my lip so hard I taste blood, sensing a presence looming behind me before their shadow appears.

"Leave me alone, Campbell." I sigh.

"What she said was unnecessary." He comments.

"It's not like she was lying." I shrug. "I was a loser then, and I'm still one now."

"You're not a loser, Hazel." He grips my shoulder.

"I know you're trying to cheer me up, but I am not in the mood for pity." My sniffles become louder. "I just want to be left alone."

"I think that's the last thing you need."

"She made me look like a fool in front of Trent!" I exclaim. "And you."

"I don't care what she has to say. You're better than her in every way."

My bottom lip trembles as my brain overrides his words.

You will never be like her.

I cast my fingers through my hair before pushing his hand off my shoulder.

"Please, from now on, just leave me alone," I ordered. "You'll be doing yourself a favor."

"Hazel, you need to stop being her punching bag!" He exclaims.

My chest tightens as I make my hands into fists. I can feel

Vicariously

the sweat gliding down my body and his erratic breaths show he's as frustrated as I am.

"I am sick and tired of you telling me what to do!" I exclaim. "You flirt with me knowing I have no interest in you, and I am sick of this back and forth we have going on!"

Tears of frustration run down my cheeks.

"You're just so afraid of upsetting her you don't realize how selfish she is!"

"I am done listening to you insulting my best friend at every opportunity."

He scoffs.

"She may be your best friend, but you are not hers." He hisses. "Don't come crying to me when she decides she'd had enough of you!"

As if he had hit me in the gut, I retreated back. I inhale and clutch the bridge of my nose.

"I don't care!" I exclaim. "I'll be fine without you."

It's his turn to look sucker punched. His jaw clenched as he gnawed on his bottom lip.

"Have it your way, Hazel."

I cry before bolting as far away as possible, but I'm unable to outrun my humiliation.

Chapter Nine

Everything around me is snow white as a blanket of melancholy exudes across the campus. The winter has become callous, intent on stifling us with its icy breath. As I clutched my books to my chest, my boots crunched through the powered ice. I gaze at the black-blossomed sky as the weeping snowflakes tickle my face and seep into my pores. The cold runs through my veins. I shiver as goosebumps crawl down my spine. The trees shiver with me in the resenting wind, their naked branches furnished with snow. The twisted twigs extend like a hand, ready to catch the snowflakes.

Thanksgiving is approaching. I couldn't be more excited about escaping this place for a while and returning to a place of nostalgia. However, there's one more hockey game to attend tonight before leaving with Nevaeh. Trent had texted and invited us to the game. I agreed. It would be a welcoming distraction from the unwanted drama. I'd planned to avoid Campbell, but it wasn't as difficult as I believed. He's been avoiding me. Life moves on.

I sigh in relief the moment I step into the dorm building. The artificial heat defrosts my body. By the time I reach my dorm room, I regain the feeling in my fingers. Maisie glances at me over the frame of her glasses.

"Hey," she states. "Are you done packing?" She gestures towards the suitcase on my bed.

"Almost," I state with a grin. "I'll pack more when I get back from the game."

Her smile drops.

"No word from Campbell?"

"I don't want to talk about him."

The night I returned from the hockey rink and the unbearable moment in the cafe, I talked to Maisie. My face deceived me, even though I had planned to avoid the conversation. She'd made it known that my choice displeased her, but agreed to let it go. It's my choice, after all.

She shrugs in defeat as I make myself comfortable at my desk.

"I need to make a call." She announces before walking out into the hall.

I open my laptop and glance at the words I've written, unsure of whether I should keep it the way it is, or scrap it. I place my head in my hands and groan. Why can I never read over my work without hating every sentence?

The door closes behind me and I jump.

"That was a quick call." I mumble.

She doesn't respond.

I glance over my shoulder and hold back a gasp as Campbell stands in the entryway with his hands behind his back.

"What do you want?" I ask.

Chapter Nine

"To talk to you."

I scoff and launch out of my seat. I fold my arms across my chest and purse my lips.

"I'm not in the mood for any of your excuses right now."

His intense eye contact becomes unbearable. I look away.

"Are you not going to let me talk?" He seethes.

I continue to ignore him. I don't want to engage in a senseless argument.

"Fine." He spits. "Have it your way."

He twists the door handle and pulls it with force, but it doesn't open. He tries again. And again. I strut to the door and attempt to open it.

"It's locked." I say before banging on the door. "Open up!"

"I don't think so!" Maisie calls from the other side. "Neither of you is leaving this room until you sort out your issues, once and for all."

I groan and march to my bed. I sit on the edge as Campbell makes himself comfortable on Maisie's.

We sit knee-deep in silence. I let out a slow, controlled breath and wiggle my shoulders to loosen the tense muscles. The air is so brittle it might snap at any moment. Or I will. I don't know how long we sat in silence, our eyes unceremoniously darting around the room avoiding each other's gaze.

"I'm sorry." He pierces the silence. "I didn't mean any of the words I said."

I don't interrupt him.

"I just hate the way Nevaeh treats you." He says. "We've had our difficulties, but I will always cherish the friendship we've built. In such a short amount of time, you've become one of the best friends I have ever had."

Vicariously

I bite my lip to hold back an onslaught of tears. I curse at how I've overreacted and taken my frustrations with myself out on him.

"I am so sorry, too." I say.

He stands up and takes a seat beside me.

"I'd always been so envious of how effortless she was at everything. I'd spent so many years in her shadow. I have no idea how I could ever escape the darkness."

He reaches over and intertwines his hand with mine. He lifts me up and connects his phone to Maisie's speaker.

I Miss You by *Blink-182* serenades the room. I giggle as he draws me in for a dance. We sway to the soothing rhythm as the tense air fades into song.

"I wish you saw yourself in my eyes." He breathes. "You have so much going for you."

I gaze into his eyes.

"You're going to accomplish remarkable things, Hazel Ellis." He says. "The only one stopping you is yourself."

I blush and drop my head.

"You're an amazing friend." He chimes. "I hope I haven't lost the honor of calling you that."

As my eyes water, I lift my head. I shake my head.

"You haven't lost it."

His eyes sparkle like the stars in the night.

"I'm willing to be your friend for the time being." He replies. "But the moment Trent messes up, I'm swooping in."

I tried not to smile, but I couldn't hold it back. I move in his arms as we twirl around the room.

"I have to confess something." He whispers as if he's in fear someone is listening in. "I never went to prom either."

I draw back and analyze his face, as if looking for signs of

Chapter Nine

dishonesty.

"Are you making this up?"

He shakes his head.

"I wasn't as confident as I am now." His smile doesn't reach his eyes. "Things happened between a girl and me. It was a disaster. I couldn't face the attention and judgment."

His eyes scan my face.

"I wish you met me when I was in high school." He says. "I think you would have liked me."

Amusement glimmers in my eyes. My stomach flutters as the tense atmosphere fades. Campbell may be frustrating, but he's had my back at every opportunity. How could I give up a friendship like that? It's time I stop being stubborn and allow someone in.

"I like you now." I say. "Just the way you are."

* * *

I glance at Trent's jersey that I'd tossed to the side. I'd forgotten to give it back to him after he'd asked me to wear it. A part of me is hoping he'd ask again tonight, but I refuse to walk in with expectations.

The crowd is livelier than ever, but I've become accustomed to the noise. I maneuver through the stadium with Maisie at my side. I'd texted Trent to meet me outside the locker room, but it seemed all his teammates kept him company.

"Hey." He greets yet his smile doesn't reach his eyes.

I pause with his shirt clutched in a tight grip. I could feel all their eyes on me as anxiety with a sprinkle of paranoia washed over me.

Vicariously

"Is everything okay?" I take a cautious step forward.

His eyes flicker to his teammates as they watch our interaction as if it were an episode of *The Hills*. He scratches the back of his neck. I could have sworn I saw one of his teammates cover their mouth to mask their laughter — my stomach clenches.

"Hazel, I'm sorry. I didn't mean for it to happen this way." The dread weighs. "I only asked you out because I was hoping to get closer to Nevaeh."

"What are you talking about?"

"I had a thing for her the moment I saw her, and I was hoping if I got close to you, I could get close to her." He shifts his weight. "And when we kissed-"

"You kissed?"

He drops his head and nods.

An influx of emotions washes over me. Anger. Sadness. Embarrassment. Alone they are deadly, but they're too powerful to withstand together. Their eyes stare at me down while some don't even attempt to hold in their chuckles.

I should have known better.

Maisie is as shocked as I am.

"I'm glad you said that, Keller." A voice pipes out from behind the crowd.

Campbell steps forward until they're eye to eye. His self-assured grin and cocky demeanor silenced the onlookers.

"She was only using you to get with me." Campbell folds his arms across his chest. "You can't believe she'd get with you when she could have me."

For once, his arrogance is helpful. Their eyes widen in disbelief. Trent's jaw goes slack. Campbell looks over his shoulder and winks at me before turning to Trent.

Chapter Nine

"You couldn't satisfy her." He chuckles at his own words before approaching me.

He reaches for the shirt in my hand, tossing it over his shoulder.

"You won't be needing that anymore." He speaks before replacing it with another shirt.

I glance at the name embedded in the back. *Atwood.*

He's giving me his shirt.

He motions for me to put it on. I obey.

"Much better." He grins as he takes in my figure enveloped by his jersey.

His grin falls as he turns to his team.

"I suggest you all get warmed up for the game." His tone leaves no room for discussion as they trample into the locker room.

He's one to be feared in their team. Even the captain followed orders.

Trent remains frozen in place, infuriating Campbell.

"You have a problem, Keller?" He seethes.

Trent shakes out of his funk and squares his shoulders.

"Right now, my problem is you." He barks. "We're supposed to be brothers, a team. Yet you're taking her side over mine."

The veins in Campbell's neck protrude. I gulp in fear as his face reddens. He marches towards Trent and grips the collar of his shirt with a menacing grip.

"We may be teammates, but if it came down to me choosing her over some egotistical douchebag, I will choose her every time." He shoves Trent. "What you did was messed up and I'm not going to let it slide."

He stumbles into the trophy case behind them, but he grips the wall for balance just in time.

Vicariously

"We may be brothers, but mess with her or anyone else like that again. I won't hesitate to draw blood."

Trent rushes into the locker room with the rest of his teammates. Campbell approaches me. I smile.

"Thank you." I glance down at my shoes, noticing I'm still wearing his jersey. "You should take your jersey back."

I reach down to take it off. He places his hands over mine.

"Don't." He orders. He places a finger under my chin and lifts my head to gaze into his sparkling eyes. "My last name looks good on you."

I blush.

A coy smile rises on his face with a dramatic wink. He rushes inside the locker room to join his teammates. Maisie has her hands in front of her face, but it isn't enough to cover the enormous grin.

"Did that just happen?" She questions in shock as we venture to our seats.

"Ellie!" Campbell calls as we make our way to the crowd.

I spun around as he jogged to us. He brushes his fingers through his tousled hair.

"How many goals do I need to score for you to go on a date with me?"

His words left me tongue-tied. I wanted to remind him of our prior conversation, but something in my heart was telling me to fight the negativity. It's telling me to let all inhibitions go. Even if only for one night.

"Let's see how many you can score, then I'll let you know if I'm impressed." I reason.

His corner lip twitches.

"We have a deal, Ellie." He grins. "I'll dedicate them all to you."

Chapter Nine

I feel as if I've floated on a cloud to get to my seat. The roaring of the crowd is nothing but background noise. Without Maisie's help, I wouldn't have located our seats. The same front-row seats as the previous time.

It's astounding how much has changed since the last time we were here.

I glance around for Nevaeh, but she's missing. I reach for my phone to text her. She reads it but doesn't respond. I furrow my brows but shrug it off as the players step onto the ice. Campbell skates around the rink, slowing down when he reaches us. He winks with a brief wave before skating back to his team. Not missing the awkward interaction between him and Trent as Campbell picks up speed and rams his shoulder into him. Trent stumbles, but regains his balance in the nick of time.

I'm enthralled as the game begins. I blink as Campbell steals the puck from the opposing team. Our school cheers as he glides along the ice, the puck being tossed back and forth from player to player until it returns to Campbell. With natural skill, he slams the puck into the net.

The team surrounds him as they celebrate their goal. My eyes widen as Campbell skates towards the tempered glass and locks eyes with me.

For you. Campbell mouths before returning to position.

As much as I want to deny it. He had me swooning.

By the third period, he'd scored three out of four goals. Each one he'd cheer with his teammates before pointing toward me with his signature smirk. My ribs were bruised from the number of times Maisie nudged me with her elbow.

With thirty seconds left to spare, Campbell seals the deal with an eventual goal. I winced from the rowdy applause as

Vicariously

we connected eyes from across the ice. It doesn't falter until his teammates surround him as the adrenaline still burns in their veins.

I glance at Maisie over my shoulder. My eyes widen as Nevaeh stands behind her with folded arms and a tight-lipped frown. She shakes her head and scrunches her nose in disgust before bolting towards the exit.

"Nevaeh!" I call, but she ignores me.

I dash towards her. She shakes off my grip and makes a beeline for the locker room. I chase after her, begging for her to stop. Once more, I hold her shoulder. She squeaks to a stop and spins around. The vile look causes me to cringe.

"I can explain." I plead.

She scoffs.

"Explain that you're nothing but a backstabbing friend." She barks.

"It's not like that at all." I insist.

Her sneer reverberates down the lonely hallway.

"Admit it, you're jealous of Campbell and me. You just had to have him!"

I don't know what happened, but it was as if something had taken refuge in my body. As if something is controlling my actions. The words spew from my mouth.

"You know what? Maybe you're the jealous one!" My uncharacteristic defense shocks us both. "For the first time, a guy likes me instead of you. And if anyone is a backstabbing friend, it's you!"

She chuckles in disbelief.

"Do you think Campbell Atwood likes you?" She places her hand over her mouth to cover her giggles. "He only follows you around because you're unattainable. The moment he gets

Chapter Nine

what he wants from you, he's moving on."

Her words sting.

"Guys always liked me more, Hazel, because I was never an antisocial prude." She spits with an ungodly amount of fury.

I close my eyes to trap the tears. I exhale. Her words sucker-punched me in the gut. She knew my biggest fears and insecurities and used them as a weapon to destroy me. She'd taken my trust and poured gasoline over it.

"Campbell Atwood doesn't care about you. No one does."

She'd just tossed a lit match into the puddle.

She glances at the jersey adorning my body and motions toward it.

"He only gave you that jersey so everyone could laugh about you, thinking you had a chance."

"That's enough!" Maisie steps up with her fists clenched at her sides.

She moves in front of me, blocking me from the shell of my former best friend.

"You cannot handle not being the center of attention." Maisie pipes up. "I've kept my mouth shut for the sake of Hazel, but I am so sick of your superiority complex!"

My body is wracked with sobs as a crowd gathers.

"I am so done being your punching bag!" I burst into a fit of rage.

It's all directed toward Nevaeh. Her eyes widened at my spontaneous combustion.

"Our entire life you've made me out to be the loser, the undesirable friend. Someone to make you look better and, like an idiot, I let you do it. I am done putting you first when all you do is knock me down." The venom laced in my words even made me shiver.

Vicariously

Campbell is front and center. He rushes toward me and I place my hands in front of me. He halts. I remove his jersey and toss it at him before bolting toward the nearest exit. Voices call for me. It only makes me run faster.

My chest burns and I embrace the pain, but I won't stop until I'm in my dorm room. I gathered everything I'd packed, needing to get out of there as fast as possible.

I need to go home.

Chapter Ten

How I made it to my hometown in one piece is a miracle. I stayed inside my car because I'm not ready to face my family's endless questions. I would have to face it, but not this very moment. My phone has been buzzing the entire drive home. Maisie must be worried out of her mind. I reach for my phone to reassure her I'm fine, but a horde of texts from an unknown number litters my screen.

Ellie, are you okay?
Please answer me.
I need to know you're okay.
Why aren't you at your dorm?
Hazel Ellis, please.

There were dozens more that were the same. All from Campbell. I ignore his texts and open Maisie's. Before turning off my phone, I ignored her pleas to talk and typed a response to let her know I made it home safe.

My parents welcome me with warm embraces, but they

don't melt my icy heart. They comment on my puffy and bloodshot eyes. I assure them the drive was exhausting. Under the pretense of needing a nap, I escape their hovering and seek refuge in my bedroom. I collapse on my bed and place a pillow over my head. I scream into it until the air empties from my lungs. My head throbbed. Exhaustion anchored my eyelids before I succumbed to sleep.

***

Thanksgiving whisked by. The weekend moved as if someone had hit fast-forward. I spent most of Sunday packing my bags to leave first thing in the morning, despite my unwillingness to return to college. Even though we live in the same town, I haven't heard from Nevaeh. I know she's been avoiding me, but I haven't made much effort. I'd spoken to Maisie to wish her a happy *Thanksgiving,* but distanced myself from the outside world and focused on the short time I have with my family.

I glanced out my bedroom window, awed by how quickly the day went. Night had fallen. A curtain of blue haze is pulled back to reveal the velvet-dark sky littered with stars. The distant light called to me, and the fresh night breeze whistled as I opened my window. I close my eyes as it tousles my hair.

Ding!

The chime of my phone pulls me from my peaceful aura. My heart misses a beat.

Campbell.

I debate ignoring the call, but I accept.

"Hello?" I lift the phone to my ear.

Chapter Ten

"You've been avoiding my texts." I bite my lip.

"Sorry." I replied.

He snorts.

"You know, you never told me if I impressed you." I could hear the smirk in his voice.

I bite my lip. However, a smile escapes.

"How about I tell you tomorrow?"

"Or you could tell me right now." He states. "I think I can survive the climb into your window."

My brows furrow.

How could he know that?

"Look down, Ellie." I drop my phone as I notice a figure in my driveway.

The artificial brightness of the street lamp shines on his face.

"What are you doing here?"

"I told you, you never gave me an answer." Even in the distance, I could see his smug grin. "I'm coming up."

"My parents are sleeping."

"I'll be stealthy." He hangs up.

I watch, opening my mouth, as he jogs toward my window. He hauls himself into a nearby tree, jumping from branch to branch like *Tarzan*. I wince every time he does. What would happen if the star hockey player broke his leg attempting to climb through my window? He sticks his head through my window and smiles widely. I move back to allow him space. He sticks one leg through but trips as he hauls the other leg inside before crashing with a thud. He glances at me wide-eyed. I could hear the approaching footsteps. I ushered him behind my door.

"Hazel," my mother knocks. "Everything okay?"

Vicariously

I open the door. Campbell pokes me in the side. I swat his hand away. He bites his lip.

"I dropped one of my books." I muster my best pout. "Sorry, I didn't mean to wake you."

"It's okay, but you should get some rest." She orders with affection. "You have a long drive tomorrow."

"I will." I state before closing the door and locking it behind me.

I sigh in relief at not being caught before punching him in the shoulder.

"Ow." He glares as he rubs the painful spot.

"How did you find out where I live?"

"Maisie."

I should have known.

He walks by me and looks around my room, approaching my bookcase and inspecting my selection of books. He picks a random book and examines the front cover.

"I was supposed to read this last year." He notes.

I peer over his shoulder as he holds my tattered copy of Catcher in the Rye.

"Is it any good?"

"It's one of my favorites."

"Why?"

I plan a million responses in my head, but each is as miserable as the other.

"Holden Caulfield is one of the most relatable characters I've ever read." I shrug. "It's as if his every thought or feeling has been my own. As if we're the same person in different universes."

He doesn't take his gaze off the book. He flips through the pages before holding it to his chest.

Chapter Ten

"Hope you don't mind me borrowing it."

I snort.

"You're going to read it?" I question in disbelief.

He locks his eyes with mine. There's no trace of insincerity.

"If it gives me a glimpse into the mysterious mind of Hazel Ellis, I'd read this entire bookshelf just to get to know more about you."

I bow my head to hide the rosiness of my cheeks. We don't speak as he dawdles around my room as if trying to memorize every inch. I watch as he picks up a framed photograph of Nevaeh and me at our high school graduation.

"I heard what Nevaeh said." My intestines twist. "I hope you know what she said isn't true."

My shoulders tense, wishing he hadn't brought this up.

"I'm not using you, Hazel." I felt him in front of me, but I couldn't look at him.

I'm too ashamed.

"I like you. I've liked you since the moment I saw you in that bookstore." He breathes out.

He grips my chin in his hand, forcing me to look into his glossy eyes.

"I need to confess something." He whispers. "When we met in the bookstore, it wasn't the first time I saw you."

I gulp at his words.

Is this the part in the horror movie where he confesses to having stalked me before kidnapping me?

"It was near the end of my freshman year. It was one of our final games. I was sitting on the bench waiting to get onto the ice and I distracted myself by scoping the crowd when my eyes landed on this girl."

The corners of his lip raise at the memory.

Vicariously

"While everyone else was watching the game as if it was the most thrilling thing they'd ever seen. This girl was sitting among them reading a book." He chuckles. "I'd never witnessed it before."

My stomach clenches.

"You could imagine my surprise when months later I walked past the bookstore and found that very girl inside. At first, I thought it was an illusion, but I could recognize that pensive face from a mile away. I was in awe of how you could drown everything out and focus on reading. You did the same thing in the bookstore."

He twirls a strand of my hair around my finger.

"It was as if some invisible force was pushing us together. I don't know what it was and I don't care, because I know walking through that door was the greatest decision I had ever made in my entire life. I had to know you, Hazel Ellis."

I couldn't look away, as if our eyes were molded into one. Campbell saw me all those years ago.

How is that even possible?

I remember that day. Nevaeh had pleaded for me to attend. We were on a campus tour and she had insisted we watch a game before going home. I took a book with me to ease the boredom.

I think back to the story he'd spoken about in the library, about the girl he'd wanted to know. *It was me all along.*

My face cracks.

Warmth blossoms in my chest as he moves closer. We press our lips together. As we have our first kiss, sparks fly - as cliche and unoriginal as it may seem. The smell of his cologne and the aromatic scent of rosemary is dizzying. Butterflies swarm in my stomach. Warmth consumes me as I lean further

Chapter Ten

into the kiss, his lips soft against mine. Our heavy breathing occupies the room as our bodies press against each other. My knees became weak as I could taste our shared breath and feel the synchronized thudding of our heartbeat. I grip his neck as he pulls me closer. As his hands travel South, I pull away. Our deep breaths mix.

"I'm sorry." He's out of breath. "I shouldn't have gotten so carried away."

I glance up at him from under my lashes with a smug grin.

"I never said I didn't like it," I tease. "I'm just not ready for that."

He grips my head between his hands and places a chaste kiss on my lips.

"I'll wait however long you want, Hazel Ellis." My heart swells at his words.

I glance at the clock on my bedside table. I stifle a yawn as it's nearing midnight.

"Will you stay with me?" I don't know where the confidence came from, but the desire to be in his arms for a while longer overrules any insecurities.

"I was hoping you'd ask."

He dawdles around my room, glancing at the outrageous amounts of photographs on my wall. He glances at one of my parents holding me as a toddler on the beach.

Our first family vacation.

"It was just after they adopted me." I confess.

He glances at me, unsure of what to say next.

"I was two years old when I got adopted by them." I explain. "They tried so hard to have children before they decided to adopt. My dad would always tell me the moment they saw me, they just knew."

I beam with pride as I trace my hands over the frame.

"What happened to your biological parents?" He questions, afraid he might have offended me.

"According to the adoption agency, they weren't the best of people. They weren't fit to take care of a child."

His face falls as he gazes at the picture.

"Sounds like someone I know." He mumbled under his breath, as if he didn't want me to hear it.

I wanted to question him about it, but I figure he'll talk when he's ready. I watch as he places the photograph in its place before glancing at a picture of my fifth birthday party with Nevaeh at my side. We grin at the camera as best as we can with missing teeth, cake splattered all over our faces.

"She wasn't always so bad," I explained to him. "She would always be my shoulder to cry on when I needed it. There was never a time that I would have to endure a hard time alone."

"What changed?" He implores.

"High school, I guess." I shrug. "We started developing different interests. I was into writing and she was into cheer, but I don't think either of us wanted to lose the comfort of a long-term friendship."

He nods his head before placing it back.

"I don't know about you, but I'm exhausted."

With a gleeful chuckle, I launch onto my side of the bed and snuggle under the sheets. I turn my back to him as he slides in next to me. I can sense the distance between us. I glance over my shoulder as he places his hands on his chest. He glances over as he feels my gaze. I blush once I notice his bare chest is on display. He raises his brow with a cheeky grin. I turn back around to hide my scorched cheeks. The room is silent. I fear he might hear my erratic heartbeat.

Chapter Ten

"You can move closer." I don't hear my voice until I have said the words.

What has gotten into me?

His chuckles make my stomach clench as the rattling sheets alert me. I become enveloped by warmth as his chest presses against my back. His arm wraps around my waist, locking me against him. My cheeks feel as if they're going to crack from my wide grin, shivering as his warm breath brushes against my neck. I can feel the rise and fall of his chest.

It's like a lullaby.

My eyelids flutter as he rubs gentle circles against my clothed waist with his thumb. I grin once more before I feel his soft lips press against the back of my head. He reaches over and draws his lips against my ear.

"Goodnight, Hazel Ellis." He whispers.

I feel myself fading as pure bliss washes over me. I'd never felt more safe or comfortable than at this moment.

"Goodnight, Campbell." I yawn before I close my eyes, as I'm lulled to sleep by the rhythmic beating of his heart.

* * *

Rough bangs against my bedroom door awaken me. Warm hands fall from my waist as I jolt up in shock. I glance over my shoulder at Campbell's angelic face. I smile, but more pounds make my heartbeat pick up.

"Hazel, are you awake?" My mother calls out.

"I am now," I call back as she twists the handle.

I couldn't be more thankful that I'd locked it.

"I'm getting ready!" I called out.

Vicariously

Campbell groans at the disturbance. I place my hand over his mouth. His eyes open as he crosses them to glance at my hand. I placed my finger over my mouth, motioning for him to be quiet.

"Hurry," my mother yells. "I made breakfast."

I strain my ears waiting for her footsteps to die out before I remove my hand from his face.

"I didn't know you were this kinky Hazel Ellis." He pokes fun.

I rolled my eyes and hit him with a nearby pillow.

"You need to get up before my parents find you." I reprimand.

He wraps his arm around my waist and drags me back down until we're at eye level. I giggle as his fingers tickle my sides.

"You know, I'm still waiting for an answer." He beams.

I pretended to be in deep thought, as if I couldn't decide on an answer.

"Did I do enough to impress you?" He implores.

"I guess you did." I sigh.

He scoffs.

"I scored three out of four." He argues.

"I would have been more impressed if you scored four." I giggle as I delight in tormenting him.

"You are something, Ellie." He rolls his eyes.

We're silent as he reaches for his shirt and slides it on. Once he's dressed, he walks towards my window and slides it open. He places one foot outside before looking at me.

"I'll see you later." He grins.

As he ducks. I pipe up.

"Yes," I replied. He draws his head back inside with a raised brow. "You impressed me."

Chapter Ten

His arrogant grin is so broad that his dimples protrude more than usual.

"It will be the greatest date ever. You have my word." He delivers a farewell wink before hoisting himself out of my window.

My stomach feels as if there's a nest of hornets inside and my face is almost split in half from the wide smile. My cheekbones burn, but I couldn't stop. I'd been fighting my attraction to him for too long, and I don't have the energy to keep pretending anymore.

* * *

I'd dreaded returning to college, dreaded facing Nevaeh and Trent and everyone else that witnessed my public humiliation, but it's as if Campbell's visit has ignited a new sense of confidence within me. A newfound positivity. It's refreshing and beyond exciting. I'd never had an opportunity for a romantic relationship, always believing I repulsed the opposite sex as if I'd had a metaphorical *kick-me* sign attached to my back. I'd always lived in Nevaeh's shadow, but I've stepped out of it. I thought back on her harsh words. The stabbing pain in my heart returned. She'd revealed how she felt about me and our friendship. I'd been nothing but her back-burner friend. *The DUFF.* I had convinced myself that I was the problem, but perhaps it had been her all along.

Yet the insecurity is still eating away at me.

I glance at myself in the full-length mirror as I scope my appearance from head to toe. What does Campbell see in me? What am I not seeing?

Vicariously

My phone vibrates in my back pocket.

As if he could hear my thoughts, his text causes my heart to soar. It's as if he knew the words I wanted to hear.

Can't wait to see your beautiful smile again, Hazel Ellis.

Chapter Eleven

The winter breeze is an icy serenade as the mellow sun magnifies the purity of the heaven-given snow. The snow-covered trees show their strength as the branches remain intact, poised to show their grace. I lift my head into the gentle breeze as the frozen air is like lace on my skin.

I enter the cafe in desperate need of something to warm me up. Nothing a hot chocolate cannot solve.

As the heat warms my fingers, I grab the ceramic mug in my hands. The cocoa touches my taste buds as I take a tentative sip. The sugar wakes me up and I moan in delight.

I open my copy of *Jane Eyre* to the bookmark and dive into the story, flying through my assigned reading. The world around me fades like static. I'd dived into two chapters before awoken by a tapping on my shoulder. I jump out of my skin.

"Sorry," the waitress apologizes. "I just wanted to know if you want another drink?"

Vicariously

I catch my breath.

"Yes, please." I breathe out.

She nods and takes my mug.

I glance around the diner, halting as my eyes befall something I had never imagined possible. Nevaeh is sitting on the other side of the diner with a group of girls I'd become all too familiar with. She's laughing along with them. *With Celeste*. The scene is like a bad soap opera - you want to look away yet can't. Another large group hordes into the diner, disrupting the peaceful ambiance. I recognize them as the hockey team. They join the group of giggling girls. There are so many they occupy two booths. My stomach drops as Campbell is one of the last to enter. I lean back in the booth and bring my book up to my face, hoping it would hide me away. I couldn't help but take a few curious peeks over the top.

As the waitress brings me another cup, I thank her. The steam is dancing from above. I take a cautious sip, burning my upper lip. As I reach for a napkin, I groan. I hadn't noticed Campbell standing at my table with a wide grin.

"Ellie," He greets me as he leans down to place a kiss on my cheek. "I was hoping to see you today." He whispers in my ear.

I couldn't repress a shiver. I couldn't even fathom a response. My lack of conversation doesn't seem to bother him as he slides into the booth across from me. I take a cautious sip of my hot chocolate to avoid any conversation. He leans forward against the table, forcing us to make eye contact.

"Are you busy tonight?"

I choke on my drink.

"Why?"

"For our date, of course."

I tap my nails against the table. My entire body stiffens. I

Chapter Eleven

glance in the group's direction. I'm surprised to find some of them are already looking our way.

Including Nevaeh.

I must have been staring for too long, because Campbell follows my gaze.

"Ignore them." He reaches over for my hand. "I have something planned for tonight."

I blush as he interlocks our fingers.

"I never said yes." I tease, and he rolls his eyes.

"We both know you weren't planning to say no."

"Cocky much?"

"Not entirely. I just know your curiosity will win."

I bite my lip. He's right. I have to know what he has planned.

"I'd kiss you goodbye, but I'll leave that for our date." He winks before hauling himself out of his seat to return his friends.

I cover my face with my hair to hide my blush, as well as the piercing daggers delivered in my direction. I hide a smile behind my mug.

As much as I wanted to deny it, I couldn't wait for tonight.

* * *

I'm walking into this date inexperienced and unsure of what to expect. I don't know the protocol. In a situation like this, I would turn to Nevaeh for advice. Unfortunately, that's no longer an option. Maisie tried to be as helpful as possible, but she has as much knowledge about dating as me.

It doesn't help that the dates with Trent were disasters.

I'm out of my comfort zone.

Vicariously

My stomach sinks as there is a knock on the door. I take a deep breath as I strut toward it. I expected to find Campbell standing with his characteristic smug grin, but no one was in the hallway. My brows furrow as I glance from left to right, as if I'm waiting for him to pop out of the shadows and yell in surprise.

A yellow *post-it* on the door captures my attention from the corner of my eye. The messy handwriting is almost ineligible, but I read it.

Meet me where it all began.

My brain relapsed until the metaphorical light bulb flipped on.

The bookstore.

With a surge of elation, I make haste for the bookstore. It's not too far of a distance, but it could have been because of my quickened movements. I burst through the doors with the widest of grins.

This time it's not only because of the books.

I scope the store and find Campbell already smirking at me. He stood in the fiction section with his hands tucked into his pockets. I approach him with raised brows.

"You look beautiful, Ellie." He states before leaning down for another chaste kiss.

This one lingers. It leaves me breathless.

"What are we doing here?" I question.

"You love books, don't you?" He beams.

I can only nod.

"Well, since you love them, I thought I should give it a chance."

My brows furrow.

"Besides, I can't look at a book anymore without thinking

Chapter Eleven

about you."

My heart palpitates.

"It's also when you're the most beautiful - at your happiest."
My heart just combusted.

My cheeks burn from the unbreakable grin. I pinch myself in disbelief that this moment could be real.

"How about we look around?" He suggests. "We each pick a book with a line for the other to read?"

I can only muster a nod, still in complete awe that this is happening. I keep waiting for myself to wake up.

Or for this to be a sadistic joke.

My pessimistic thoughts take over again. Appearing at the most inconvenient of times. I shake it off and scope the vast amount of literature. I trail my fingers across the spines as I bite my lip.

How am I supposed to choose?

My eyes fall on *To Kill A Mockingbird*. I flicked through the pages.

"Find anything?" Campbell's warm breath tickles my neck.

"Yes." I maintain my composure.

He hid the book behind his back. I notice him repressing a grin. I roll my eyes and hand him the book, pointing out the line.

"People generally see what they look for and hear what they listen for." He reads aloud.

I shrug.

"I don't know. It always resonated with me." I explain.

The back of my neck burns. I couldn't maintain eye contact. He lifts my head with a wide grin before extending his book of choice out to me. I scoff.

"You're kidding," I raise a brow. *"The Cat in the Hat?"*

Vicariously

I'm in utter disbelief. He feigns offense.

"That's a classic!" He exclaims. "Used to read it every night before I went to bed."

I roll my eyes.

"Just open it to page five."

I scroll to page five to find a piece of paper wedged in the spine. His familiar messy scrawl appears. I dropped the book as I clutched the note in my hand.

Let's write our own love story.

I gaze at him. For the first time since I've met him - Campbell Atwood seems flustered. He bounces on the heels of his feet, awaiting an answer.

"When Trent messed up, I made a promise to myself that I would never give another guy the chance to hurt you again. So what do you say, Ellie?" He questions. "Can I call you my girl?"

I waited for the punchline. Waited for someone to appear from behind the shelves filming. For a crowd to gather around, laughing and mocking me for thinking someone like Campbell Atwood would ask me out. It never happened.

"Yes." I replied.

I felt ridiculous until his smile became as wide as mine.

"So, can I kiss you now?"

I don't reply. I grip the back of his neck and attach our lips. I shiver as he tucks my hair behind my ear. He gripped my head in his hands as he pulled away. My legs give way as he gazes into my eyes, unable to comprehend that the look is for me. I'd never imagined I could have someone look at me the way he is right now.

"I was nervous you were going to say no." He confesses. "I'm happy the next time you wear my jersey, you'll be mine."

Chapter Eleven

My breath hitches. His mischievous grin softens as he brushes his thumb against my cheek.

"How about we finish the rest of our date?"

"There's more?"

He shrugs.

"I'm starving." He grins before grabbing my hand.

He drags me out of the store as I glance down at our interlocked hands with the widest of grins. Campbell insisted on ordering takeout, claiming we needed to enjoy our meal with a better view. I didn't question him.

We sat in his truck as the gentle lullaby of *Blink-182* paraded through the speakers. I hum along to the melody as I glance out the window at the deep forest. The trees look as if they're moving at an inhuman speed.

The sky was becoming a cauldron of black as the night expanded like angel wings. I glance forward as the headlights lead us into the new dawn night.

He pulled into the parking lot of a deserted park. The glowing yellow-white of the moon loomed over the features as it became surrounded by an ethereal glow.

I glance at the river ahead as we step out of his truck. I watch in awe as it seeps and slithers, jumping for joy over the timeworn rocks. The reflection of the moon against the current captures my attention.

"Beautiful, right?" Campbell grins, sitting in the car's trunk.

I joined him, unable to keep my eyes off the view. We eat our food as the ripples of the water glide over the rocks. The crickets chirp. Everything is perfect.

"How's the novel coming along?" Campbell makes small talk.

"Great." I grin.

Vicariously

"Will I ever get to read it?"

"No." I replied.

"Why not?"

"I don't let anyone read my work." I shrug.

"Is there a specific reason?"

I sigh as I watch the ghostly reflection of the moon shimmering in the water.

"I've never been confident in much, especially with my writing," I admit. "I'd lost hope of success a long time ago."

He slides closer to me and wraps his arm around my neck, drawing my head onto his shoulder. The butterflies in my stomach are rampant as he places a gentle kiss on the top of my head.

"I wish you could see yourself through my eyes." He admits. "You'd never doubt yourself again."

I wrap my arms around his waist in a loving embrace as we revel in each other's presence.

"Maybe one day you can write a book about me." He quips.

I giggle and glance up at him through my lashes.

"Who says I haven't already started?"

I could have sworn I felt his heart skip a beat before his supple lips caressed mine. My stomach clenches as he litters my neck with kisses. The ambivalence of emotions makes my head rush. The mix of nerves and pleasure is all too consuming. My stomach flutters as his lips brush against mine. It's as if he's kissing away every doubt in my mind. Every insecurity. He pulls back and places his forehead against mine.

"You are remarkable, Hazel Ellis." I'm consumed by his ocean eyes.

His eyes flicker around. The faintest of smiles appears.

"Maybe this could be our place." He pipes up.

Chapter Eleven

"I thought the bookstore was our place." He chuckles.

"There's no rule stating we can't have more than one place."

He reaches over for my hand. He intertwined our fingers together as we relished in the momentary tranquility before returning to the disquieting rush of college.

* * *

Snowflakes flutter down from the sky with grace and elegance and land on the Earth. I admire the blanket of snow along the ground spreading like an angel's wings. I gaze at the bench I would sit on to read, to find a cushion of snow covering it.

The campus looks like a winter wonderland, as if the winter goddess has placed her ever-loving hand over us and sprinkled her magical dust. The winter leaves are soggy and weighed down by the snow, falling to the ground with a farewell kiss to the fall.

Some may think I'm foolish, but I've always felt that winter has a distinct scent. Every inhale smells like menthol, as if the pure air washes out all the harmful toxins of seasons past. The damp pine trees make the air smell fresh. I ignore the cold air stinging my face and reach down for a handful of snow. Even through my gloves, my fingertips tingle from the frost-bitten snow.

A frozen ball of ice splatters against my face. My ear numbs from the cold. I glance around in search of the culprit, but there's no one in sight. I gaze up at the ashen clouds sailing above in a wind-charged, effervescent sea.

Another snowball collides, this time against my shoulder.

I duck behind the bench and monitor my surroundings in

Vicariously

search of the culprit. I screech as arms wrap around my waist, hoisting me from the ground before I'm tackled into the ice.

"You should have seen your face." Campbell bellows as he collapses beside me.

He clutches his stomach unbothered by the frozen particles seeping through his clothing. I shiver as the cold invades my veins. I reach over and slap him on the chest with a frown.

"You're so mean!" I pout as I sit upright.

He launches up and grips my waist once more, yanking me back on the cold ice as he tickles my sides. My giggles echo with the breeze as I attempt to wriggle from his hold, but his grip is too strong.

"S-stop!" I say as the giggling intensifies.

My abdomen aches from the uncontrollable laughter. Seeking pity on me, his tickles die down, but he doesn't release his hold on me.

"You don't like the cold." He says.

"Not all of us spend every single day in freezing temperatures, Campbell," I reply.

He reaches his gloved hand to my cheek and brushes the snow out of my hair and face. My reindeer red nose feels as if it is about to fall off at any moment. However, as he reaches over to place a kiss on the tip of my nose, my entire body warms up.

The cold seems bearable now.

"If you hate the cold so much, why are you out here?"

I shrug.

"Looking for inspiration." He stands up and dusts the ice off his pants before extending his hands out to me.

I grab onto his hands as he lifts me into his arms. He wraps them around me, protecting me from the brutal breeze.

Chapter Eleven

"You're overthinking again." He says, gazing into my eyes. "Let's have some fun. You can go back to worrying later."

"What do you have in mind?" His eyes sparkle with mischief as he raises his left brow. "We have to make a snowman, it's the rules."

I gaze at him.

"Is that so?"

He nods.

"It's a good thing I have everything we need."

I hadn't noticed the bag at his feet. I glance inside to find everything we need to decorate a snowman.

"Why would you carry this around?"

"I was coming to find you so we could build one together. I just saw an opportunity to splatter you with a few snowballs, and I couldn't resist." He says.

I roll my eyes.

"I guess we're making a snowman." He tosses his hands into the air and cheers.

We got to work, but it has been so long since I built a snowman. My arms ached from the exertion, but I power through intent on making this snowman with Campbell. He seemed so carefree, as his delighted grin never wavered. During the shoveling of snow, I would get distracted and take a moment to appreciate the childlike glee on his face. He's as determined to finish this snowman as he is on the ice. My fingers felt like icicles as my gloves became soaked in melted ice, but I didn't care. I was having way too much fun.

Once we were done, we took a step back to gaze at the atrocity before us. It had already begun to collapse and disfigure. Its head lulled to the side before it landed on the ground with a *splat.*

Vicariously

I cupped my hands over my mouth. Our widened eyes gazed at each other before we burst into a fit of laughter. Our unrestrained giggles echoed through the silent campus as my eyes watered.

How did we mess this up?

Our laughter dies down as the calmative wind glides past us. He wraps his arms around me from behind and places his chin on the top of my head. Neither of us speaks as we watch our creation melt away, piece by piece.

"I used to build a snowman every year with my mom on her birthday." He says. His voice is reserved, as if he's afraid that talking about this could ruin the mood.

I place my hands over his in silent comfort, willing him to continue. He releases a shaky breath.

"She would have liked you." He says, drawing me closer to his chest. "Things between her and my dad were never the best growing up. She always made me promise that if I ever found something that seemed real, I should never give it up."

I smile at his words as I bring a hand to my lips for a gentle kiss. My silent reassurance.

"I wish I could have met her." I say. "I know she'd be proud of you."

"She'd have liked you as much as I do."

The peaceful silence is soothing. The only thing to be heard is the rustling wind through the pin-drop silence. Nothing but a melodious symphony. Despite the bitter cold, the silence holds warmth. Comfort.

"She had this snow globe of a miniature hockey player surrounded by snow. She'd leave it next to her bedside, but before every one of my games, she'd shake it and tell me it's for good luck." I can feel his smile on my head. "She'd always

Chapter Eleven

say as long as the snow is falling inside, I could never lose."

I turn in his arms to gaze into his tear-soaked eyes. He turns his head to hide it. I reach for his jaw and draw his face near mine.

"It's okay to miss her." I whisper. "I would never judge you for having feelings."

His face reddens as he hides it in the crook of my neck. I twirl the hairs on the back of his neck around my fingers. His shoulders rattle until he succumbs to the peacefulness. He pulls away as I soothe the fallen tears from his reddened eyes.

"Thank you for making me feel safe enough to be vulnerable in front of you." My heart leaps with joy. I brush my thumb over the ridges of his cheeks.

"I will always be here for you."

Chapter Twelve

As if it were an unspoken rule, the frat is hosting another party to prepare for tomorrow's away game. When Campbell mentioned it, I found it strange to host a party before a game. I couldn't imagine playing with a raging hangover, but it's a pregame ritual. However, I know it's only an excuse to get wasted and have random hookups.

The good old college life.

I shove past the horde of people, gasping as a figure rams into my shoulder. I rubbed the injured spot as Celeste towered over me, her eyes as fiery as the pits of hell. Her squad of minions is standing behind her - with a recent addition. Nevaeh.

I gulp as I'm surrounded.

"Who keeps inviting you to these things?" Celeste demands with her hands on her hips.

I open my mouth to speak, but my tongue dries out. My face feels flushed as my hands shake at my sides.

"I do." Campbell slides in front of me, blocking me from

Chapter Twelve

their hateful scrutiny.

He glances at me over his shoulder as if he's scoping the damage inflicted. He turns back to them. I can see his muscles tense from underneath his shirt.

"Campbell," Celeste scoffs. "You're going to move on from me with her." She spits as if I'm some ogre.

"It was about time I upgraded." I found it difficult to hide a giggle at her slack-jawed expression.

She looked ridiculous.

I make eye contact with Nevaeh. Any sense of warmth has faded from her eyes. Her icy gaze gives me chills.

"Now, if you'll excuse us - we're going to find some more interesting people to hang out with." He sneers before gripping my hand.

He ushers me through and upstairs. I don't question him until we're inside a cluttered bedroom. He closes the door behind us. I analyze the mess.

"I never scoped your room out the last time I was here."

"You had your reasons," He grins. "I talked my way out of having to share."

"How did you do that?"

"It helps to be one of the best on the team."

I snort at his lack of modesty. I sit on the edge of his bed, elated to be away from the numbing music and judgmental stares. He leans against the door with his arms folded across his chest. I attempt to ignore his smirk. It only gets wider.

"What?" I question.

He chuckles before taking a confident strut forward.

"Just admiring how beautiful you are." I scratch my arm and cover my face with my hair.

His footsteps come closer until his tattered *Converse* appears.

Vicariously

He crouches in front of me and grips my head in his hands. He gazes into my eyes.

"Why do you do that?"

"Do what?"

"Always hide away every time I compliment you."

I shrug.

"I'm not used to it."

"Well, you need to because infinite compliments are coming your way." He grins. "Because you seem to get more beautiful every second that ticks by."

My heartbeat picks up speed. If my heart continues palpitating, he's going to kill me with compliments. A strand of his hair casts over his eyes. I brush my fingers through his locks before gripping the back of his neck for a kiss. He meets me halfway as he reciprocates. My entire body tingles as he hovers over me. My head meets with the soft cotton sheets. His arms wrapping around me feels forbidden. He pulls away and gazes into my eyes before claiming my mouth again. This time, his kisses are hungry and intense. I'd lost all sense of control. By the time I realized my fingers, they'd already tugged on the hem of his shirt. He pulls away.

My heart dropped into my stomach as he rejected my advances.

The insecurity takes over my mind again.

"I want to take this further," He states as if he'd sensed my inner turmoil. "I don't want our first time to be in a frat house with an intoxicated crowd downstairs."

His explanation makes my heart feel lighter. He wanted this to be as perfect as I did. His gaze is far away, like he's in deep thought. He leaned down and placed a quick peck on my lips before hoisting himself off the bed.

Chapter Twelve

"Wait here," He pleads. "I'll be right back."

He rushes out of the room. I puff out my chest before releasing a deep exhale as I gaze at the snow-white ceiling. I wasn't sure how long he was gone, but three songs had played downstairs before he returned. His dimples are on full display. Like a child on Christmas morning, he extends his hand. I placed my hand on his before he hoisted me into his arms.

He remains silent as he leads me downstairs, through the drunken crowd, and out of the frat house towards his truck. He opens the door for me and rushes to his side. His grin never faltered. I gaze out the window at the familiar path. A nostalgic sense of déjà vu infiltrates my mind.

I can't believe three weeks have passed since we were last here.

Once the car is motionless, I bolt out the door and rush towards the river. The weather had changed since our last visit.

It has frozen over. The soothing flow of the water has turned to ice.

I hear Campbell's footsteps before his arms wrap around my waist. He pulls me against his chest, surrounding me with his natural warmth.

"What are we doing here?" He chuckles at my impatience.

"This is our spot, remember?"

I hum as his grip tightens. He leans down to my ear.

"I have a surprise." Without releasing me from his hold, I chuckle as we wobble towards his truck.

He kisses the back of my head before approaching the trunk. He lifts it to reveal a comfy-looking bed made of a thick mattress covered in silk sheets. I swoon at the rose petals scattered around.

It's so cheesy, but it makes my heart pound. He bites his lip with a frown.

"Is it too much?" He questions. "I don't want to get ahead of myself. I'd be more than happy to spend the night just holding you. I just wanted an escape from all the noise."

His worried babble is just too cute. I had never seen him in this light. His openness is admirable.

"It's perfect." I breathe as the aching pit in my stomach makes me second-guess my words.

"I've messed this up, haven't I?" He must have picked up on my distress.

As much as I didn't want to confess the truth, I couldn't have him thinking my change of mood was because of him.

"You did nothing wrong," I assured him. "This is all me."

His eyes softened with concern. He doesn't speak as he waits for me to elaborate.

"I'm just scared that this will be the moment you realize you've made a mistake." I hadn't realized I'd started crying until a warm tear rushed down my cheek.

He leaps towards me with inhuman speed as he attempts to wipe away my tears, but more keep falling. He pulls me into his chest, wrapping an arm around my waist, and the other combs my hair with his fingers. I sob into his chest. He doesn't stop me. He continues to let me soak his shirt until I'm drained.

I risk a peek into his eyes. I'm taken aback by his passionate gaze. It's as if I had taken the stars out of the sky and stored them in my eyes.

For the first time in my life, I felt beautiful. Worthy.

I lean up and place a kiss against his jaw. Even on my tiptoes, I couldn't reach his lips. He grabs my waist and pulls me closer, leaning his head down. Time stopped in a collision of senses

Chapter Twelve

as our lips connected. My knees give in. If it weren't for his firm grip on my waist, I would be a mere puddle on the floor. I break our kiss and bite my bottom lip as it tingles. I could still taste his lips on mine.

A newfound sense of confidence floods my veins as I climb through his trunk. I motion for him to join me. He hesitates before hoisting himself inside. He draws nearer. I close my eyes as our lips reunite. I trail my fingers under his shirt, his smooth skin radiating heat. Every negative thought melts away. Every insecurity is nonexistent. I slither my hands up his chest and toss his shirt.

"Are you sure you want to do this?"

I gaze into his intoxicating eyes.

"Yes," I replied. "I do."

I waste no time in attaching our lips again. Every inch of him consumes me like a drug.

He's a deadly narcotic and I'm an addict.

He trails his hands along every fraction of my body, igniting an unfamiliar thrill, heightening every sense. My skin scorches beneath his touch. He presses himself closer to me. Despite his warmth, I shiver in delight.

I never thought this moment would arrive. The moment I'd bared myself to another person.

Mind. Body. And Soul.

However, as I lay there offering every vulnerable part of myself, I didn't feel insecure. He scoped every inch of my body as if *Michelangelo* himself sculpted it, gazing at me as if hypnotized by a siren's song.

He lathers my neck in kisses as he crawls his hands down my legs. I gasp as his hands slither between my legs, touching me where no one has ever before.

"You're so beautiful." He speaks as our eyes lock, never stopping his movements.

I gaze at his reddened cheeks and disheveled hair from where I'd grip it. I lather his neck in kisses.

"Hazel."

The way he whispers my name could make me commit the most unspeakable sins.

Heat rose from my stomach to my chest as our bodies became one. His lips brushed over mine and my body reacted to him with every thrust. My toes curled as his hypnotic smell invaded my nostrils, making me desire him more. A final gentle thrust ignites a kaleidoscope of pleasure. Our eye contact never wavers as our heavy breaths fill the silence. He brushes a lock of hair out of my eyes before placing a searing kiss on my lips.

He pushes himself up and my body craves his warmth as a shiver of a breeze enters the trunk. As if he could read my thoughts, he drapes a thick blanket over us before locking me in his arms. I place my head on his chest as I'm lulled by the rise and fall of his chest. His erratic breathing slows down. He'd fallen asleep.

My eyes become heavy as he tightens his grip around my waist. My eyes flutter before I'm soothed by the sound of his heart.

His heartbeat is my new favorite lullaby.

Chapter Thirteen

I am doomed to be in this purgatory of insecurity and indecisiveness. Doomed forever to the shadows, witnessing other's successes. I groan as I slouch over my laptop, my fingers hovering above the keyboard, but I'm unable to write. The self-doubt has reared its ugly head again, infecting me with its pessimistic thoughts. Like a devil on my shoulder, it whispers into my ear.

Why bother trying?

I skim through the paragraphs I've already written. The words I believed to be a work of art are the most absurd sentences I'd ever seen. My stomach twists as I resist the urge to click *delete*. I'd spent the entire morning willing myself to write over five words. I'd done anything else to avoid this imminent moment. My inspiration evaporated as soon as it appeared, leaving me to wallow in despair.

I'm losing myself. I'm losing my will to keep pulling myself back up.

Vicariously

My mind drifted to Nevaeh. We haven't spoken in months - the longest we've ever gone without speaking in our friendship. She'd replaced me with a group of girls that find pitiless pleasure in tormenting me.

It made me feel replaceable. Worthless.

I'd always feared I'd leave this Earth with no one caring I was gone. However, Campbell has begun to diminish that fear.

I smile at the thought of his name. My body is still tingling from the thoughts of *that* night. I'd always wondered what my first time would be like - I never expected much, however, Campbell raised the standards above and beyond.

I attempt to soothe the kink in my neck. I'd been hunched over my desk for far too long. I glance at the time on my phone.

Two hours until the game.

Maisie bursts through the door with an exhausted groan. She tossed her bag to the side before extending a blue polka dot box with a ribbon in my hands.

"I bumped into Campbell on the way up." She grins. "He wanted me to give you this."

I yank on the ribbon and toss the lid onto my bed. His spare jersey is folded underneath a cream-colored paper.

Wear this tonight. Can I see you before the game?

"What's the big smile for?" Maisie grins as she glances over my shoulder and snorts. "And you said he wasn't into you."

I got ready in a daze, admiring the jersey in my full-length mirror. There was about an hour until the game, yet I couldn't wait a moment longer to see Campbell. I drag a lifeless Maisie out of our dorm room. It would be one of the last home games. I wanted to make it meaningful. However, it seems I wasn't

Chapter Thirteen

the only one with the idea.

An enormous crowd had already gathered in the grandstands, anticipating what was supposed to be the season's biggest match rivalry. I know the way to the locker room like the back of my hand. Maisie didn't feel like tagging along, and opted to relax in her seat.

My anxiety grows as I draw nearer. Outside this locker room, I have not had the best of encounters. I hasten my steps, only to collide with someone rounding the corner. My biceps take most of the impact as I groan.

"I'm so sorry!" The voice replies in panic.

Rounded forest green eyes lock with mine.

"It's okay," I'm flustered. "I was in a rush."

He gazes at me with a simpering smile. I feel uncomfortable and take a step back. My attention falls on his hockey jersey - he's from the opposing school. I clutch my arm and shift my weight from one foot to the other.

"Somewhere you need to be?" He questions.

"To see me." Campbell replies, standing beside me.

"This your girl, Atwood?" His smirk deepens.

Campbell's shoulders square.

"That's none of your business, Maddox." He seethes.

The guy raises his hands with an arrogant grin. His eyes contact mine before Campbell steps in front of me.

"You better get out of here before I break your nose." Campbell chuckles. "Wouldn't want a repeat of last time, would we?"

His words frustrate the mystery guy and his jaw tenses. I intervene and move between them and place my hands on Campbell's chest, yet they don't break eye contact.

"Campbell, let's go." I plead. "You have a game to focus on."

Vicariously

"Your girl has a point." The guy grins. "Guess I'll see you on the ice."

My jaw drops.

He's not a fan - he's the opposition.

I wait until he's out of earshot before turning to Campbell.

"Is he a friend of yours?"

"Something like that." He replies.

I glance at his clenched fists. His knuckles are ghostly white. I reach for his hands and brush my thumbs against them. He loosened his fists and intertwined his fingers with mine, but I can sense the tension.

"Who was that?"

He sighs.

"Jonah Maddox, we went to high school together." He clears his throat. "We played on the same team."

"So, what's with all the hostility?"

"We may have been teammates, but he was not my friend."

I nod my head and squeeze my hands. He directs his gaze on me.

"Forget about him. You need to focus on beating him."

He couldn't hold back a smile. It widens as he notices the jersey.

"That jersey is perfect for you." He compliments.

"Good luck." I release my grip on his hands, but he tightens them.

"I need a good luck kiss." He teases.

I roll my eyes but lean up to connect our lips. I planned to keep it brief, but he placed his hand on the back of my head, holding me in place. We only break apart at the sound of someone clearing their throat. His teammate is standing with his hands behind his back.

Chapter Thirteen

"Hazel, I want you to meet Nathan - my favorite teammate."

"Aw, I'm honored." Nathan jokes before gazing at me with a welcoming grin. "He talks about you all the time."

Campbell punches him in the arm. My eyes twinkle in delight.

"What does he say?" I question.

"I know everything about you. He's even started reading hordes of books. I've never seen him read in the two years I've known him. Not even textbooks."

I grin as Campbell becomes flustered.

"We've got to get out there." Campbell speaks before turning back to me.

"You're going to crush them." My words garner a smile.

"I'll look for you in the crowd when I score." His confidence never seems to falter.

I squeeze his hand before rushing off to join Maisie. I grin in delight as we get a front-row view of the action, but my smile wavers as Jonah skates past with a hurried wave in my direction. Maisie glances at me. I pretend not to notice. I could feel his stare. He is looking at me over his shoulder. Our eyes lock as he winks before turning around. I huff and fold my arms over my chest.

The game started civilly, with neither team scoring during the first period. As we waited for the players to return, I kept myself occupied chatting with Maisie or scrolling through my phone. The cheering of the crowd alerted me to the players returning. I tucked my phone into my pocket.

Campbell skated past as I blew him a kiss. I noticed his wide grin before he turned. Jonah skates in front of him. I watch as they have a verbal exchange. Jonah spoke for a few more seconds before smirking and skating away. I could see the

Vicariously

frustration exuding from Campbell. His frustration grew as one of the opposing members stole the puck. They cheered as he took the shot and scored. Campbell taps his stick against the board.

Jonah slides next to him and whispers something in his ear. My eyes widen as Campbell shoves him against the board. The crowd gasps. Jonah only chuckles before Campbell delivers a harsh blow to his jaw. My eyes water as Jonah gets a few shots in before they collapse on the ice, each taking turns punching the other. The players get involved and yank their teammates away from the altercation.

Campbell attempts to escape their hold, but their grip on him is too firm. His coach points an accusatory finger at him before pointing to the locker room area. Campbell takes off his helmet and tosses it to the ground before stomping off. I hesitate on whether I should check up on him or allow him to cool down.

"I'll be back."

Outside the locker room door, I bite my lip as I knock.

"Go away!" He bellows.

"It's me!" I called out.

Harsh footsteps echo from under the door. His wet hair falls into his eyes as his frame leans against the doorway.

He must have taken a shower to cool down, and I might have had an internal debate for longer than I thought.

"Come inside." His voice is hoarse as he moves to the side.

I hesitate in the doorway. The thought of entering a locker room doesn't strike me as a worthwhile experience. He must have sensed my apprehension and chuckles.

"There's more than one room in here. I promise you won't see anything scarring."

Chapter Thirteen

With a roll of my eyes, I enter. He grips my hand and drags me into the furthest room.

"It's where we relax before a game." He states.

I admire the large television and abundance of gaming systems.

He took a seat and placed his head back with a groan. His entire demeanor exudes anger as his knuckles turn white. I approach him, fearing how he may react. As if he could sense my erratic thoughts, he lifts his head to look into my eyes. He reaches forward, grips my hands, and yanks me onto his lap. I squeal as I straddle his waist, my cheeks burning red at our position.

"What happened?" His jaw clenches as his eyes flicker with fiery fury.

I knew I shouldn't have brought it up, but the curiosity was unbearable. I couldn't wait any longer to understand what could have set him off. I take in his tattered appearance. An enormous bruise is darkening around his right eye. The bottom of his lip is bleeding. I reach over to touch it, pulling away as he winces.

"You and everyone else saw what happened." He grumbles. "He deserved it."

I sigh and brush my fingers through his hair.

"He must have said something pretty serious to set you off."

"He mentioned you." The words blurted out.

I freeze.

"Told me all the things he wanted to do to you. I lost it and punched him." He shrugged.

The air became restricted.

"You hated him before this drama. What happened between you both?"

Vicariously

He avoided my gaze, but I needed an explanation.

"Campbell, please." I stress.

He sighs.

"I found him in bed with Celeste last year during an away game." He scoffed. "It's when we first started dating. He's made a habit of sleeping with my girlfriends."

The mention of Celeste has my stomach in a knot, but I push it aside and focus on him.

"Our teams always had a rivalry, but it became more personal." He explains.

"That's why you got so upset, because it made you think history would repeat itself." I drop my head.

"No," He seethes. "You're nothing like Celeste."

He grips my head between his hands, willing me to look into his eyes.

"No one talks about you like that, especially not in front of me."

My stomach flutters. I didn't know how to respond. No one has ever punched someone for me. It's all surreal.

"Are you upset with me?" He questions, glancing at me like a lost puppy.

"Why would I be?"

"I don't know." He shrugs.

This time I'm the one to grip his head in my hold, willing him to look into my eyes.

"No one has ever done that for me before." I whisper.

"I'd do it all over again if I could." His voice is hushed as the intensity of our gaze grows.

Every emotion in my body amplifies, every feeling, every thought of him. It's all-consuming. As if we'd shared a telepathic thought, we both lean in. Our lips brushed, so soft I barely felt it, yet it sent a shock wave through my veins. It was like an adrenaline rush.

I surrender under the sensuality. What had started with a gentle and unhurried touching of the lips became need and desire - as if we needed this as much as we needed air. He littered my neck in kisses as my groan echoed in the room.

My brain could not function coherently. I couldn't care less about getting caught. Not at this moment. Not when the desire to be connected to him again is so strong.

I've become addicted to him and I need my fix.

His lips are like marshmallows. I parted mine, allowing his tongue to slip inside. He gripped my hips and drew me closer to him. The only sounds to be heard were our heavy breathing and pressing lips, followed by the hasty fumbling of our undressing. All that remained on my body was his jersey. I reached for the hem to remove it, but he placed his hands on mine.

"Leave it on." He commands as he gasps for breath. "I want you to ride me with it on."

I could only nod.

He pressed our lips together again, neither of us fearing getting caught. The only thing on our minds is each other. I didn't know it was possible to convey so much feeling in a kiss, but it was as if Campbell was pouring his heart and soul into it, as if he was projecting his feelings and desires. My heart hammered in my chest as I raised myself for us to unite once more.

I didn't think it could have been better than the first, but that theory is tossed out the window. Every single aspect of this moment is an upgrade.

Perfection.

Vicariously

"You make me feel things I've never felt before." He groans into my ear as he grips my hips to guide me, thrusting them up in sync with mine.

The entire action is foreign to me and I feared that I'm doing it all wrong, but the moment he tilted his head back with an animalistic groan ignited a newfound desire and confidence within me.

I couldn't help but feel an overwhelming sense of love as he kept me safe in his hold. His gentle whispers of reassurance made my head rush. His arms wrapped around my waist as our eyes locked. I was once again drowning in them. Every thrust brought us closer in ways I'd never imagined possible. Each second, my heart grows heavier.

This is what being in love must feel like.

I'd come undone at the very thought. My body felt light as a wave of euphoria ignited through me. He placed his forehead against mine as our hot breaths mixed. He tucked a strand of my hair behind each ear before placing a loving kiss on my forehead.

"Hazel, I -" The irate voices of his teammates interrupted him.

With wide eyes we redress. I'm thankful no one peered into the room for the next few minutes.

I wanted to know what he was going to say.

Once satisfied with my appearance, I wrapped my arms around his neck in a loving embrace. He returned the gesture by wrapping his arms around my waist in a stronghold.

"You'll get them next time." I deduce by the grunting of his teammates that they had lost.

He places his head on my shoulder, kissing just below my ear.

Chapter Thirteen

"Can't wait to kick his ass again." He muses.

I didn't want to laugh, but it escaped. I pull away and place a hand on his cheek.

"Console your team. I'll see you later."

He places his hand over mine before pulling it to his lips to peck my palm. We exchanged a brief smile before I rushed out of the locker room pleading none of his teammates saw me.

Once I make it into the hallway, I beam until my face burns. For the first time in my entire life, I'm happy.

* * *

I believed you could only find love between the pages of books. The love that's consuming and infinite. I'd always imagined love to be fictional.

And I always believed I would never find someone that could love me.

I spent so much time suffering in silence, consumed by self-loathing.

Until I met Campbell.

Every moment I'm with him, I feel as if everything about myself is beautiful and worthy. He'd loved me before I ever loved myself, and for that, I will be eternally thankful. I'd wake up every morning with a smile because he'd be the first thing on my mind. Knowing that I would see him again gave me constant motivation to get up every morning.

I glimpse at the words on the screen with an unusual sense of confidence. I'd found my inspiration to write. I have pushed the negative thoughts to the back of my mind as the story is

Vicariously

coming to life.

Maisie saunters into the room with a loud yawn.

"I'm exhausted!" She exclaims.

The weekend had approached and the hallways were rowdy, as most people were packing for the away game. They filled the nearest hotels to maximum capacity. My stomach has been in knots about going, but Campbell claimed he needed me there.

His good luck charm.

Even days after he'd said it, the stampede in my stomach is still rogue. I'd never felt more special. More wanted.

Maisie had fallen asleep by the time I'd finished writing a chapter. She'd expressed her disinterest in traveling to watch the game, so I left her a note and grabbed the bag I packed this morning. It wasn't much since it was only a night. I skipped the steps, halting in surprise as Campbell stood at the bottom.

"I thought you already left with the team."

"And leave you to travel on your own?" He scoffs before grinning wide. "I'd rather spend the drive with you."

I blush as I reach the last step.

"Well, we better get going then."

I pipe up as he places his hands on my waist.

"So, not even a hello?" He teases.

"Hi," I roll my eyes. "Can we go?"

He smirks before grabbing my bag. He exits the dorm building. I have to speed walk to keep up with him.

I fixate my gaze outside the window as we drive away from the campus. A woolen white duvet of snow covers the entire forest trees, as the gentle humming of the music surrounds me. Artificial heat warms my numb fingers. I notice Campbell glance at me from the corner of his eyes. I ignored it at first,

Chapter Thirteen

but it became unbearable.

"Why do you keep looking at me?"

He seems nervous. He bites his lip as he keeps his eyes on the road.

"So, I may have booked a room with one bed." He admits. "I only realized after I booked it."

My eyes widened. Despite our many compromising times together, we'd never shared a bed. Or bedroom. This feels too real. Too serious. However, it seemed enticing.

A night of just the two of us. No distractions.

"I don't want you to think I did it for an ulterior reason." The panic in his voice is clear.

I shake my head.

"I know you didn't, and I'm okay with it." I place a hand on his knee.

His shoulders slump. He sighs, as if he'd been panicking about telling me this for a while. I'd almost fallen asleep, but we reached the hotel.

The hotel fills with a chaotic abundance of college students. I stay close to Campbell as we venture to our room. They directed a few glances our way, so I lowered my head and allowed Campbell to lead me.

I sigh as he shuts the door behind us. I place the back of my head against it and twirl a strand of hair around my finger as I take in the homey room. Just big enough for two. He tosses our bags to the sides and tucks his hands into the front of his pockets. He raises his brow at me.

I ignore his stare and glance outside the window to be greeted by the bleak night sky. The day had escaped us as the long travel had left me exhausted. I peek at the double bed like a snake ready to pounce. The negative thoughts appear

Vicariously

uninvited in my brain as the insecurity gnaws at me.

Campbell's hands on my arms shock me back to reality. He gazes down at me.

"I didn't book this on purpose." He reassures once more. "I can sleep on the floor."

"No!" I interject. "I'm just being silly."

He slides his hands down my arms and interlocks our fingers.

"You're not," He replies. "I never want you to be afraid to tell me anything."

I nod my head as my tense muscles relax.

"I don't know about you, but I'm exhausted."

He grins and nods his head. We don't speak as we prepare to turn in for the night. I exited the restroom and found him outside on the balcony. He's leaning against the railing as he gazes at the night sky. I join his side, only to be pulled in front of him as his arms wrap around my waist. He sways us as we marvel at the beauty of the night. I close my eyes as he kisses the back of my neck, letting his lips linger. I shiver.

"Do you ever get nervous before big games like this?" I question.

I can feel the vibrations of his chest against my back as he chuckles.

"No one has asked me that before." He breathes. "I guess I'm darn good at hiding my feelings."

I place my hands over his in silent encouragement to continue speaking.

"I guess I'm just afraid it could all cut off. As if I don't keep up the charade, it will go away."

I hum.

"If opportunity doesn't knock, build a door." I muse.

Chapter Thirteen

"Where did that come from?"

It's my turn to chuckle.

"It's a famous quote." I state. "If you aren't afraid, it's not worth it." I lean my head against his chest. "We fear losing the things we love. If we don't, then we never loved it."

He places his chin on my shoulder. My stomach somersaults as his comforting breath fans the side of my face. We remain silent as we absorb each other's soothing warmth. My eyes flutter.

Campbell chuckles once more and leads me inside towards the bed. I close my eyes as my head rests against the silk pillow. The bed dips as his arm slides around my waist, gripping me flush against him. His natural heat seeps into my back and throughout my entire body. He brushes my hair away from my face before placing a tender kiss on my cheek.

"Goodnight, Hazel Ellis."

Chapter Fourteen

My eyes flutter open for no reason other than my dreams have come to a blissful conclusion. The shut blinds block any rays of sunlight. My eyes are grateful. Campbell's grip on my waist tightened through the night, but I wiggled around to face him. I glanced at his tousled hair, pushing the strands away that had fallen over his eyes. His chest rises and falls as his breathing is slow, his nostrils flaring. I trace my fingers across his angelic face, giggling as his nose scrunches at the sensation. I lean over and kiss his cheek, closing my eyes at the feel of his skin against my lips. Once I open them, I see his eyes flutter. A smile graces his face as his eyes seem more mesmerizing in the mornings. I grab his hand and intertwine our fingers together.

"I could get used to this." He jokes.

I roll my eyes, feeling flushed. It's as if the kaleidoscope of butterflies in my stomach has increased in size.

"I'm spending most of the day training, but you're welcome

Chapter Fourteen

to watch." He offers.

I mull it over.

"No, thank you. I might catch up on some writing."

He kisses my forehead before getting ready for the day. I feel cold despite the copious amounts of blankets. It isn't long before he's gone and I'm left alone to dwell on my thoughts. I reach for my laptop and open the document.

My fingers hover over the keyboard. Nothing comes to mind.

I force myself to type the first thing I can think of, only to delete it seconds later, repeating the daunting process until frustration kicks in. I slam it shut more forcefully than necessary and get ready for the day, needing an escape from this claustrophobic room. With my laptop tucked under my arm, I rushed through the lobby and sauntered into the hotel cafe. I find the most isolated table and return to my failed attempts at writing something decent.

"Can I get you anything?" I jump as the waiter appears at my side. "I'm sorry." He apologizes. I can sense he's holding back a grin.

"It's my fault." I sigh as I clutch my chest.

"So we beat on, boats against the current, borne back ceaselessly into the past."

"Excuse me?" I question in confusion.

He points to my copy of *The Great Gatsby* on the table. I blush.

"It's one of my favorites." I smile widely.

I'd met no one else that liked it. Or reading.

"Mine too."

I glance at his name tag.

Ben.

Vicariously

He clears his throat as he shifts his weight.

"Right, I forgot." He grins. "Can I get you anything?"

"Just a coffee, thanks."

He nods. I watch him walk off before turning back to my laptop screen with a frown. I wrote a sentence by the time Ben returned with my drink.

"Do you go to school here?"

"Nope, just here to watch hockey."

He smirks.

"So I guess that makes us rivals." He teases.

"I guess that does." I grin. "Guess we shouldn't be talking to each other."

"I'm willing to risk it." He chuckles. "I'm on my break in five if you'd like some company?"

"Why not?" I replied. "I'd love to know what other books you like."

He excuses himself. I'd never had someone I could talk about books with and understand where I'm coming from.

He returns with another cup of coffee for me and one for him. He slides into the booth across from me.

"I'm Ben, by the way." He responds. "We never introduced ourselves."

"Hazel."

"And since we've been talking about books - I should admit my full name is Benvolio."

I snort thinking he's kidding, but he keeps a straight face.

"You're serious." I note.

"My mom is into Shakespeare." His face is flushed. "And she felt Romeo was too pretentious."

I lean back in my seat and fold my arms across my chest.

"So, your mom is into reading too?"

Chapter Fourteen

He nods his head.

"She's a high school teacher, but she spends her weekends writing as much as possible." He explains. "I guess I got her writing gene."

"You write?" My eyes widened in shock.

He looks down embarrassed.

"I write too!" I exclaim.

His jaw hits the table.

"Are you kidding?"

I point toward my laptop.

"I came here to work on my book, but don't have any inspiration."

He scratched the back of his neck.

"Mind if I look?"

My chest tightens as I glance at my interlocked fingers. I've let no one read my work, but it would be helpful to get an opinion from a fellow writer. I bite my lip as I slide my laptop toward him. He scrolls to the top.

I twirl my thumbs and tap my foot as I watch his eyes flicker across the screen. It feels like an eternity has passed before his eyes lock with mine.

"Well?" I question as he does nothing but stare.

"Your writing is incredible." He gushes. "You have a way with words."

"Really?" I am in disbelief.

"I'm being serious, I'm not just saying it to be nice." I couldn't wipe the large smile off my face.

"You're the first person I've ever let read my work." I admit.

His smile widens as much as mine.

"I'm honored."

I take a sip of my coffee before my phone vibrates against

the table.

Campbell.

My eyes skim over the text that pops up on the screen.

Where are you?

I hadn't noticed how much time had passed. He must have returned to the hotel. The game starts in two hours.

"I have to go." I gathered my things. "It was great meeting you!"

"Maybe I'll see you at the game tonight?"

"We shouldn't be talking to each other." I grin. "We're mortal enemies."

"How Romeo and Juliet." He chuckles.

"It was great meeting you, Benvolio." I giggle before rushing out of the cafe.

The second I enter the room, Campbell leaps off the bed with open arms.

"Where did you go?" He questions.

"Downstairs." I shrug as I place everything aside. "How was practice?"

"Brutal." He groans. "But I'm ready to kick some ass."

I chuckle at his natural cockiness. He wraps his arms around my waist.

"Want to get something to eat before the game?" I question.

A childish grin rises onto his face.

"I know something I can eat." He wiggles his eyebrows. I shove his chest. "I meant food options, Ellie!" He exclaims. "You and your dirty mind." He scolds.

I roll my eyes and raise a brow.

"Okay then, what did you have in mind?"

"I don't know." He shrugs.

I scoff.

Chapter Fourteen

He returns his hold around my waist. His eyes glance into mine as they soften.

"Thank you for coming with me." He utters. "You're my good luck charm."

My heart flutters as I wrap my arms around his neck.

"I did nothing." I argue.

"You do more than you think." He coos. "You've given me a reason to keep fighting. I'd started losing my purpose for playing, but now I play to win for you."

There's so much love and admiration in one gentle stare. It felt like my heart was about to combust.

"You were great before we ever met." I state.

"Now I'm even better." He squeezes my waist. "I'm a better person."

I attach my lips to his, overcome by emotions. He inhales before pulling away.

"Every time I kiss you, it's like the first time again." He whispers against my lips as he grips my hand in his.

He raises my hands to his chest and places them over his fluttering heart.

"You're the greatest adrenaline rush."

He leans down and kisses my jaw as his hands slither to the hem of my shirt.

"There's not enough time for that. You have a game soon." I whisper, but I don't stop his movements.

"I'll cancel everything for you." I can feel him smirk against my neck.

He places his forehead against mine as he closes his eyes. I placed my hands on his cheeks, willing him to bless me with his ocean eyes.

"Hazel," He stares into my eyes with an unrecognizable

intensity. "There's something I've been wanting to tell you."

I don't move. I don't speak for fear of interrupting the moment.

"I-" The sound of his phone ringing cuts him off.

I groan and toss my head back as he reaches for the device.

"The team needs me back." He speaks. I nod my head with a pout. "Let's go."

I hadn't expected to arrive so soon, but it beats sitting alone in the hotel room pretending to write. I lean over the barrier and inspect the glossy smooth ice.

Too bad it's going to get ruined soon.

Campbell is inside the locker room with his teammates for their coach's traditional pep talk and revision of strategy. I blow air through my lips as I slump further over the barrier.

"Hazel?" The voice piques my interest.

"Ben," I greet with a wide grin as he glances at me as if deciphering whether it's me. "What are you doing here so early?"

"My brother is on the team." He states as he tucks his hands in his coat pockets. "I could ask you the same question."

"I'm here to support my boyfriend, Campbell." I shrug.

Sometimes I still feel strange describing Campbell as my boyfriend. I guess I haven't come to terms with reality yet. Ben nods his head and joins me against the barrier.

"I thought we shouldn't talk." I mock.

He shakes his head with a chuckle.

"It's a risk I'm willing to take."

We remain in silence for a moment.

"Did you get any more writing done?" He questions.

I shake my head and glower at my shoes.

"It will come to you." He reassures me.

Chapter Fourteen

I smile at him in thanks.

"Ellie!" Our heads shoot towards Campbell approaching us but as soon as he spots Ben his brows furrow.

"Ben, this is Campbell." I introduce. "Campbell, this is Ben. We met at the cafe. He works there." I explain.

Campbell straightens his posture as if sizing him up, but Ben doesn't notice. He extends his hand.

"It's great meeting you." Ben replies. "Your girlfriend is an amazing writer."

I gulp. Campbell's eyes dart toward me.

"You've read her work?" He questions through clenched teeth.

"I guess she needed another writer's opinion."

"So, you're a writer too?"

"Yeah, we bonded over our love for *Gatsby*."

I couldn't distinguish if Ben was oblivious to the hateful glaring, or if he is gifted at keeping his composure.

"Sounds like you both have a lot in common." Campbell's fists tighten.

I choose that moment to intervene as I place my hand on Campbell's chest. His heart thumps under my palm.

"Well, we need to go, but tell your brother I wish him luck." I state before pushing Campbell away.

"Are we leaving so soon?" I'm thankful he waits until we're out of earshot to speak. "He hasn't gotten around to proposing."

"Now is not the time to be jealous." I sneer.

"I'm sorry," He mocks. "How ridiculous of me not to get upset."

He spins around to glare at me with his arms across his chest.

"I met him this afternoon!" I exclaim. "I'm never going to see him again after this night."

"You let him read your work." He yells with equal frustration. "A literal stranger got to read it while your boyfriend hasn't even read a sentence! I know I'm not knowledgeable in literature, but I thought it would be nice if you could have trusted me to read it."

I did not know he wanted to read my work. I thought he was being a nice and supportive boyfriend.

"I didn't know it was that important to you." I defend.

"Why wouldn't I?" He tosses his hands in the air before dropping them at his sides. "Is it so outrageous to think that maybe I wanted to support you?"

My eyes trickle with tears. The guilt eats away at me like acid.

"Atwood!" His teammate's voice bellows as he pokes his head outside the locker room door. "It's time to get ready."

His jaw is tense.

"I need to go." He replies.

I grip his arm.

"I'm sorry." I apologize.

He sighs and reaches down to place a kiss on my forehead, but I can still feel the awkward tension between us.

"We can talk about it later." He states before marching through the doors.

I close my eyes and brush my fingers through my hair. My vision becomes blurred by tears. I decide it's best to let things cool down, so with that thought in mind, I trudge towards my seat wishing a win could smooth things over.

Chapter Fifteen

The game has gone into overtime. Stress is a silent killer. I can't help but feel responsible for Campbell's lack of focus. We'd never argued before, especially before a game. I don't know what to say or do. I'm new to everything a relationship entails. This is out of my comfort zone.

"Trouble in paradise?" A taunting voice whispers into my ear.

Celeste.

"I do not know what you're talking about." I feign ignorance.

"Please," she scoffs. "No one knows Campbell better than I do."

I ignore her and focus on the players, but she cannot take a hint.

"This is the part where he ignores you. He did it every time we had a minor argument, he ran away from conflict."

I continue to ignore her.

"And if you're thinking it's going to be different for you, you're fooling yourself." She continues to dig. "Campbell will never change. That's why we broke up."

"Funny," I reply. "I thought it was because he found you in another guy's bed."

She chuckles.

"I guess he never told you about our agreement. We were never exclusive. He saw other people just like I did, but we'd always crawl back to each other."

It felt as if my heart had stopped beating. My heart told me not to believe a word coming out of her mouth, but my brain betrays me. She struts off with a satisfied grin.

The crowd around me bursts into celebration, but it's background noise for me. As if everything is moving in slow motion. Every insecurity rises to the surface.

I tried to warn you. The voice in the back of my mind chimes. Tears welled in my eyes as I watched Campbell celebrate with his team.

The crowd is suffocating. I need to get as far away as possible. My legs react the moment the thought enters my mind. I don't stop moving until I'm engulfed by the outside air. My eyes reproduce more when I wipe the tears with my hand.

The night is as morbid as my thoughts. The dark sky lacks light as the expanse of gray clouds masks the bright stars. Everything is bland. There is nothing but pure misery. I feel the icy breeze as my entire body becomes numb. I rebuke my harsh thoughts.

You should have known better.

None of it was ever true.

I wrap my arms around myself and lean against a nearby

Chapter Fifteen

bench. I close my eyes and take steady breaths, but it does nothing to ease the invading thoughts. I ignore the crowds as they flock out of the building to their vehicles, gazing into the abyss, hoping I could take flight with the galaxy. Hoping I could look down on the world instead of being looked down on.

"Ellie," Campbell's quavering voice breezes with the wind. "I've been looking for you for ages."

I don't turn, don't move. I couldn't let him see me like this.

His footsteps become more distinct. The second his hand touches my shoulder, I bury my face in my hands as agonizing sobs wrack my body to the core. His arms wrap around me, drawing me flush against his chest. I wanted to push him away, yet I craved comfort. I soak the front of his shirt in tears as I press further against him. No words are said. He just lets me cry.

Once I've calmed down, I pull away and wipe away the remnants of tears. He runs his hands up and down my arms.

"I run away once things get like this." He admits.

My stomach fills with dread. He pulls me closer and leans down until we're at eye level.

"I don't want to do that with you." He breathes. He brushes his thumb against my cheek. "I want you. Only you. Every part of you. The worst and the best." He states with the utmost sincerity. "For the first time, I want to work things out instead of running, because I know I couldn't stand losing you."

I gaze at him, doe-eyed. He tucks a strand of my hair behind each ear. He grips my head and brushes his lips against mine, so soft I hardly detect it, but it surges like static.

"You're my lighthouse, Hazel Ellis."

He remembered.

Vicariously

I'm overcome with a wave of emotion as I launch into his arms. I press my lips to his with as much love and emotion as I can muster. However, he pulls away far too soon.

"I need to show you something." He breathes.

I nod my head in confusion as we walk to his truck. He rummages through his backpack before tucking something behind his back. Vertical wrinkles appear between his eyes as he leans against his truck. He takes a big breath before handing the object to me. I take a quick glimpse at the worn copy of *Wuthering Heights*.

"It's how we first met," I reminisce, smiling. "I was holding a copy."

"This *is* the copy." He replies.

"What do you mean?"

He runs his hand down his face.

"After you left the bookstore that day, something told me to go back inside and buy it." He trails off as he looks at the book. "I needed something that would remind me of you every day."

He gazes into my eyes.

"I needed to know you."

I inspect the book. The spine broke from the many times it's been opened. As I flip through the pages, I notice some highlighted sentences.

"What's this?" I question as I read a line.

"If he loved you with all the power of his soul for a whole lifetime, he couldn't love you as much as I do in a single day."

His face is flushed.

"Why did you do this?" I question.

"I've read through that book a million times, and the more I got to know you, the more things I highlighted that reminded me of you."

Chapter Fifteen

My eyes widened.

"You annotated a book for me?"

He nods with a sheepish grin.

"Isn't that what a guy does when he's in love with a girl?"

I chuckle, trying my best not to sob in pure joy.

"I'm not sure, but it seems unlikely."

It's his turn to chuckle. I gaze at the book in awe at the copious amounts of highlighted quotes. I grip it to my chest with the widest of grins.

"Just for the record, I'm in love with you, too."

I was on cloud nine as we rode back to the hotel. I couldn't tear my eyes away from the book as I flipped through the pages. My heart fluttered with every annotated line. However, Campbell took it from me once we were alone in the room.

"I keep it with me everywhere I go." He explains before returning it to his backpack. "I look at it before every game for motivation."

It felt as if my heart was going to burst from inconceivable happiness. He struts towards me and attaches our lips. I'm taken aback by the unexpected intensity, but I reciprocate. I sigh in delight as my body hits the soft sheets, his body hovering over mine. He dips his head and grazes his teeth along my collarbone. My breath hitched at the sensation. He pulls away to gaze into my eyes, looking for the slightest hint of hesitation. I cup his face as he brushes his lips against my forehead. His hands soothe down the ridges of my back, so soft, as if afraid I'm going to break.

"You don't always have to be so gentle with me." I squeak as his eyes pop open.

"What do you mean?" He smirks, already knowing what I meant but wanting me to say it.

Vicariously

"You know what I meant." I mumble as my cheeks flush.

"Do you want me to be rough with you, Ellie?" He chuckles, but his eyes darken.

I nod my head before I'm taken by surprise as he tosses me further up the bed. He's hovering over me and pinning my hands to the bed with cat-like agility. He seems to enjoy the dominant role.

Why did I not suggest it sooner?

As every article of clothing disappeared, he'd gaze into my eyes, waiting for any sign of uncertainty, but I'd craved him more than I thought possible. He never broke our gaze. My head felt flushed as he trailed kisses down my abdomen to between my legs. He gazes up at me with a devilish grin and I spread my legs wider, pleading for him to give me what I desire most.

One gentle lick had me gripping the sheets as the unknown sensation coursed through my body. Every nerve in my body ignites with desire.

I'd always feared being intimate with somebody. To let them see every vulnerable inch of me, but at this moment I would let Campbell Atwood do whatever he wanted to me.

He went from gentle and predictable to erratic and rough in a moment. I launched my back off the bed with a silent scream. His chuckles flitter through the room.

A curious finger massages the inside of my walls as if searching for the most pleasurable spots.

"Just relax, Ellie." He whispers as I tense up. "You're doing great. It's just us, baby."

Baby. He'd never called me that before. It sounded so foreign, but so sensual.

I groaned as the pleasure disappeared, opening my eyes to

Chapter Fifteen

lock with his.

"We're just getting started." He grins as he reaches over to attach our lips.

He bit my bottom lip, eliciting a groan, allowing his tongue to slip inside.

We became one, tethered together in the most intimate way conceivable. My mind becomes fogged from every thrust as my hands drag down his back. His hips brush against my nerve endings as he reaches all the right places.

"You're the best I've ever had." He whispers into my ear as I wrap my legs around his waist.

We groan in unison as he sinks deeper.

"Harder." The command slips from my mouth with no regrets.

He obliges my request.

His declarations of adoration in my ear were the most beautiful melody to befall my ears. The room fills with our silent moans. I'm lulled into an almost hypnotic trance as our lips connect. My eyes become watery at his constant declarations of love. I pull him closer to me, encompassed by his warmth.

For the first time in my life, I feel loved.

As we come down from our highs and catch our breath, he chuckles.

"Who knew you had a kinky side to you?" He jokes and I shove his chest.

His laughter dies down before his face turns serious.

"You are a goddess in my eyes, Hazel, and I never want you to doubt the effect you have on me ever again."

Chapter Sixteen

Hockey games have become a procedure for me, so have the parties the night before. I'd become accustomed to the loud music and intoxicating slurs. I lean against the wall, watching two frat boys wrestle each other on the floor. They knock over a vase, yet they ignore it or they're too drunk to notice it had fallen.

"So, this is where you're hiding." Campbell grins as he places his arm against the wall above my head.

He leans down for a kiss. I pull away, but he grips my chin and pulls me in for another. I could sense him smiling.

"What's got you in such a good mood?" I questioned, moving away.

He places his other arm on my side, trapping me between him and the wall.

"I'm always in a good mood when I'm with you." He flirts, knowing it's enough to make my cheeks flush.

He chuckles as he caresses my reddened cheek with his

Chapter Sixteen

knuckle.

"I'll be right back." He pecks the corner of my lip before rushing off.

I resume my casual stance against the wall as I scroll through TikTok.

"I was hoping to find you here." A familiar voice pipes up.

I freeze.

"Trent," I mutter. "What do you want?"

"What's with the hostility?"

"Are you going to ask me that?" I scoff in disbelief.

"You're not still holding a grudge, are you?" I step back, only to collide with the wall.

I attempt to shrink away from his unnerving gaze as he steps closer. My hands shake at my sides. I close my eyes as if it would make him disappear. A painful grunting noise sounds followed by a thud.

I gasp as I find Trent on the ground, clutching his jaw. Campbell is standing at his feet, nostrils flared and a dark protruding vein in his neck. His teammates rush to the scene.

"What's wrong with you, Campbell?" One of them scolds as they help Trent up.

"No," He growls. "What's wrong with *him*?"

He steps to strike Trent again, but someone catches his arm in time.

"Enough," the guy I recognize as their captain yells. "You're supposed to be teammates."

Campbell yanks his arm out of their grip.

"Teammates or not, he better not come anywhere near my girlfriend again!" He bellows.

"Trent, you need to step in line." Their captain orders. "That's Campbell's girl and you're going to respect her. It's what a team does."

Campbell's icy gaze softens. With a deadly scowl, Trent bolts toward Campbell, as if he hadn't heard a word their captain said.

"Don't make me hurt you!" He hollers.

Campbell cracks up.

"If anyone is getting hurt, it's you."

Their captain steps in between them.

"If you can't put your differences aside, I'm kicking you both off the team."

Campbell snorts.

"You don't need to do that." He states. "I quit."

My heart stops, along with everyone else in the room that's witness to the exchange. Campbell doesn't wait for them to recover. He grips my wrist and drags me upstairs and to his bedroom. He shuts the door with a purposeful slam. I lean against the door as the shock numbs my entire body. I only jolt back to reality as his hands grip my waist.

"Did he hurt you?" He questions with an opposite emotion to the one downstairs.

He'd gone from aggravated to delicate in a nanosecond.

"No." I choke out.

He twirls a strand of my hair around his finger.

"You can't just quit." I utter as guilt poisons my body.

"Don't worry. They'll come crawling back to me tomorrow." He grins. "They know they can't win without me."

My corner lip twitches.

"I should have hit him harder." His face stiffens.

I brush my thumb against his forehead to soothe away the frown lines. His face softens under my touch. His shoulder slumped. He leans down to place his forehead against mine.

Chapter Sixteen

Our eyes lock.

"I was thinking." He whispers. "Tomorrow is the last game before the break, and I was hoping you'd maybe want to come home with me."

My breath hitches.

"To meet your family?" I question.

He nods.

"It's just my dad and stepmom, but I'd love for you to see where I grew up."

My heart soars at the invitation.

He wants me to meet his family. He wants to share his past and allow himself to be vulnerable.

"I'd love to." I declare, before sealing the deal with a feverish kiss.

* * *

The nerves only struck once Campbell pulled his car into the parking lot of his home. I gaze at the monstrous house in awe. It looked more like a palace than a home. He grins as we exit the vehicle.

"When were you going to tell me you're rich?" I place my hands on my hips.

"My dad is rich." He corrects stretching to connect our hands. "He's a jerk, by the way."

I don't question him as he drags me down the long path and into their home. I glance at the Victorian interior, expecting a butler to materialize.

"Campbell!" an elderly woman exclaims as she embraces him in a hug.

Her perfectly manicured nails demand attention. She glances at me over his shoulder. Her eyes sparkle.

"You must be Hazel!" I'm surprised as I'm hauled into a firm embrace.

"It's a pleasure to meet you, Mrs. Atwood."

"Please, call me Gina." She states. "Let me see what's taking your father so long."

I watch as she rushes off into another room. Campbell rubs the back of his neck.

"I like her more than my dad." He whispers into my ear.

I roll my eyes and stiffen as his stepmom returns with his dad trailing behind. Campbell doesn't release his firm grip on my hand.

"Hey, dad." His father barely acknowledged his forlorn greeting. "This is Hazel."

He glances at me before focusing his attention on his phone.

"Lovely to meet you, Hazel." He states as he types away. "If you'll excuse me, I have a call to make."

He marches off. Campbell scoffs at his retreating figure.

"He's been busy." Gina apologizes.

"Don't make excuses for him." Campbell mutters before tugging me up the spiral staircase. We wander down a long hallway, passing a few closed doors, until he opens one on the left.

Hockey posters and trophies litter the room. I glance at a framed picture of a younger Campbell showcasing a medal around his neck.

"That was freshman year of high school." He glances over my shoulder. "Even as a kid, I was good."

I chuckle at his words.

Typical Campbell.

Chapter Sixteen

He wraps his arms around my waist and places his chin on my shoulder. I inspect every picture. He only had a few of him showcasing his hockey achievements. I wanted to question why he doesn't have any family pictures but decided against it.

"We need to take photographs together so I can frame them." He points at his shelf of images. "Everything I love goes on this shelf."

My insides turn to gelatin. I turn my head to gaze at him, not bothering to hide my burning cheeks. He gazes at me, as if my very existence was enough for him to smile. I lean forward and caress his lips with my own.

"Thank you for inviting me here."

"I want you to see every aspect of me." He states.

"Maybe next time you can come with me to my hometown." The words slipped before I could register them.

His eyes widened as if he hadn't expected me to ask.

"I want you to see every aspect of me," I add. "It's only fair."

His grin expands.

"Nothing would make me happier."

He wraps his arms tighter around my waist as we bask in each other's warmth, neither of us wanting to leave the comfort of his room.

"Where am I sleeping?" I question as the thought enters my mind.

I can feel him smirking. He leans closer until his lips touch my ear.

"Your choice." I shiver before turning into his arms to peer into his eyes.

"You're telling me your dad and stepmom would let us share a room?" I raise a brow.

Vicariously

He scoffs.

"You underestimate how little my dad cares about what I get up to," He winks. "My stepmom tries to be cool to win me over."

He places his hands on my lower back and draws me nearer.

"There's a spare bedroom if you're not comfortable."

I weigh my options, but I know I'd end up in his bed.

What's the point of delaying the inevitable?

"It wouldn't be the first time we've shared a room." I replied.

He grins.

"I was hoping you'd say that."

His warm lips envelop my own. I part mine, allowing his tongue to slip inside. My knees buckle. His firm grip on my waist prevents me from falling.

"Campbell," His stepmother calls as her footsteps are in earshot. "Come downstairs for dinner."

He pulls away with a groan as our heavy breaths meld together. He pouts his swollen lips.

"Let's go." I roll my eyes with a jovial giggle.

We exit his bedroom, but he places his hand on my shoulder. I turn and glance at his agonizing gaze.

"Whatever my dad says, ignore it."

I don't have time to question what he means before he bolts downstairs. I followed him. The walk seems longer than necessary until we're in the dining room. The table seems as if it stretches from one side of the room to the other. It could seat Campbell's entire hockey team. His dad and stepmom are already sitting at one end. Campbell attempted to sit at the opposite end, but I dragged him closer to the delight of his stepmom.

"You've lost a few games." His dad scolds him instead of

Chapter Sixteen

greeting him.

"I'm surprised you took the time to notice." Campbell grunts.

"I didn't pay your tuition for your hockey career to fail before it ended."

I cower at the unusual dinner discussions.

Sorry. His stepmom mouths as we make eye contact.

"I'm one of the best on the team." Campbell leans further over the table.

"You should be the best." His dad hisses.

I jump as Campbell slams his hands against the lavish wooden table.

"And you wonder why I never come home during the breaks." He hollers.

"Don't be dramatic." His father rebukes.

"How about we enjoy some dinner and get to know Hazel." Gina interjects.

His father stabs his plate of salad with his fork. Campbell leans back in his seat with folded arms, looking like a child would after being scolded. I reach for his hand and interlace our fingers together. I squeeze his palm, pleased to see his shoulders slump. He squeezes back with a beaming grin.

"So, Hazel, Campbell mentioned you're majoring in creative writing." Gina attempts to make conversation.

I'm speechless by the information that Campbell has mentioned about me to his stepmother. What else has he told her about me?

"I've always wanted to be a writer." I grin.

"Not the best career choice." His dad chimes.

"About as possible as a professional hockey career." Campbell glares at his father.

Vicariously

I'd lost my appetite. I stare at my plate with a forlorn gaze. I'd thought Campbell was overreacting about warning me, but it seems worse than he let on. His hands slide into mine. He takes me by surprise as he hauls me out of my seat.

"Where are you going?" His dad calls, but he ignores him and guides me to the front door.

He grabs two coats from the rack before handing me one. It's quite large, but I'm enveloped by the citrus of Rosewood. The moment we're in his truck, he dashes off. I try to take in as many of the views as I can. Every home in the neighborhood is as gargantuan and ostentatious as the other.

Neither of us speaks, but the silence is soothing. He reaches over the console and places a comforting hand above my knee.

Perhaps more for his comfort than my own.

I place my hand on top of his. He glances at me before returning his gaze to the dark road. I hum along with the melody, raising the volume.

My eyes widen at the myriad of colors before us and the dazzling flickering lights. I bolt out of his truck the second he halts. The carnival grows luminous against the gray sky.

"I used to come here every year. It's one reason I asked you to join me," He explains. "It's the only time of the year it's open."

I glance at him with childlike glee.

"I haven't been to a carnival in forever." I cannot take my eyes off the lights.

It's mesmerizing.

"Well, let's not waste another second." He grips my hand in his as we bolt like eager children.

I giggle as I attempt to keep up with his hasty pace. He steers us toward a random food stand.

Chapter Sixteen

"This is the greatest funnel cake you will ever taste," He states. "I'm not kidding."

I take his word for it, watching in fascination at his complete change in character. He bounces on the heels of his feet as we wait in line. He's like a kid on the morning of their birthday. It's as if the tough and arrogant persona has taken a break for the day. The other side of Campbell is unveiling itself.

The moment he's given the funnel cake, he lugs me to the side and holds it out to me. I take a dramatic breath before breaking off a piece. I groan as my taste buds become overthrown with flavor. He gazes at me with the biggest of grins, eager to hear the verdict.

"You were right." He raises his hands in celebration before taking a piece of his own.

I'm sad the moment the funnel cake finishes, but there's so much more to experience.

"This might be super cliche," He states as he swings our interlocked hands. "But I want to win a stuffed animal for you."

I became giddy at the idea. As silly as it may seem, I'd always dreamed of having a guy win a stuffed bear for me. I almost pinched myself, not believing this could be real. I take a deep breath to keep my composure before following him to one of the infinite amounts of games. I cheer for him on the sidelines as he tosses the balls, knocking down the targets. I refrain from squealing as a giant fluffy bear falls into my arms.

"What's its name?" He questions.

A million different names speed through my mind, but one stands out.

"Puck." I grinned, satisfied by my hockey reference.

He chuckles in delight.

Vicariously

"It's the perfect name."

We continue to stroll through the carnival. The animated laughter of children drowns out the various songs playing from the speakers at each stall. My nostrils become invaded by the most delicious scents of the abundance of food. Everything is a sensory overload in the best way possible.

I spotted an isolated photo booth. I gasp and drag Campbell toward it. He groans but follows.

"We have to take pictures of this day," I insist. "Our first photo with Puck."

As much as he wanted to pretend the thought of it all was torture, I know he loves it. However, I never expected the booth to be so claustrophobic.

"Looks like you'll have to sit on my lap." Campbell teases.

"Or Puck could sit on yours." I suggest.

He chuckles. I squeal as he yanks with force. I land on his lap as he wastes no time securing his arms around my waist. However, I'm facing him instead of the camera.

"This isn't how the pictures work, Campbell." I chastise.

He seems unbothered.

"I'm not one for rules." His arrogant grin resurfaces. "Besides, I'd rather stare into your eyes than the camera."

He always knows what to say to get out of trouble. I wrap my arms around his neck as he pulls me in for a kiss. He pulls away as our foreheads touch.

"I'm sorry about my dad," He whispers. "I thought he'd behave for one night."

"It's okay," I twirl my fingers around the locks of hair behind his head. "You warned me."

We welcome the peace. The brief escape from the outside noise. A moment where it's just the two of us.

Chapter Sixteen

"I'm sorry your dad's a dick." He chuckles.

"I'm used to it." He shrugs.

I play with the hairs on the back of his neck.

"Everyone needs a family." My voice is hushed.

He reaches his hand to my cheek, brushing his knuckles against it. I close my eyes.

"All I need in my life is you, Hazel Ellis." He states before capturing my breath with an adoring kiss.

As he deepens the kiss, it's as if the shock waves of delight return, shooting down my spine. I grip his hair as he pulls me closer to prevent me from falling off his lap. I could feel his warm body beneath me as he caressed my thighs, and I placed my hands on his stiffened shoulders.

"You're tense." I whisper against the kiss.

"Then loosen me up." He says.

"In a photo booth?" I tease.

"I'm ready for you anywhere."

I giggle as he grips the back of my head to draw me in. I trail my fingers down his chest and run my nails down his thighs evoking an involuntary shiver. He groans into my mouth as I brush my hands over his growing length.

"Fuck, Ellie." He moans into my mouth. "Don't be a tease."

I palm him over his jeans. His head falls back, knocking against the wall but he doesn't wince.

The merriment of children outside breaks us from our bubble. I'd forgotten where we were for a moment. My cheeks flush, but Campbell seems smug. I roll my eyes and attempt to climb off his lap, but he holds me in his grip. I look into his eyes as he frowns.

"I never thanked you for coming with me." His voice is mellow. "I wouldn't have come here if it wasn't for you."

185

Vicariously

I brush my thumbs against his cheeks.

"I'm sorry you had to experience it, though." His shoulders droop in exhaustion.

"I'm glad I did," I breathe. "I want to know every part of you, no matter what."

I push back the strands of hair that have fallen into his eyes.

"It makes me love you even more." I declare.

This time it seemed I was the one to take his breath away. As if he'd lost his composure for the first time. He places his lips against mine as if conveying his love for me through actions. As if words weren't enough.

"I do not know how I survived this entire time without you, but I am thankful I never have to live another day without you again."

My eyes water at his declaration of love. My heart swells as I gaze into his eyes. I never knew it was possible to love someone as much as I love Campbell. It's as if he consumes my every thought. I could not believe that someone like him could ever love me. How had I gone from being in the shadows to being loved by one of the most perfect guys in existence?

"There's just one issue." My smile falters.

"What?"

"I have a raging boner right now." We burst into laughter, so much my stomach aches.

"Guess you'll be the one carrying Puck."

His grip on my waist tightens as his eyes darkened with lust.

"Please," He whines. "Help me."

My stomach flips at his desperate plea. The desire he has for me shocks me to my core.

I want to try something new. He'd always been taking care of me during our intimate moments, and it was time I returned

Chapter Sixteen

the favor.

I lift myself off his lap and kneel in front of him. He gasps and pales as if he'd seen a ghost.

"Ellie," He exhales. "You don't have to do this."

I push his legs open and gaze at him from under my lashes.

"I want to." He hardened even more at my words.

He lifts his hips while I unbutton his pants. I pull his jeans down, along with his briefs until they're at his ankles. As I reached his length, I became dizzy.

"Hazel." He moans my name as I wrap my fingers around him. "You're a fucking, goddess."

His chest heaves as I run my fingers along it before reaching over for a tentative kiss. He bit his clenched fist as if the simple action had him on the verge of coming undone. I placed my lips at the tip before sliding my lips down, only reaching halfway. He gripped the back of my head, moaning words of encouragement as I bobbed my head.

"I can't believe we're doing this in a photo booth." He groans.

I pull my mouth away as I stroke his length in my clenched fist. His head falls back as he lifts his hips. I repeat my actions, becoming bolder each time. I relax entirely as I manage to take more of him down my throat.

"I'm so close." He groans. "Why is everything you do so perfect?"

I pull my lips away and speed up my thrusts. It isn't long before he's a writhing mess, groaning in orgasmic bliss. As I reach into my bag for some *Kleenex*, I avoid him. I give him one to clean up with.

I leave him alone to compose himself. The icy breeze soothes my scorched face. He steps out of the booth, but I keep my gaze on a popcorn stand ahead of me.

Vicariously

"Ellie," His hand envelops mine, as he lifts my head to stare into his eyes. "You just had my penis in your mouth, no need to be shy."

I burst into a fit of giggles at his unexpected reply. My eyes water as my stomach burns. He chuckles as he pulls me into his chest, placing his chin on my head.

"You were amazing," He says. "Everything about you is amazing."

He kisses the top of my head.

"Before we leave, I need to kiss you at the top of the Ferris wheel."

He releases his hold on me, but I yearn for his warmth. With Puck in my arms, we stroll toward the Ferris wheel. I gaze at the stars sprinkled in the murky sky. It's not a long wait as most people have already left. The families have gone to tuck their kids in for the night. Campbell hands Puck to the bored-looking middle-aged man before gripping my hand. I triple-check that we're both attached before we ascend to the sky. The stars seem closer, brighter. I can't help but gaze at them in wonder as I admire their carefree beauty and unwavering confidence. His arm slithers behind me before curling around my neck. He pulls me closer until my head rests on his chest. My stomach somersaults as he pecks the top of my head. Everything is like a dream. Absolute perfection.

* * *

I wake up with goosebumps littering my body. Campbell's side of the bed is icy. I glance around the bedroom with a frown and grab a hoodie he tossed over his desk chair before descending

Chapter Sixteen

the stairs. Distinct sounds of yelling bellow through the long hallway. I follow the noise.

"When were you planning on telling me this?" Campbell's father roars.

I'd never experienced so much rage from one person.

"Never." Campbell sounds too calm.

"You're going to give this all up for some girl?" His dad questions in disbelief.

I risk a glance into their living room.

Campbell's entire body tenses.

"I'm not giving anything up!" He argues. "And she's not just some girl!"

Are they talking about me?

"You are sacrificing your hockey career to chase some unrealistic fantasy!"

My stomach clenches.

What would this all have to do with me?

"I am done talking about this." Campbell seethes.

"Well, I'm not!" I didn't think his father could raise his voice even more.

Neither notices me as Campbell bolts out of the room with his father charging right on his tail. I press myself against the wall as if I were a chameleon able to camouflage. Campbell rushes towards the door and bolts outside. His dad slams it behind them with a brutal shock.

"It happens a lot," Gina's presence was unexpected. "Don't take it personally."

"Were they arguing over me?"

"I don't think it's my place."

"Please."

She sighs.

Vicariously

"Campbell and his father always planned on him moving to Toronto after college for hockey," She explains. "He dropped the bomb on his father this morning that he'd rejected the offer."

My throat tightens.

Why did he never tell me?

"Why would he do that?"

She gazes at me in bewilderment.

"For you, of course."

I wish I could camouflage myself at this very moment.

"I don't understand."

She gazes at me and brushes my hair from my cheek with affection.

"I think you need to talk to him about it."

She smiles before returning to the living room. I return upstairs in a daze as if I were on autopilot.

Hours had passed by the time Campbell entered his room. I'd avoided going downstairs for fear of encountering his father's rage. I opted to sit on the edge of the bed. Neither of us speaks. He locks the door behind him and leans against it. We'd never experienced such tension between us.

"You heard, didn't you?" He deduced.

I can only nod.

He sighs and kneels in front of me. He laces our fingers together.

"You never mentioned Toronto." I mutter.

"I'm sorry," He exhales. "I just didn't think it was important."

"From what I've been told, it's your life plan."

"You spoke to Gina." He notes.

I glance over his head at the mundane wall. Anything is better than having this conversation.

Chapter Sixteen

"You're giving up hockey for me." I replied.

He releases his hands from mine and places them on my cheeks, leaving me no choice but to gaze into his pleading eyes.

"I'm not giving up anything," He leans closer to me. "I can play hockey anywhere."

I close my eyes as they burn. I attempt to move from the hold, but my efforts are futile.

"Hazel," He pleads. "Look at me."

His eyes are glossy.

"I once told you hockey was the only thing that made sense in my life." He cries. "I didn't know it then, but I do now. My life never made sense until I met you. I was always selfish, I only cared about my best interests, but now I love someone beyond comprehension. Someone for which I would give my life. I'd give up everything for you in a heartbeat and never look back."

A lone tear glides down my cheek.

"I can't ask you to sacrifice anything for me."

He smiles as strands of tears escape his hold.

"I wouldn't be sacrificing anything," He promises. "I have everything I need right here."

He stands up and nuzzles me back against the covers. He hovers over me, enveloping me in his natural warmth.

"As long as I have you, Hazel Ellis, then I have everything I could ever want."

I close my eyes and bite back a gasp as he trails his lips down the path of my neck.

"You're so beautiful." His voice vibrates against my skin.

I couldn't help but shiver as he pulled back to glance into my eyes. He never breaks the contact as the edge of my baggy shirt glides up my body as he brushes his hands across my skin. I lift myself as he removes the garment, tossing it to the side. Our eye contact never wavers. He trails his hands down my abdomen until he reaches my inner thighs. He connects our lips to drown out my gasp. I grip the back of his head as I arch my back as a foreign sense of rapture ignites through my core.

"Every time we're in this predicament, I fall in love with you all over again." His words are hardly audible, but they're enough to make my breath hitch. My body reacts to every touch. Each bruising kiss. I place my hands on his chest for a comforting reassurance that he is here. That every pleasure and declaration of love is sincere. He gazes at me as if I were the most angelic thing he'd ever seen as if he was the one that couldn't believe I exist.

I lean forward and place a lingering kiss under his jaw. My stomach burns with pride as the simple action elicits a deep moan. He brushes his nose against mine.

"Thank you for showing me what it's like to be loved." He speaks before pulling me until I'm flush against his chest. "I'd always had admirers, but I've never had someone love me. I never felt like I was ever worth loving."

As his eyes open - I'm greeted by a divine arctic blue. My fingertips glide along his chest. His stomach tightens under my daring caress. I gaze at him through my lashes.

"I'd never had a guy even so much as acknowledge my existence," I admit. "I'd never felt beautiful until you."

"Those other guys were fools." He smirks. "Their loss is my gain."

I cast my eyes downward. He places his hands on my bare waist, dragging me further up the bed. My head meets the soft

Chapter Sixteen

pillow. I bite my lip as he places kisses down my abdomen. To every tender touch, my body responds. The sound of our labored breathing fills the space. His bare flesh rubs against mine, igniting every cell in my body. We'd been in this situation before, but every time is like the first time. The excitement never dwindles. The intensity amplifies with every moment we're together. I wrap my legs around his waist, needing us to be even closer. His natural fragrance and skillful touches make my head swim.

"I love you." He whispers before we once again join as one.

Our breaths collide as our simultaneous moans echo throughout the room.

"I love you too." I breathe out as I wrap my arms around his neck.

Every moment is better than the first.

Chapter Seventeen

I woke up feeling weightless. As if Campbell has kissed away every stress, every point of pressure. His arms are locked around my waist as his warm breath caresses my neck with each exhale. I snuggle further into the sheets, not wanting to leave the insatiable comfort. My mind begins to wander as I trace my nails up and down his arm. I stare into space.

"That feels nice." He utters, followed by a yawn.

I grin but don't stop. He places a hand on my hip and I quiver as his warmth seeps into that spot.

"What is on the agenda for today?" I turn around in his arms.

His eyes are half open as his long lashes caress his cheeks. He pulls me closer and interlocks our legs.

"I want you to meet some of my old friends." He mentions. "They're having a small get-together tonight at my best friend's house. I think you'll like Logan."

Chapter Seventeen

"Will they mind me crashing the reunion?"

"He insisted you come with me." He puffs. "When I told him about you, he told me I couldn't come without you."

He had spoken about me to his friends.

"I'd love to meet them too." I grin.

"Well, I say we don't leave this bed until tonight." He smirks, and I gasp.

"Let's have a Gilmore Girls marathon!" I cheer.

He scrunches his nose.

"Not what I had in mind." He mumbles.

"Please." I pout.

He avoids my gaze, but he relents with a groan.

"You're lucky I love you, Ellie."

He gets out of bed and brings his laptop with him. As his arms pull me closer to him, I don't waste time snuggling into his chest. I trail my finger along his bare chest as goosebumps rise, and he does the same with my exposed hip. He kisses me on the head and leaves his lips to linger.

"Tristan reminds me of you." I tell him once we reach the scene where he and Rory are talking at the party after Summer broke up with him.

"Is that so?" I can hear the smile in his tone.

"He appears a bit of a jerk, but underneath the *I don't care* exterior, he is a softie." I lift my head to look at him. "Just like you. That's why Tristan is my favorite."

"Well, then I'm happy you think we're similar." His radiant grin makes my stomach flutter.

I return my head against his chest and snuggle further into him, loving how he exudes warmth. My eyelids flutter. However, the unimaginable comfort is too delightful to fight as I fade into sleep, lulled by the soothing cradle song of his

Vicariously

heartbeat.

***

Logan's house is as colossal as Campbell's. It seems everyone in this neighborhood is wealthy. Multiple cars are parked in front of it, but I find myself excited to meet his friends.

He doesn't bother knocking, walking straight through the door, dragging me along with him. He waltzes to the outdoor area where the distinct sound of laughter invades my ear drums. As soon as we step outside, we're greeted by whoops and hollers. I bite my lip to hold back a smile at the unusual greeting.

"Finally!" A guy shorter than Campbell draws him into an eager hug. "I was wondering if you were going to show up."

"You begged me to visit." Campbell punches his shoulder before drawing his arm around my waist. "This is Hazel."

His eyes fall on me with a benign smile as he extends his arms out for a hug, which I return.

"I have to admit, I didn't think you were real." The guy chuckles. "When he told me he was bringing a girl back, I called his bluff. I'm Logan, by the way."

I peer at Campbell as he scratches the back of his neck. More guests approached us for a welcomed reunion. My mouth slackens as they all embrace me as if I were a lifelong friend.

"You are so gorgeous!" A petite girl greets. "I'm Moira."

"I'm Hazel." I greet, already feeling at ease by her comforting aura.

"This is Mckenzie." She points to another gorgeous girl.

"Hi." Mckenzie embraces me.

Chapter Seventeen

I take note that they're the only two girls in a herd of guys. Moira grips my hand and drags me towards a campfire. The flames were so high it was as if they were trying to touch the stars. I stood before it as it heated the wintry air around us.

"We've been so excited to meet you." Mckenzie states. "Campbell has never introduced a girl to us before."

"Really?" My natural inquisitiveness takes over.

"It's true," Moira states. "I've known him my entire life. He never once introduced someone as his girlfriend."

I glance over my shoulder with a knowing grin. He stood with his group of friends as they chatted among themselves. It's the most carefree I've seen him in a while.

"How did you meet?" Mckenzie taps her legs in excitement.

I smile at the memory.

"We met in a bookstore." They glance at each other and gasp.

"Campbell Atwood was in a bookstore?" They squeal in unison.

"Are you talking about me?" He calls out.

"Yes!" the girls exclaim in sync before focusing their attention back on me, waiting for me to elaborate.

"He approached me about a book which he later confessed he used as an excuse to talk to me."

"Smooth, Campbell, real smooth." Moira mutters.

My heart leaps with joy as the pair engage in genuine conversation with me. They'd attempted to include me in their group discussions and had taken the time to get to know me. I could hardly conceal my delight as they reminisce about their high school moments.

They are the kindest souls.

I'm giggling along with them as Mckenzie relays a story

about her embarrassing first day of college before being joined by the rowdy guys. Campbell sits next to me, so close our legs are flush together. He tosses his arm over my shoulder and places a quick kiss on my temple.

They screech in delight and I hide my face in his shoulder. He shakes with laughter.

Logan insisted we couldn't let the campfire go to waste and brought a giant platter with everything we needed for s'mores. After I'd burned three of them, Campbell demanded he made one for me.

I thank him before a devious thought enters my mind. As our gazes lock, I scoop some melted marshmallows on my finger and sucked it off.

He gulps as he watches me before I moan in delight. His eyes darken before I break our gaze and converse with the girls once more. As Moira falls into a story of something that happened last week, Campbell leans down to place his lips at my ear.

"You're a tease, Hazel Ellis." He growls. "And I fucking love it."

* * *

Two chapters into my book, I felt a presence in the doorway. Campbell looked at me with wonder as he leaned against the wall.

"I could watch you read for hours." He says as approaches his side of the bed.

He leans his back against the wall and I move closer to him. "You could?"

Chapter Seventeen

He nods his head and twirls the end of my hair between his fingers.

"You could do literally anything and I would think you're the most angelic thing I've ever seen."

He never fails to take my breath away. For someone who claims they aren't good with words, he speaks like a poet.

"When do I get to read your work?"

I giggle. He's adamant.

"Soon." I promise. "You'll be the first to read the completed version."

"Do you promise?" He asks as he holds his pinky out for a *pinky swear.*

I interlock our pinkies, giggling at his immature behavior.

"I promise."

He reaches over and places his lips against mine.

"I will hold you to it, Ellie."

We revel in the peaceful silence as I'm lulled to sleep by his soothing actions of twirling my hair.

"My friends loved you." He says.

I open my eyes and peer at him from under my lashes.

"They did?"

He nods his head with a gentle smile.

"They're happy that I'm happy." He says. "I can't remember a time I've been this content with life."

My heart flutters at his confession.

"You make me happy too."

He pulls me into his chest and places multiple kisses all over my face. I giggle at the ticklish sensation.

"I vow to make sure you're always this happy. It's a promise I never intend to break."

Vicariously

* * *

I glance at the sky through my dorm window. The heavens are overcast with clouds as the brutal breeze strips the trees of their remaining leaves. I'd already begun shivering before even leaving the building. Maisie joined me at my side and offered me a mug of freshly brewed coffee.

"I needed this, thank you." I grip the mug with both hands as the steam defrosts my fingers.

"I'm so excited to go home for winter break." She gushes.

Maisie had lived in California her entire life. She'd always state how much she missed the sultriness, but mostly the beach. The cold has been nothing but unkind to her.

However, I have been ambivalent about returning home for the break. Campbell would join me as I'd been waiting to share stories about my hometown with him - but it's Nevaeh's hometown too. I hadn't spoken to her in months, but we will bump into each other.

The downfall of small-town living.

Campbell had been a nervous wreck since he'd agreed to spend the holidays with my family and me. The paranoia has overruled his every thought. I found it adorable. He'd wanted to learn every detail about my family, hoping to find something to impress them, despite my reassurances that they would welcome him with open arms. They would express their excitement every time I spoke to them on the phone.

After wishing Maisie a joyous holiday followed by a farewell hug and a promise to keep in touch during our time apart, I waltzed out with my horde of luggage.

Campbell greets me at the door and helps load it up in the

Chapter Seventeen

back of his truck. He doesn't speak as his face seems set. I smirk but choose not to confront his strange conduct until we at least get into the car. I turn my body to look at him. He stares out the window. My hand touched his knee as I bent to console him, but he didn't acknowledge me.

"Are you still worried?" I question, afraid of disrupting his thoughts.

"Not at all."

I groan.

"Campbell, I told you they will love you. Why are you so stressed?"

He doesn't speak. He doesn't move.

"Because," He licks his bottom lip. "Because I love you."

He gazes at me like a fragile puppy.

"What does that have to do with anything?"

"I know how much family means to you, and I don't know how I would handle them not liking me. I care about you so I want them to approve of me."

I squeal before reaching over for a heartfelt kiss. He's taken by surprise before returning the kiss.

"They'll love you as much as I do." I reassure.

He takes a moment to compose himself before setting off.

I couldn't wait to be home.

Chapter Eighteen

My town is enriched with history. Generation after generation has seen this town flourish, but it never lost its tradition. The origin is still ingrained. The wind twirls through the streets as the rain gushes upon the rooftops. I revel in the nostalgia. It has been months since I've been home, but I'm grateful that nothing has changed.

We drive past *Tilly's Bakery* - one of the many businesses in this town filled with history and tradition. Tilly Maxwell is the fourth generation to run the bakery. They have the best triple chocolate muffins in existence.

I cannot leave without one. I note as we drive past various businesses before I direct Campbell into my street. His posture stiffens. I repress a giggle. His eyes widen as he spots my family standing outside, ready to greet us. The moment he halts the car, I bolt into their arms.

"We've missed you so much!" My mom exclaims.

Chapter Eighteen

I giggle in their embrace, overjoyed to be home.

They glance over my shoulder as Campbell hovers in the background.

"This is Campbell." I grip his hand and drag him to join us.

"Pleasure to meet you." He replies before extending his hand.

He's taken aback as my mother yanks him into a loving embrace. His hands float in the air before he wraps his arms around my mom. She holds him at arm's length with a wide grin.

"Welcome to our family."

My father shakes his hand and pats him on the shoulder.

"Thank you for having me." He replies in awe of the unusual behavior.

They help us with our bags before dragging us inside to escape the vengeful cold. They gave us a moment to get settled as I ushered him upstairs.

"By the way," I pipe once we're out of earshot. "There's no way they're letting us share a room."

He chuckles.

"I thought as much." He states.

I direct him to his bedroom.

"I'm right across from you." I inform him before rushing into my room, hoping to hide anything embarrassing.

"Ellie," He knocks on my door after a few minutes. "Can I come in?"

I waltz to my door and open it. He pokes his head in with a childish grin.

"I couldn't wait to see your room now that I don't have to sneak around in it." He brushes past me.

I dawdle at the door as he inspects every inch of my room.

Vicariously

He glances around my desk until his eyes befall copies of my short stories. He reaches for them.

"Don't read those." I bite my lip. "I wrote those when I was thirteen."

My eyes lock with his.

"You wrote when you were thirteen?"

I shrug and glance down at my tattered *Vans*. I wasn't fearful of him reading it, I fear him hating it. Campbell's opinion means so much to me. I'd hate for him to dislike my passion. I tread closer.

"You can read it on condition that you don't laugh."

"Why would I laugh?"

I shrug once more. He doesn't hesitate to make himself comfortable on the edge of my bed. His eyes follow the words on the pages as I chew my bottom lip. He places the pages on the side but does not show his thoughts.

"Well?" I question.

"I can't believe you wrote that at thirteen." He breathes. "It's incredible."

As much as I wanted to accept the compliment, my mind forbade it.

He's just saying that.

I don't take my eyes off my shoes, not even when he comes into view. He places his finger under my chin, forcing me to look into his dejected gaze.

"Stop doing that."

"What?"

"Telling yourself you're not good enough."

My shoulders fall. My eyes widened.

How did he know?

"I've noticed it every time I compliment you." He places his

Chapter Eighteen

hands on my waist. "As if you convince yourself you're not worthy of anything."

He towers over me, craning his neck to keep our gazes locked.

"I'm not worthy of you." He speaks.

I freeze.

"Every moment I'm with you, I become a better person. I admire you, Hazel Ellis. I'm the one that will never be worthy of your love, but I'll do everything in my power to show you why you're the greatest thing to enter my life."

My vision becomes blurry. I choke back a sob. Time stops as his lips meet mine in a fervent kiss. My knees buckle as he invades all my senses. His hands glide to the back of my thighs, lifting me and wrapping my legs around his waist. I place my hands on the back of his neck, gripping his strands in a firm grip.

"Hooking up in your childhood bedroom," He grins against my lips. "How scandalous."

I gasp, pulling away.

"I killed the moment," He groans. "Didn't I?"

I giggle and nod my head. He places me back on the ground with a gentle kiss.

"We better go before my parents wonder what we're up to." I wink.

His playful demeanor becomes tense. He's still nervous about spending time with my family.

Wait until he meets the rest tomorrow.

Our dining room is no comparison to his, but he seems delighted by the intimacy. He takes a seat next to me at the table.

"So, Campbell." My dad starts up a conversation. "I heard

you play hockey."

"All my life." He replies.

"I'm impressed. I've heard a lot about you." My dad pipes up. "You should be proud."

Campbell's jaw goes slack. I frowned. Why does he seem so surprised by the comment?

"Thank you." He seems flustered.

He reaches for the glass of water and takes a large gulp. We filled the dinner with laid-back chatter as they took the time to get to know Campbell. I noticed his uncharacteristic behavior the entire time. I only bring it up as we're climbing the stairs to turn in for the night. Before he could rush into his room, I grip his wrist.

"What's going on?" I question.

He avoids my gaze.

"Nothing," He shrugs. "I must be more exhausted than I thought."

I raise my brows.

"Please just leave it alone, Hazel." His tone holds a hint of frustration.

I take a step backward, dumbfounded by his sudden change. With a heavy sigh, I stalk into my room. I shut the door and lean against it. The doubts invade my mind once more.

Was it the best idea to invite Campbell home?

Our contradicting lives have become clear.

Has it put him off?

Has he realized I'm so below him on the social hierarchy?

The insipid thoughts infected my brain as I tossed and turned. My covers have fallen. There's no light except for the alarm clock on my bedside table.

1 AM.

Chapter Eighteen

I groan, as not even an inkling of sleep is present. My phone screen illuminates its surroundings as it vibrates off of my table. I catch it just in time.

Are you awake?

I'm sorry.

I responded.

You're forgiven.

It isn't long after that, I hear a subtle tapping on my door. I launch out of bed and yank him into the room before my parents see him. I lock the door behind him. He hovers by the door.

"I am sorry." He states.

His voice cracks as if he's on the edge of tears.

"What's going on?" I question.

He doesn't reply. I approach him and grip his hand. I motion for him to join me on the edge of my bed. He keeps his eyes set across the room.

"Campbell, you're scaring me."

He glances at his clasped hands.

"I'm not used to this, that's all." He utters.

"Used to what?"

"A family."

My heart shattered at the devastated frown on his face. I place my hand over his.

"Your family has treated me better in a few hours than my dad has my entire life." He confesses. "For the first time in my life, I feel as if I belong somewhere. It terrifies me."

"Why would it scare you?"

He doesn't reply. He keeps his head down as his overgrown curly locks cover his face. My stomach twists as his tearful eyes lock with mine.

"I fear losing it." His voice cracks. "It's everything I've wanted and now that I have it, I feel like I don't deserve it. I don't deserve you."

Tears well up in his eyes before they burst through the walls. His body shakes as he drops his head into his hands. I comb my fingers through his hair, allowing him to let everything he'd been bottling up erupt.

"My mom died in a car accident my junior year." He confesses. "It didn't take my dad long at all to move on. I guess I always viewed family as something replaceable."

My own eyes burn as I reach over to caress his cheeks. I lean over and kiss away a single tear.

"You deserve so much and more." I declare with the utmost sincerity. "I love you and you may have never had a family, but you have one now - if you want it."

His sniffles fill the room as the tears die down. He places his head on my shoulder and I coax my fingers through his hair. We remain in a loving embrace until he pulls away to gaze at me. The corner of his lip rises.

"I want everything with you." He proclaims, before placing his lips on mine.

As if he's trying to convince himself that this is all real. He pushed away. I found myself lost in his orbs, before he pulled me in, once again claiming my mouth. The kiss became hungry and intense. It made my knees weak. His fingers sink into my skin as if it has a mind of its own. His arms wrapped around me in a firm embrace, as if afraid I would vanish.

I place my palms against his chest. His heart is beating at an abnormal pace. He inhales as I drag my nails down his bare chest. Our eyes remain locked as we share our natural warmth. I take him by surprise as I push him down onto the

Chapter Eighteen

sheets before straddling his waist. I lean down as my locks create a protective barrier around us, shielding us from our surroundings. I couldn't help but admire his striking features.

I'm in awe that someone as beautiful as him could love someone like me.

His hands glide down my spine, not stopping until they reach the back of my thighs. I shiver at the delectable sensation.

This moment feels different. More passionate. We take the time to appreciate each other. Mind. Body. Soul. His hand cups the back of my head as he draws me in for a desperate kiss, as if he needs me like oxygen. As if my lips were his life support.

"Seems we're going to hook up in your childhood bedroom, after all." He grins as if this was the cure for his sadness all along.

His tongue explores every inch of my mouth. I pull away to catch my breath as his hand slithers between my legs. I shudder at the sensation brought upon by his skilled fingers. I admire the rise and fall of his chest, as if he's receiving as much pleasure as I am.

"I love you." His hoarse voice fills the silence.

"I love you." I whisper before reaching down to connect our lips to block out our moans as our bodies collide again in an explosive act of intimacy.

I groan as he digs his nails into my skin before he places his hand over my mouth.

"Quiet, Ellie." He taunts. "Wouldn't want your parents hearing us, would you?"

I shake my head.

"I love it when you ride me." He breathes against my neck.

Vicariously

"I get to see every magnificent inch of you."

I stroke my hips as he tilts his head back.

"Hazel." The sound of him groaning my name ignites a new desire in me.

My stomach tightens as he meets my thrusts. He hits all the right spots as if he has mesmerized my pleasure spots, launching me into pure ecstasy. I collapse on his chest as he caresses the back of my head.

"Do you know how much you mean to me?" He asks.

I shake my head.

"I could write an entire novel about how much I love you and it will never be enough."

* * *

I woke up alone. I found it best since my parents would not take well to finding Campbell in my bed first thing in the morning. I made myself as presentable as possible, considering my entire extended family would join us for the day. I'd been ecstatic for them to meet Campbell, but it's been his worst fear. With a pep in my step, I skip downstairs but halt as I hear my mother in the kitchen talking to Campbell.

"This is the happiest I've ever seen her." My mother states.

"I can assure you, it's the happiest I've been." His response has me beaming with pride.

"She's been through a lot." I can sense the sympathy. "Hazel has always doubted herself, but it's as if you've brought out this confident side. It's refreshing."

"She's better influenced me than I have her."

They're silent for a moment. I debated entering the kitchen

Chapter Eighteen

and pretended I heard nothing until my mother spoke again.

"She loves you."

The silence reappears. My stomach twirls with impatience.

"I'm madly in love with her."

My eyes water at his words. I wipe them away before they escape. I take deep breaths until I keep my composure. Campbell and my mother fall into a light conversation about the family and what he could expect. I used that as my opportunity to appear.

"Good morning." My mother greets me as she continues to ice her cupcakes.

Campbell glances at me over his shoulder with a broad grin. He cocoons me in his arms as my back is flushed against his chest.

"Good morning, Ellie." He whispers in my ear.

I place my hands over his in silent greeting.

We filled the rest of the morning with idle chatter until my family arrived like animals at the watering hole. My grandmother embraces Campbell once she sees him, and she's not the only one. My entire family greets him with warm embraces and pleasantries. I could see by the gleeful look on his face that he was enjoying every second of the attention.

We make ourselves comfortable outside as my dad and uncles stand around the grill under the pretense of cooking, but we've all learned it's their ideal gossip spot. I watch as Campbell sits next to my grandmother, absorbing the ample attention she's giving him.

"I'm proud of you, cousin." Layla, my oldest cousin, pipes up beside me.

"What do you mean?" I glance at her with raised brows.

"He's gorgeous." She shrugs. "Never let him go."

I roll my eyes at her words, but cannot hold back the smug grin.

"Wouldn't dream of it."

She leaves before he approaches me. I have never seen him smile so much. He snuggles against me as I'm flush against his chest. He leans down to my right ear as his hot breath fans against it.

"I need you to promise me something." He whispers.

"What?" I responded.

"Promise me we're coming back here for every holiday."

I beam at his words. He'd not only embraced my family, but also admitted that he sees us together in the future. I wanted to squeal and tell everyone in attendance, but I maintain my composure.

"I wouldn't want it any other way."

My cousin's daughter, Sabrina, rushes toward us. I expect her to leap into my arms, but she brushes past me and goes to Campbell. My brows furrow in surprise as he lifts her up and her childish giggles flutter through the wind.

I raise a questioning brow as Campbell turns to me.

"We've become best friends." He explains with a shrug as he tickles her side.

If she continues to giggle, she might combust. I can't help but smile at their exchange.

I've always been a sucker for a guy that's good with kids.

"I want you to have this." She says as she places a unicorn bracelet in his hands. "I made it for you. You can wear it for good luck at all your hockey games."

He gasps as if it's the most amazing work of art he's ever seen. He places it on his wrist and beams with adoration.

"It's perfect." He says. "Now I will think of you every time I

Chapter Eighteen

play."

Her toothless smile widens as he embraces her before setting her down. She rushes off to play with the rest of the kids. He doesn't take his eyes off the hot pink bracelet.

As our eyes connect, I notice they'd become watery.

"I am never taking this off." He grins as he wraps his arm around my waist.

His lips tremble as he leans his chin on my shoulder.

"Thank you for bringing me here." He whispers.

I cast my fingers through his hair and placed a kiss on his temple.

"I'm glad you enjoyed it."

"I *loved* it." He leans his head back. "I've always wanted this, and it makes me even more excited about my future with you."

He tilts his head for a kiss, sighing in delight against my lips.

"Let's not let the rest of the day go to waste." He suggests before placing a kiss on my lips.

* * *

I'm overloaded with nostalgia as I enter *Tilly's Bakery* with Campbell hot on my heels. I could smell her cinnamon buns before I even stepped foot inside. They are as decadent as any gateau.

This place holds so many memories. It had been my first summer job. It was my junior year and my family kept our vacation local. I'd walk to her bakery every morning to catch the delicacies fresh out of the oven and I would write for hours until she approached me and offered me a job as a waitress. I accepted, delighted I would have money and something to do during the break.

The aroma of freshly baked cookies invades my nostrils and I moan in delight. If I could eat the air, I would. I approach the counter to find Tilly standing with her oldest daughter, Maggie, as they placed the cookies out to cool. Her eyes sparkle in delight as she notices me.

"Hazel!" she exclaims, rushing towards me as fast as her aging legs could allow. I meet her halfway with extended arms.

"I am so happy to see you." I beam. She's always been like a grandmother to me.

Her eyes fall on Campbell hovering in the background, witnessing the exchange. I motion for him to come closer.

"This is my boyfriend, Campbell." I say with a timid grin.

He welcomes her hug as she dotes over him, just like a grandmother would.

"You are so handsome!" She grips his cheeks and I bite my lip to stop a giggle from escaping.

"It's a pleasure meeting you." I scoff at his uncharacteristic display of manners. He'd have an arrogant comeback lined up most of the time, but I admire how gentle he is with her.

"I'll bring you your favorite." She says as she motions for us to sit at the counter.

Campbell is nothing short of delighted as she places two large chocolate shakes and a plate of triple chocolate chip cookies fresh out of the oven. I grab a cookie and take a huge bite out of it. I close my eyes in delight as the familiar taste envelops my taste buds. The chocolate chips melt on your tongue. I open my eyes to find Campbell already gazing at me. His eyes sparkle with amusement.

"What?" I take a smaller bite.

Chapter Eighteen

"Everything you do is fascinating to me." He remarks before reaching for a cookie. He takes a bite and has the same reaction as me. "This is so good." He says through a mouthful.

I scoff with a slight grin as we demolish the plate of cookies, wolfing down our chocolate shakes. We are going to suffer an outrageous sugar rush.

Snickers capture my attention as a trio of girls enters the bakery. My heart plummets into my stomach as I notice Nevaeh and the familiar faces of Taylor and Kelsey - the *it girls* of my high school. Campbell preoccupied himself with the menu and didn't notice them. I gulp and place my hand on his knee.

"I'll be right back." I bolt for the restroom and place my head in my hands.

Out of all the people in the world that could have walked into the bakery, it had to be them. I take a deep breath before trailing out of the restroom. I halt in my tracks as I notice the trio surrounding Campbell. He's leaning against the counter as they chatter away. His eyes seem glazed over as he folds his arms across his chest. I watch as Kelsey twirls the ends of her hair, just like Nevaeh. She tilts her head to the side as she places her hands on his biceps. I see red.

I storm toward the *pretty committee*, not even flinching as they look down on me. Campbell seems scared for his life, as if he's afraid I'm going to lash out at him for being surrounded by beautiful women. His eyes could pop out of the sockets they're so wide. I grip the collar of his shirt and place my lips against his in a heated kiss. A kiss that sends a message.

He's mine, back off.

He juts out his chin as his smug grin surrounds most of his face. I avoid him for the time being.

Vicariously

"Hazel, when Nevaeh mentioned you had a boyfriend, I couldn't believe it." Taylor says with a scrunched nose.

"Well, I'm right here." Campbell chimes in before I could.

She responds with a conceited grin.

"That's so kind of you." She says. "I doubt a virgin could keep up with an Adonis like you."

Is she flirting with my boyfriend right in front of me? The nerve.

He gazes at me in mock horror. I giggle, knowing what he's thinking.

"I'm certain she's not a virgin, considering we've fucked before." He smirks. "Multiple times, in fact." He brushes his locks through his hair. "And let me tell you, I've never had it as good as Hazel and I never will."

Their jaws drop open. I can feel Nevaeh's piercing stare, as if she were wishing I would instantaneously combust. The corner of my lip rises. Campbell intertwines our fingers and tilts his head to the side.

"I hope you have a lovely day."

We hold in our laughter until we're outside the bakery. We clutch our stomachs, not caring about the strange looks we're receiving. Their ridiculous faces keep appearing in my mind. I wipe the tears away as the laughter fades.

"It doesn't get as good as me?" I say, attempting to tease him, but he's unbothered by my attempt at embarrassing him.

"It's the truth." He says as he twirls my locks around his finger. "You've put me off any other women, Ellie."

Now I am blushing. I think back to what he'd said when we were spending the day with my family, how he'd mentioned spending more time with them in the future. I wanted to question him on it, but I'm afraid it may make things tenser between us.

Chapter Eighteen

What if it was a slip of the tongue? Or he'd reconsidered. What if he'd regretted it the moment he said it?

"What's on your mind?" He grips my hands. "I know that look."

As I look at our interlocked hands, I bite my lips. As I debate on bringing it up or not, I sway our hands to the side.

"Can I ask you something?"

"Always." There's no sense of hesitancy in his voice.

"You mentioned wanting to spend more time with my family?" I say.

"I did."

I inhale for courage.

"So, that means you see a future with me?"

The smile on his face was like a sudden beam of light, illuminating the darkest edges of my inner turmoil.

"I see eternity with you, Hazel Ellis."

I could hardly contain my happiness as I stood on my tiptoes to attach our lips together. He bites my bottom lip before pulling away with a chuckle. His eyes gaze into mine as our foreheads touch.

"By the way," He breathes. "You're sexy when you're jealous."

Chapter Nineteen

I'd never felt comfortable in my body. I'd always resorted to baggy clothing and covering up as much skin as possible, but I see myself in a new light ever since I met Campbell.

He makes me feel beautiful and desirable, reassuring me I'm the most beautiful girl in his eyes. Words cannot express how appreciative I am of his reassurances. He was the weapon against my fearful thoughts. He's always ready to chase the negativity away. I'm thankful for him.

With a defeated sigh, I flip through my textbook. I'm supposed to be studying, but everything is a distraction.

My mind keeps flickering back to Campbell as if I'm some love-struck middle schooler. He'd been preoccupied with practice, so we have seen little of each other for a few days. We'd been exchanging texts and phone calls, but it was not the same as seeing him in person.

I've been missing the feel of his arms around me. His

Chapter Nineteen

warmth and the intoxicating scent of *Rosewood.* I miss him.

I may be acting ridiculous considering it's only been a few days, but I yearn for him.

I flip through my textbooks, marking things I feel are important, but I'm not registering the information. As I lift the book above my face, I roll onto my back.

There are no text messages on my phone. Maisie is gone for the weekend to visit her sick grandmother, and I have no other friends.

Pretty tragic.

I drop my book to the side and gaze up at my barren ceiling. My thoughts run wild as I think back on everything that has happened so far this year. It's been a tumultuous year so far and it's nowhere near done. I drop my head to the side to gaze at Maisie's made bed and groan.

A devious idea pops into my mind and I engage in an internal debate on whether I should go through with it. I scour through my wardrobe in search of something that I wanted to throw out but never did. My fingers brush over the lace and I haul it out of my closet with shaky hands.

I glance at the black and red lingerie, biting my lip in thought. Nevaeh made me buy it during our college shopping spree, insisting I would need it one day. I thought she was absurd, but now I am thankful that she'd forced me to buy it.

My chest feels tight as I try it on, glancing at myself in the mirror. I take in every angle of my body, fearing how terrible I look.

But I know Campbell will love it.

The thought is enough for me to build up the courage to reach for my phone and open my camera. I point it toward the mirror and snap a picture of my reflection. I analyze the

Vicariously

picture, noticing how awkward I look. This is supposed to look sexy. I move to my bed and collapse against the pillows. Before I raise the phone, I take a deep breath. I bite the tip of my finger as I snap a few shots.

I analyze the pictures until I find one that's decent enough to send. Butterflies rumble in my stomach as I search for his contact. I write the words *I'm Missing You* under the image. My fingers hover over the send button.

Once it's sent, it's out there forever.

I trust Campbell. I know he's not the type of guy to show anyone, but what if one of his teammates glimpses at his phone? I shrug off the concerns and click send before I could talk myself out of it. I gnaw on the corner of my lip, waiting for a response.

He must still be busy with practice.

I redress over the lingerie and sit on the edge of my bed. My heart races as I tap my foot against the floor. I pace back and forth around the room, on the verge of pulling my hair out.

Ding!

I launch onto my bed as I reach for my phone. My heart hammers in my chest as Campbell's name flickers on the screen.

Holy shit.

I giggle at his reply, feeling a wave of confidence wash over me.

Do you like it?

I wish I could have witnessed his reaction, or been able to read his mind to know what he thought when he opened the text. My phone chimes.

I LOVE IT!

I'm overcome with joy at his words. He beats me to it when

Chapter Nineteen

I think of what to text next.

You would look better without it on, though.

My body feels flushed. I should be used to his boldness by now, but he still surprises me at every opportunity.

If only you weren't busy with practice...

I giggle as he types back.

I've never hated hockey as much as I do right now.

The humor leaves my body as another text follows.

Don't even think about taking it off. I have an idea.

As I ponder what he could have planned, I am left pining for him. I distract myself by cleaning up around the room. However, my mind keeps running back to Campbell and his mysterious plans.

I return to my textbook and flip back to the last chapter I'd read. I'd gotten through five pages before there was a knock at my door. I rush toward it and swing it open. Campbell is leaning against the doorway with the widest smirk I'd ever seen.

"What happened to *keeping it on*?" His voice is hoarse.

"It's underneath my clothes." I flush as my neck feels hot.

He brushes past me and into the room.

"Did I interrupt your studying?" He questions as he picks up my *creative writing* textbook.

"I haven't been able to focus much." He slides off his team jacket and tosses it on Maisie's bed.

"I think I can help with that."

I tilt my head to the side.

"You're going to help me study?"

He approaches me and grabs my waist. My stomach tenses at our intense eye contact as his eyes seem dilated.

"You were my tutor. Now it's time I tutor you."

Vicariously

I draw my eyes to his mouth as my palms become sweaty.

"How about I ask you questions and if you get them correct, I'll remove an article of clothing."

My eyes pop out of their sockets.

"What if I get a question wrong?"

"You take off your clothes, of course." He doesn't miss a beat.

I nibble on my lip, something I've been doing often in his presence. I admire him in his faded black shirt and jeans, but the backward cap on his head gets me worked up.

"You have a deal."

Pleased with my answer, he takes a seat on my bed and motions for me to do the same. I sit in front of him and place my hands on my lap. He skims through my book in search of a question.

"What are the three types of dramatic poetry?"

I pretend to think it over, but I already know the answer.

"Dramatic monologue, soliloquy and lyrical." The smug grin falls, but only momentarily.

"A deal is a deal." He reaches for his cap.

"No!" I exclaim. "Leave the cap for last."

He rolls his eyes, but his smile is prominent. I watch in desire as he reaches for the hem of his shirt and lifts it to reveal his glistening abdomen. My heart hammers against my chest.

"Name three poetic devices."

My brain has turned to jelly as I forget to speak. I'm distracted by him and the outrageous aching between my legs.

"I forgot."

He places the book down with a cocky smile.

Chapter Nineteen

"A deal's a deal, Ellie."

I roll my eyes as I reach for my shirt, lifting it to tease him. His eyes widen as he glances at the lacy material.

"It looks even better than in the pictures." He says, his eyes seeming far away.

"Next question." It's my turn to be smug.

He shakes his head and breathes out through his nose before glimpsing through the chapters for another question. It gets to where we're left in only our underwear, and his backward cap is still placed on his mop of hair.

"Hazel." He says. "Where were you when I needed you for my finals?" I giggle at his words with a shrug. "I've never loved education more."

His gaze burned into me and it was as if something had been ignited inside me. Deciding to be a tease, I stood up and slid my straps down my arms. I reach behind my back and loosen the back. I was tempted to look at Campbell, but I knew if I saw the desire in his eyes, I would lose all my nerve. I toss my bra to the side and he takes a sharp inhale of breath. I reached for my final shred of clothing and slid it over my thighs and let it drop to my ankles. I kicked the discarded material to the side.

I approach him and straddled his lap. I was so close to him that I could feel the heat of his body. My heart raced as our eyes met and we held contact. I could feel him throbbing beneath me. I press my lips to his, enticing him with the promise of more.

"You amaze me." He gasps through ragged breathing. "You're always keeping me on my toes."

I grind my hips against his in reply. He groans and wraps his arms tighter around me. Our eye contact never wavers.

Vicariously

"You bring out this side of me," I whisper against his lips as I continue to thrust my hips.

"Ellie." He gasps. "I need you right now."

I halt my movements. His eyes pop out of his head.

"Why did you stop?" He growls.

I shrug in response.

"Stop being a tease."

"Or what?"

He reaches behind my head and grips my hair, drawing me closer until his lips brush against mine.

"Now is not the time for games, Ellie." His minty breath brushes my face.

"I feel like playing." I say with a sinister grin.

With cat-like agility, he tosses me onto my back and hovers over me. He reaches to remove his cap, but I place my hands over his.

"Please don't take it off." His dark eyes flicker with a hint of amusement, like stars among his darkened pupils.

With a curt nod, he reaches to slide his briefs down his spindling leg. He trails a finger down my chest while maintaining eye contact. My veins burst with desire for him.

It's as if he'd heightened my senses with every fiery kiss. I hungrily attach our lips together as I wrap my legs around his waist.

"I think I may be a bad influence on you, Hazel Ellis." He grins between our kisses.

"I'm only bad for you." I say as I lather his neck in kisses.

"You know the words to get me going." He says with a shaky breath.

He spreads my legs further to make himself comfortable, never once removing his lips from mine. I'm feeling faint

Chapter Nineteen

from the lack of oxygen, but I don't care. The only thing I care about is engaging in this act of unbridled passion with him.

The moment he slides into me, I arch my back and rake my nails down his spine. As he places my arms at my sides, I am overthrown by passion.

I gaze up at his rosy face, admiring the backward cap attached to his head. The most delicious moan came when I clutch the sheets as his thrusts sped up.

"Campbell!"

"I love it when you moan my name." He growls into my ear. "I can never get enough of it."

My veins feel scorching, like molten lava. It's as if the galaxy was above our head as I get lost in the galactic pleasure.

"I'm nearly there, Ellie." He groans as our highs approach.

We collapse on the bed, completely spent. His arm curls around my waist.

"I am wearing this cap every day if this is the reward I get." I hit his hand as I snuggle further into him.

He trails his fingers down my arm, creating goosebumps. The loving gesture lulls me into slumber.

Chapter Twenty

The deafening music pulsed from the frat house, becoming more ear-splitting the closer you get. I wanted to turn around and save myself a migraine, but this party wasn't like the others. It's important.

It's Campbell's birthday.

I'd spent weeks of preparation searching for the perfect gift to give him. What do you give someone that already has so much? I'd developed an ulcer from the stress until it popped into my mind like a metaphorical light bulb hanging above my head. *The perfect gift.*

On the makeshift dance floor sweaty, drunken students, coiled together, jumping to the base of the music. I kicked a pile of beer cans as I become hazy from the smoke fumes. The smell of nicotine has a way of making me feel nauseous. A large group gathered around a beer keg as someone delegated themselves as the *honorary server.* However, he seemed to have been sampling most of it for himself. His intoxicated eyes

Chapter Twenty

couldn't find the cups, as most of the beer splattered on the ground. I ventured into the quieter part of the home. The living room filled with people crowding around the chairs as Campbell and Shaun, their frat leader, were engaging in a battle of hockey on the *Xbox*. I lean against the wall as the spectators cheer their respective players on. I couldn't help but admire how adorable Campbell looks with his tongue poking out from the side as he concentrated on winning.

Our eyes lock for a moment. I expected him to continue playing, but he paused the game, much to the disinterest of the crowd. Horizontal wrinkles appeared between my eyes as he approaches me and lifts me off the ground. I giggle and wrap my arms around his neck.

"Happy birthday." I whisper into his ear.

"Thank you, baby." He places me down and kisses me.

More groans resonate in the room.

"You can make out later, Atwood. We have a game to finish." I chuckle as he grips my hand and drags me with him.

He returns to his seat and pulls me onto his lap. I tense as he wraps his arms around me and reaches for the controller.

"Watch me kick his ass." He whispers into my ear.

I could only focus on their game for a while before my mind strayed. I couldn't believe that he was being affectionate to me in front of his friends. *Is that pathetic of me to think?* Trent barely acknowledged me when we *dated,* but I suppose it's because he never liked me. *He wanted Nevaeh.*

The thought may have upset me in the past, but being with Campbell has shown me everything that was wrong with Trent. Campbell has never failed in showing me how much he cares and helped me see how I deserve to be treated. My stomach tingles as I snuggle further into his hold, beaming with love as he seems proud to show me off in front of his friends. My attention returns to the game as Campbell is leading by one. He taps away at the buttons with his tongue stuck out. I smile at the sight.

"Why are you staring at me, Ellie?" His concentration never falters.

"You're so cute when you're concentrating."

"I'm not cute, I'm sexy."

I roll my eyes and scoff.

"Whatever helps you sleep at night."

"The thought of you helps." He grins.

I feel my posture beginning to sink. I place my hands on his knees and push myself up onto his lap. He groans into my ear as his grip on the controller tightens. Mischievous thoughts take over my mind as I grind myself against him once more. His knuckles turn white as he misses a goal.

"What's going on with you, Atwood?" One of his frat brothers questioned.

"Sorry." He utters through strangled breaths.

He lines his character up for another shot. I take it as my opportunity to grind against him again. The puck goes nowhere near the net. The crowd around us groan as most had placed their bets on Campbell.

"What do you think you're doing?" He growls into my ear, but I pretend I didn't hear him. His breath brushes against my ear, igniting shivers down my spine. "I'm thinking I've corrupted you, Ellie."

I decided it was best to stop distracting him. After all, I want him to win. It doesn't take him long to make up for the goals he'd lost, placing him back in the lead. He scores another goal before the game ends. Shaun tosses his controller onto the

Chapter Twenty

table as a flurry of mixed responses reverberates in the room. Campbell secures his arms around my waist and kisses my cheek.

"I can't believe you're letting us around your girl, Atwood." A guy with dirty blonde hair says. "We were thinking you wanted to hide her from us."

Chuckles infiltrate the room.

"I didn't want to punish her by making her spend time with you." Howls followed Campbell's retort, like a pack of hyenas.

I witness the exchange in delight. The unknown dirty blonde acknowledges me.

"I'm Willis." He says. "We've been nagging him to meet you, but he was too concerned you'd run off the first chance you got."

"The night's still young." They met my remark with cackles as they reach over and shove Campbell.

"He talks about you all the time." Another speaks before downing a can of beer. "You've got him whipped."

They all crack their imaginary whips before rolling into fits of laughter. They're either drunk, or the house has been infected with laughing gas. The latter seems very unlikely.

"You would understand if any of you had a girl." They feign offense as they place their hands over their hearts.

"You get one girlfriend and now you're better than us?" Willis says as he wipes away an imaginary tear.

"If you find a girl even a quarter as amazing as mine, you'd understand where I'm coming from."

My ears burn at his confession. His *public* confession. This wasn't a declaration of love in private. He'd done that countless times. This was a declaration of love in front of his teammates. His friends. He doesn't seem the slightest bit ashamed. Instead, he grips my head and draws me in for a kiss. They applaud the action and I pull away. I've always hated *PDA*. There is nothing more revolting than having to watch a couple eat each other's faces.

"Whose up for another round?" Shaun questions.

"I will."

The words escape before I could stop them. As *Cady Heron* would say - *word vomit.* The perk of being a social outcast is that I would spend most of my nights on the *Xbox* if I wasn't reading. While most people were going out, getting wasted, and losing their virginities, I opted to isolate myself from the teenage *rights of passage.* It always seemed like a mistake, but an opportunity has arisen for me to show off my hidden talents.

"I don't want Atwood to beat me for making you cry." Shaun teases.

I snort.

"The only one that's going to need comfort is you." The group chuckles at our banter.

I wait for Shaun to start the game. Campbell draws me closer to his chest and brushes his lips across my ear.

"A part of me wants to get revenge on you." He says. "The other wants you to kick Shaun's ass."

I turn my head. Our noses touch.

"We have all night for revenge." I wink.

"I didn't think it was possible for you to turn me on any more than you already do, but you holding the controller in your hand does things to me."

As the game begins, I suppress my laughter. I lean forward in Campbell's lap with furrowed brows as I press the buttons at such a speed it would make *The Flash* jealous. Cheers erupt

Chapter Twenty

as I score a goal. Shaun drops his head in defeat.

"You were saying?" I question, feeling smug.

"The game isn't over yet." He says as we continue our competition.

It's as strenuous as if we were on the ice. If this is the pressure I'm feeling virtually, I cannot imagine the pressure they withstand realistically.

"You can do this, Ellie." With a sudden boost of confidence from Campbell, I score three goals to Shaun's two.

I tilt my head back and pump my fists in the air. The whoops and hollers boom around the room. I glance at Shaun as he strives to hold his smile back.

"I let you win." He says.

"My girl kicked your ass." Campbell intervenes. He reaches over to pat Shaun's back. "That should teach you to never underestimate her."

He hugs me from behind and lathers my cheek in a kiss. I shriek and swat his hands away, but he's relentless. Everyone breaks away into their own conversations. I turn my head to look into Campbell's eyes.

"Have you enjoyed your birthday?"

"Having you with me has made it so much better." He places a kiss on my scrunched nose.

"I have a present for you." I say.

"Is it you?" He waggles his eyebrows. I chuckle in amusement.

"It's even better."

"How could it get any better than you?"

I lean closer as if I'm about to share confidential information.

"Follow me upstairs and you'll find out." His breath hitches

Vicariously

as I stand up. He licks his lips and gets to his feet.

"Where are you going?" Shaun asks.

"No offense, bros, but I've had enough of you. I want to end my birthday with my girl." They whine, but he ignores them as he ushers me upstairs and into his bedroom.

He locks the door behind him before rushing toward me and attaches his lips to mine like an addict needing a fix.

"I've been wanting to kiss you ever since you arrived." He reaches for the ends of my hair. It seems to have become a habit for him. "What's this rumor about a present?"

I reach up and kiss his jaw before approaching my backpack on his bed. There is a dark red bow on top of a box in red and white. He holds it in his hand. He takes a seat at the edge of the bed and unwraps it. I gnaw on my bottom lip suddenly concerned he'd hate it.

He opens the present and gasps. He lifts the snow globe out of the box and inspects it. He says nothing. He's only focused on the object in front of him. I notice a trail of tears flowing down his cheeks and my stomach clenches in fear I'd upset him. Did I overstep my boundaries? He places it back into the box and sets it on his bed before his head falls into his hand. His shoulders shudder with each muffled sob.

"I didn't mean to upset you." I say as I panic.

This was an awful idea.

With lightning speed, he launches toward me like a rocket and smothers me in his arms.

"I love it so much." He says through tears. Some fall onto my head, but it's irrelevant. I wrap my arms around his waist as we take comfort in each other.

"I know it's not your mom's, but I'm hoping it's similar."

"It's perfect." He cups my head in his hands and places his

Chapter Twenty

warm lips on my forehead. "You're perfect."

"It's still your birthday, and you get to do whatever you want." He smoothed my hair down, coaxing his hands down my shoulders and to my hips.

"What I want most in the world is to end the night with you in my arms."

I reach my hand behind his neck and pull him down for a chaste kiss.

"Your wish is my command." I breathe against his lips, intent on ending the night the way he wants.

* * *

Morning arrives as a mother's gentle hand as I bask in the bliss from the previous night. Campbell's sheets envelop me as if he were beside me. Waking up comes slow and relaxed. I raise my arms above my head, stretching my tense muscles. Curious about what Campbell's gotten up to, I force myself out of bed and cover my scandalous outfit with his hoodie. I tiptoe downstairs. One of his frat brothers could find me any second. I strain my ears for any sign of where he might be, drawing my attention to hushed whispers in their kitchen. I approach with my back against the wall as a mixture of voices echo. I recognize Campbell's rough morning voice.

"Hazel is cool." A voice says. I smile.

"She's the best."

"I still cannot believe you're not single anymore." Another voice chuckles. "Don't you miss it?"

"Miss what?"

"The old Campbell." Someone says. "The random hookups

and never being tied down."

The silence makes my stomach turn.

"Not even a little." Campbell says. "I can never go back to that guy again, not when I have Hazel."

"I can't picture wanting to give that all up. We're in college. We're supposed to be young and wild."

Campbell's laugh brushes off the walls.

"I'm still young and wild." He says. "I just get to experience it with the love of my life."

They make hurling sounds, and I refrain from scoffing at their immaturity. I know it's wrong to be listening to their conversation, but how can I resist?

"Wait until you find someone. You'll regret making fun of me." Campbell says.

"I'm never falling in love."

"I said the same thing, and then I met Hazel." I bite my lip to hold in a squeal. Could he get any better?

I tiptoe back upstairs and wait for him to join me. I didn't want to risk getting caught. I fall onto his fluffy pillows and close my eyes. His door creaks. I sit upright and smile as he has a tray full of breakfast in his hand.

"You made all of that?" I ask.

"Of course not. We ordered it."

I bite into a bagel and moan. His eyes lock on me and I felt self-conscious.

"What?"

"You know," he says. "It's rude to eavesdrop."

I choke on the bite in my mouth.

"How did you know?"

"I saw your shadow." He chuckles.

My cheeks are as red as the ketchup on my plate. So much

Chapter Twenty

for being stealthy.

"Sorry."

He caresses my cheek.

"It's okay, Ellie, it's not like I lied to them." He says. "I meant every word."

"You must love me." I say, attempting to make light of the situation, but his intense expression doesn't change.

"More than life itself." He bends for a kiss. "Thank you for making my birthday the best I've ever had."

"How did I do that?" I ask as his smile widens and his dimples are more noticeable.

"By being mine."

Chapter Twenty-One

I've always wondered what makes an excellent writer. Is it the grammar? The spelling? The plot? I've concluded that everyone holds a different opinion. I believe being a talented writer entails so many unique elements. Every story is unique. The most important thing a writer can do is to remain true to themselves. A writer's authenticity amplifies the story. The words we write showcase our thoughts.

However, someone that has never attempted to sit down and write will never understand the emotional trauma it inflicts. It's easy to read a work already written and to give your opinion, but once you attempt to bring pen to paper, your words of judgment become your reality.

No book is perfect. No story is written perfectly. However, every story is perfectly foretold, even if it takes a few drafts.

I'd always doubted myself as a writer, doubted my abilities, my talent. I've gotten so into my head about writing the perfect story I've forgotten it's been perfect from the start,

Chapter Twenty-One

because it's mine.

Yet the erratic and deceiving thoughts in the back of my mind always attempt to power through, tainting me with its negativity before I get the strength to push it back. Doubt has always been my *kryptonite* and I fear it always will be - because even Superman feared the very thing that could destroy him. It's why he always ran from it.

The harshest critics are the ones that never walked in your shoes.

As my vision begins to blur, I stare at my laptop screen. I've been hunched over my desk for most of the morning when a sudden wave of inspiration hits. Before the pre-game party at Campbell's frat, I wanted to write as much as possible. They're playing against their biggest rivals tomorrow night. *Jonah's team.* He'd been bragging about destroying the opposition. I found it best to indulge his arrogance.

My phone vibrates against my desk.

Can't wait to see you tonight!

I bite my lip and type a response before returning my focus to my story. My fingers glide over the keyboard as I bring my story to life. I attempt to drown out the negative thoughts. It's not that I fear anyone reading my work. I fear them hating it. I fear failing before even trying. My biggest fear has always been failing at the one thing I love doing.

I shake all the concerns away as I continue to write.

I'll never know until I try.

* * *

From the moment I entered the sultry party, I searched for

Vicariously

Campbell, only to come up short. A girl and I collided. I apologized, but she only delivered a glare. I ignore it and continue my search. This time I collided with a hardened figure. I soothe the spot under my ribs where I was elbowed.

"I'm sorry, I must have not recognized you without your boyfriend." He bellows over the thunderous tones of some song I'd never heard of before.

Jonah towers over me with a sadistic smirk, as if he could sense how uncomfortable I feel around him. He's enjoying every second of my cowering. He leans down until he's at ear level.

"You look beautiful tonight." Shivers run down my spine, but not in a good way.

My bottom lip quivers. I take a cautious step back as he steps forward. We repeat the process until my back is against the wall.

Literally.

He placed his hands on either side of my head, trapping me in. I'm too frozen to breathe. My chest tightens as his face draws nearer. His smirk widens.

"Do I make you nervous?" I don't speak. "I don't know what a pretty girl like you is doing wasting their time with someone like Campbell Atwood."

A wave of confidence strikes like lightning.

"You say it like the real douchebag isn't standing before me."

The thing about lightning is that it's gone as soon as it strikes.

His forehead crinkles in frustration before it's masked by the sickening smirk.

"You don't like me." He notes.

Brilliant observation.

"I promise I'm the better choice."

Chapter Twenty-One

That's debatable.

Before I could react, he bent the rest of the way down, attaching our lips. My instincts kick in as I pull away. The palm of my hand collides with his cheek before sprinting into the crowd. I shove people aside until I'm engulfed by the fresh outside air. I place my hands on my knees as I take large gulps of oxygen. Hot tears cascade down my cheeks and fall at my feet.

"Ellie." I sob harder at the sound of Campbell's voice.

With a stream of tears, I watched as he left his group of friends and rushed toward me. His hands grip my shoulders.

"What's going on?"

I didn't want to tell him what had transpired. I couldn't. I know the chaos that would ensue if Campbell was to learn the truth. My body shakes as I calm myself down.

"Hazel," His voice is firm. "What's going on?"

I shake my head.

"Hazel," He hisses in frustration. "Who did this?"

I wipe my eyes.

"I'm serious." He insists. "Give me a name. They're dead."

His gaze flickers over my shoulder. His entire face contorts into an insurmountable rage. With superhuman speed, he rushes past me. I remain frozen as he tackles Jonah to the ground, gathering a large crowd. They block my view, snapping me out of my stupor. I push through the crowd with as much strength as I can muster. I'm just in time as Campbell's fist collides with Jonah's jaw. I plead for him to stop, but the jeering crowd drones my voice out, sighing as his fraternity brothers push through and haul him away from Jonah. He attempts to wriggle out of their clutches, but they overpower him.

Vicariously

"Let me go!" He bellows. "Who even invited him?"

"That would be me." Celeste emerges from the crowd with her posse shadowing.

Including Nevaeh.

I hadn't seen her in ages. She avoids my gaze.

"Well, take your date and leave." Campbell seethes.

"What were you thinking, Celeste?" One of Campbell's frat brothers questioned.

Jonah straightens up and gazes at me with a sickeningly sweet grin.

"Hazel wasn't complaining when my lips were on hers." His wicked grin makes my blood boil. "It's not my fault Atwood is dead weight."

It's as if the world paused. As if every single person in attendance was digesting the words. My face contorted with rage. It's one thing to insult me, but the moment he'd attacked Campbell, all I saw was red. Before I could even think what I was doing, I bolted towards him and kneed him in the balls before delivering a harsh slap across his face. Everyone around me groans as he drops to the floor in pain. I gasp and place my hands over my mouth.

Did I just do that?

I turn to Campbell - his face as shocked as mine. We burst into simultaneous laughter.

"You stupid bitch."

Campbell's venomous glare returns before he's launching for Jonah. I cry out for Campbell, pleading for him to back off, but he's consumed by rage. A larger group steps and pulls them apart. They drag Jonah away, but I only care about Campbell. He's dragged upstairs and I follow him into his bedroom. His frat brothers exit the room leaving us alone.

Chapter Twenty-One

I close the door and lean against it. He's hunched over on the edge of the bed. His hair is gripped between his fingers. His knuckles are bloody. I cringe as the images of the fight reappear in my brain.

I venture into his connected restroom in search of a first aid kit - anything to distract me. I kneel before him and place my hand on his knee. He takes a deep breath but doesn't move. My eyes prickle with tears. My incessant sniffling must have alerted him as he lifted his head. His once-dark eyes returned to their alluring state. He brushes his thumb along my cheek, wiping away a lone tear.

"I'm sorry." I choke out.

His round eyes gaze into mine.

"Why are you sorry?" His voice is hoarse from the verbal dispute. "I should be the one apologizing. I never wanted you to see that side of me."

He bows his head in shame.

"You did nothing wrong," I assured him. "You were looking out for me."

He doesn't acknowledge my words.

"I didn't kiss him." I don't know why I brought it up, but I needed him to know.

For my sanity.

The silence is a steady killer. Every second constricts my airway until I feel as if I'm going to choke.

"I know," He mutters under his breath. "I know."

He lifts his head.

"You do?" I breathe.

He nods with a hint of a smile under the scowl. He doesn't break our connection.

"I've never doubted your love for me, Hazel Ellis." He

reaches for a strand of my hair and twirls it around his finger on instinct. "Besides, you're far too intelligent to downgrade from me to him." I giggle at his attempt at lightening the mood. "I'm sorry he did that."

I lean on my knees and grip his head between my hands. My eyes admire his distinctive features.

"I'm happy I have you to turn to when things get out of control." I murmur.

"You always will." He seals the vow with a kiss but winces as he realizes he'd split his lip.

He breathes out a laugh.

"You kicked the guy in the balls." He cackles. "I always knew my girl was a badass."

My heart flutters at the words *my girl*. I reached for the first aid kit. Neither of us speaks as I tend his wounds. He barely winces as I lather the alcohol on his knuckles.

"You make an excellent nurse." He grins.

I suppressed a laugh but continued swabbing at his wounds. He gazes at me from under his enviously long lashes. He places his hands on my waist.

"I'm so glad I get to kick his ass on the ice tomorrow." He muses.

I scowl.

"Do nothing that could get you in trouble with the team." I warn.

He grins with a shrug.

"No promises." He pulls me further between his legs. "You know what could make these bruises heal quicker?"

"What?"

"A kiss." He smirks.

I lean down and press my lips against his. I pull away,

Chapter Twenty-One

making him frown.

"Is that all?"

"I don't want to hurt your lip."

He chuckles.

"The only thing I feel when you kiss me is butterflies." He grins. "I promise I won't feel any pain."

I grip his cheeks between my hands and lower my head. Our lips brush against each other. I giggled as he tugged my arm. I straddle his waist. We gaze into each other's eyes before his carefree expression hardens.

"I promise you, I'm never going to let anything hurt you again."

I gaze at him, tucking strands of his locks behind his ears.

"I know," I whisper.

An affectionate smile rises on his face. I can't help but admire his dimples.

"What's with the smile?" I ask.

His smile widens.

"I'm just thinking how grateful I am for that bookstore."

There's a stampede in my stomach. I couldn't wipe the broad smile off my face.

He dipped his head, grazing his teeth along my collarbone. I shiver as he embraces me in his arms. He places his lips against mine with purpose. The sounds of our quick breaths and moans infiltrate the delightful silence. I pull away to catch my breath. Heavy puffs escape his kiss-bruised lips. We took a moment to indulge each other's bodies, neither of us in a rush. We exchange gentle touches and reassurances as our disrobed bodies reciprocate natural warmth.

He hauls me into his arms as he drags me toward the restroom counter. He hovers over me and connects our lips once more, my lust-fogged mind seems unable to fathom a coherent thought. He spins me around as I glance into the large mirror, our eyes locking through the reflection. He moves my hair away from my neck and trails his lips along the length of my neck. The only noise was the sound of his name falling from my lips.

I groan. He pushes my head down until I hover over the counter. He grips my hips from behind.

"Look at me." He orders.

I glance at him in the reflection as his lustful eyes lock with mine. He doesn't speak as he brushes his hand down my spine and I bend further with a moan. His hand slithers along my side and down my stomach. It clenches at the sensation. His fingers dawdle between my legs. The moment his finger brushes against my lips, I close my eyes with a gasp.

"Don't stop looking at me." He orders out of breath.

I struggle to keep my eyes open as his skillful fingers work magic between my legs. The pleasure becomes too much and my legs give out, but he wraps his arm around my waist to keep me upright. He pulls my waist out and spreads my legs further as I feel his length brush against my outer walls.

"Please." I beg through hooded eyes.

"Please, what?" He asks with a cocky grin.

"I need you inside me." I plead.

His eyes soften.

"Anything for you, baby."

Our moans mix as he slowly enters me from behind. He grabs my waist as he controls my movements. With every thrust, we were both teetering on the edge of release.

"You take me so well." He growls as his eyes flutter. "Keep looking at me, I want you to see how good you make me feel."

Chapter Twenty-One

His arms pulled me closer to his heated body, holding me as if I were porcelain. I'd never felt so loved and appreciated.

"You're fucking amazing, Hazel Ellis." He groans.

After words of adoration and rhythmic thrusts, we came undone. Exhaustion crashes over us as we take a moment to catch our breath.

I lean against the counter as he moves away. The sound of running water infiltrates our silence. I glance over my shoulder as he approaches me, soothing my hair out of my face.

"Let's get you cleaned up." His words are gentle, a contrast to the commanding, lustful words he'd used prior.

I smile in appreciation as we step in. We stand for a few seconds, letting the water cascade down our faces. He brushes his fingers along my body, but nothing about the moment is sexual. Our eyes lock as we relish the intimacy. I close my eyes as I let his shampooed hands rake through my curls. As the water washes the suds away, his hands ghost over my waist as he pulls me closer.

"I love you." He whispers as he soothes the aches away.

"I love you too." I say as I reach up to attach our lips.

Things between us could not get any more perfect.

The exhaustion washes over me as we enter his bedroom. I sigh in delight as the covers caress my skin and his warmth seeps through me. My heart feels as if it's going to burst with love as we fall asleep in each other's ardent holds.

Chapter Twenty-Two

I watch in awe as Campbell glides along the ice. His unspeakable amount of confidence never ceases to amaze me. He absorbs the roaring crowd as he scores moving his team into the lead. His teammates gathered around him, patting him on his helmet before they skated back into position. I try not to get too excited as it's only the first period, but this is the best I have ever witnessed him play.

I know his desire to beat Jonah has been his best source of success.

I step away from the tempered glass as Jonah skates towards me. He waves before joining the rest of his team. None of it goes unnoticed by Campbell.

"Hazel." A voice calls jogging down the stairs to join me. "I thought I spotted you."

"Ben!" I exclaim. "I thought I'd see you here."

He shrugs.

"I was hoping to see you, too." He muses.

Chapter Twenty-Two

The first-period ends. I'd been so preoccupied with my conversation with Ben that I hadn't noticed the players had already exited the ice. I frown at having missed Campbell.

"Are you still working on that novel?"

"It's near completion." I grin.

"I hope I get a sneak preview?"

"Of course!" I exclaim. "If you have nowhere to be after, we could grab a coffee and you could read the new chapters."

"Sounds like a plan." He grins.

"What are we planning?" I freeze, believing I'd imagined Campbell's voice, but his hands on my waist prove I wasn't.

He's adorned in his gear except for his helmet, as if he'd rushed to join us.

He most likely bolted the second he spotted me with Ben.

"Hazel is going to let me read the newest chapters of her book." Ben chimes.

My heart sinks into my stomach. I expect Campbell to burst into a fit of rage, but he smiles a genuine smile.

"Sounds great." He beams before leaning down to place a kiss on my cheek. "I better get back, but I'll be looking for you from the ice." He promises.

I stare in astonishment as he vanishes.

What just happened?

I turn back to Ben. Throughout our conversation, my mind kept darting back to Campbell's reaction. The players return to the ice. Ben excuses himself before returning to his seat. I bite my bottom lip as Campbell and Jonah crouch across from each other, engaged in a heated discussion.

Talk about déjà vu.

The events happen in a blur, like scene selections of a show. Jonah gains possession of the puck, but before reacting,

Campbell rams him into the glass. The sound reverberates through the stadium as a large crack forms along the tempered glass. Jonah falls to the ground with a harsh slam after Campbell *accidentally* kicks him. I wince at the impact. With a sense of urgency, their teammates rush toward them before a full-on brawl ensues.

The hollering of the crowd gives me a migraine. The cheering doesn't halt until my eyes follow Campbell entering the penalty box. He's seated before walking up to the ice and yelling at Jonah, who seems far too smug for someone that just got beaten down.

The third period is filled with just as much turmoil. They're heading into overtime.

My nails were almost non-existent. It's too much pressure and I'm not the one on the team. Even from the other side of the ice, I could see the determination on Campbell's face. The desire to watch Jonah and his insufferable team lose.

Time had slowed down once he'd stolen the puck from one of Jonah's teammates. My heart hammers against my rib cage as Jonah is hot on his tail. I'd hardly registered Campbell taking the shot until everyone around me launched out of their seat in elation. I join in their celebration as Campbell's teammates bombard him with congratulations and high-fives. My smile cracks as he departs from them and skates toward me. He places his hand on the tempered glass. I giggled and placed my hand against the glass.

"That was all for you, baby." He calls over the roaring spectators.

My heart stumbles at his arrogant grin.

I was overflowing with anticipation as I waited for him outside the stadium. I wrap my arms around myself as I

Chapter Twenty-Two

bounce on the edge of my heels.

"What a game, right?"

I glance over my shoulder as Ben approaches with a wide grin.

"Too bad my team kicked yours' butt." I tease.

He chuckles.

"I wouldn't get too cocky."

He tucks his hands into his front pockets.

"Ready for that coffee?"

"Sure," I grin. "I'll just say goodbye to Campbell, then we can get going."

As if summoned, he rushes towards me. He wraps his arms around me, raising me off the ground. I giggle and wrap my arms around his neck.

"Congratulations!" I beam.

"Thank you, Ellie." He glances from the corner of his eye. "Hey, Ben."

"Hey," He clears his throat. "Good game."

"Thanks."

I bite my lip.

"I'm going to grab a coffee with Ben and talk about books."

He nods his head. I can sense his displeasure, but he opts to remain unbothered.

"Have fun." He grips my head and secures our lips together.

I kiss him once more before retrieving my laptop bag from his truck and taking off with Ben.

I sigh in delight once we enter the barren cafe. I grab a seat further back, knowing how crowded it will get. I open my laptop and the document before handing it over to Ben.

"I'll get us some drinks." I excuse myself as he delves into my work.

Vicariously

Before I could reach the counter, a familiar voice called my name. I freeze in my tracks as a distressed Nevaeh approaches me. Her eyes are watery as she wraps her arms around herself.

"Can we talk?" She croaks.

I debate on whether I should leave or help her out. My mind told me to ignore her, reminding me how she'd abandoned me, except my heart wouldn't let me. She'd once been my best friend. That's hard to let go. I nod my head as we take a seat at a table near the entrance.

My eyes dart around the cafe as she twirls her thumbs. My legs shake as I wait for her to speak up. She's the one who wanted to talk, after all.

"I'm sorry," she gasps as her eyes prickle with tears. "I don't know what came over me."

I drop my head. A lock of hair falls over my face. I don't bother tucking it away.

"I haven't been a friend to you." She states. "You have been nothing less than the perfect friend. I ruined it."

She wipes away fallen tears.

"I've missed you so much." She gasps through her weeping. "I only hope that there is a time when you can forgive me because I miss my best friend."

My chest tightens at her pain-stricken demeanor. My ambivalent thoughts cloud my judgment. I'm uncertain what to do, but I know that despite all her wrongdoings, Nevaeh is my oldest friend.

Our history is far too long to give up.

"I may not forgive you right now," I gulp. "But I would like to mend things between us."

She smiles at my words and stands up. She hauls me up and wraps her arms around me in a tight embrace.

Chapter Twenty-Two

"I missed you." She exclaims in my ear.

We pull away as she wipes the remnants of her tears.

"How about I call you tomorrow so we can hang out?" She questions.

"Sounds great." I replied.

She squeezes my hands before strolling out of the cafe. I take a deep breath as I digest what just transpired. It's only then I remember Ben. I order our coffee before rushing to our table.

"I'm so sorry." I apologize.

"It's okay." He chuckles. "I noticed you were distracted."

"That was an old friend." I explain.

"I loved what you've written so far." He grinned.

I beamed with pride. Nothing is better than a fellow author appreciating your work.

"Thank you." I grin.

He takes a sip of his coffee before leaning back in his seat.

"So," He pipes up. "What's the plan for the rest of the night?"

I raise my brows with a shrug.

"I do not know. What about you?"

"Well, what's your boyfriend up to?"

I glance at my phone to look.

"He's at his frat house." I sigh. "It's party central over there."

"Do you think they'd care if I crashed?"

I bite my lip in thought. Campbell knows I've developed a friendship with Ben. He had no issue with me getting coffee with him, so why would he care if I brought him to the party?

"I don't think there would be an issue at all."

* * *

Vicariously

The celebrations were in full swing. It's as if the usual guest list had doubled in size. Everyone was in the greatest of moods. It was a much-needed victory. I notice a group of Campbell's frat brothers gathered around in the kitchen, but it doesn't seem he's with them. I motion for Ben to follow me as we shove through the crowd.

We walked out to the backyard. I wrap my coat tighter around myself. I hadn't realized there would be such a drastic drop in the weather. The familiar laughter flutters in my ears as I notice Campbell standing around a fire pit with an assembly of unfamiliar people.

As if he could sense my staring, he turned in my direction. I beam with pride as his eyes light up. He approaches us.

"I did not expect to see you at all." He wraps his arm around my shoulder.

"Ben wanted to come." I shrug.

His smile drops as he glances at Ben.

"Well, welcome." The corner of his lip rises in an artificial grin.

I place my hand on his chest.

"Go back to hanging out with your friends." I insist. "I'll be fine here with Ben."

He hesitates as he scans my face for any sign of hesitancy, but seems satisfied. He leans down and places a chaste kiss on my forehead before returning to the group.

"Want to grab a drink?" I question.

"Sure," Ben replies. "I just need to make a phone call first."

I nod.

"See you inside." I smile before returning inside.

It's only at this moment that I've realized I don't know anyone or the people I know I am not fond of. I scour the

Chapter Twenty-Two

kitchen for a bottle of water, but they're hidden under the copious amounts of alcohol on the counter.

Multiple chimes of phones reverberate over the music, including mine. I tug it out of my back pocket. It's from a number I don't have saved in my contacts. The moment I open it, my blood runs cold.

Hazel Ellis - a wannabe author in the making.

The words ignite a sense of dread. I open one of the multiple attachments and drop my phone. A copy of my various digital journal entries and cringe fan fiction I'd written over the years is available for everyone to read. Journal catalogs dating back to the worst times of high school, including a short story I'd written about a boy I'd had a crush on in my sophomore year. Even the covert details about my adoption. I opened the rest of the attachments to find every story I hold dear to my heart but had wanted private. I freeze as laughter echoes throughout the house as people read all my embarrassing stories. My thoughts and desires.

My eyes brimmed with tears as I could feel multiple gazes scorching my body. I close my eyes as I attempt to hold back a sob.

"How tragic." The wicked voice echoes. "It must suck to have everyone think your writing is laughable."

I gaze toward Celeste as she hovers in the doorway with her entourage and Jonah. My eyes widen as Nevaeh materializes and stands at her side. Amusement glitters in their eyes.

"How could you?" My voice is raspy from the tears. "I thought you wanted to be friends again."

Nevaeh scoffs.

"I lied, big deal."

My hands shake at my sides as their captious eyes dissect

me.

"How did you get this?" I glare at Celeste. "This was personal."

Jonah steps forward and self-approvingly folds his arms across his chest.

"My brother helped." He chuckles. "You've met Ben, right?"

He enters at the mention of his name. It's only now that I notice the resemblance. How did I miss it?

"You played me." I growl as I deliver a deadly glare.

Too bad he didn't drop dead.

"I did." He shrugs.

I wipe away the hot tears.

"You didn't think he'd be interested in your stuff, did you?" Celeste ridicules. "Just because Campbell saw you as his charity case doesn't mean everyone else will."

I wince as her words stab my heart.

"I find it pathetic how you thought Campbell could care about you." She sneers. "If your writing proves something it's that you're a nobody. Campbell is way out of your league and always will be."

More eyes seem to befall my deadened appearance. I must seem a mess. I bite my lip so hard that I taste blood. My stomach churns at the metallic tang. My eyes glance from person to person before my legs bolt for the nearest exit. The laughter follows me as if I'm moving in slow motion. The door seems further than usual as I shove people aside in desperate need of escaping.

I couldn't be there for another second.

I only stop running once I'm alone out front and I lean against the streetlight as my gut-wrenching sobs awaken the silence. My head throbs from the uncontrollable crying. The

Chapter Twenty-Two

dehydration is kicking in.

"Ellie!" I can hear Campbell's voice call out.

I sob even more.

"Ellie." He coaxes curling his arm over my shoulder. "Hazel, look at me."

I yank my body away from him and create an appropriate distance.

"Please, just leave me alone." I cry. "I don't want to deal with this."

I clutch my stomach as it burns from the unabating blubbering.

"I'm going to kill them for what they did to you." He seethes. "That Ben guy better run back to campus."

I chuckle and clutch my hair in my hands.

"It won't change a thing!" I wail. "You can beat up as many people as you want, but it will never change the fact that I'm a nobody!"

He jerks back as if I'd just struck him.

"What are you talking about?"

"I'm talking about us!" I motion between us. "We don't work. We never did. I was a fool for thinking otherwise."

His jaw clenches.

"Did someone say something?"

"Does it matter?" I sigh. "It's the truth."

"How can you say that?" His angered voice leaves a bitter taste in my mouth.

"I'd always thought about it." I shrug. "The thought was always taunting me in the back of my mind. People would always look at us when we're out in public, wondering how someone like me had someone like you on their arm." I close in on myself. "I'd been fooling myself for too long."

He scoffs in disbelief.

"I don't give a damn what anyone has to say about us!" He bellows. "I am in love with you and don't need anyone's permission or acceptance to be with you."

His confession was near perfect, but it did nothing to ease my burdening thoughts. He takes a step forward. I step back. He shakes his head as tears brim in his eyes. His bottom lip quivered.

"I'm not afraid to fight for you, Hazel Ellis." His voice quavers. "I already know we'll spend the rest of our lives together."

I wanted to believe him and his words, but my unyielding insecurities rose to the surface. A guy like Campbell Atwood deserves someone better than me. He deserves someone that doesn't overthink everything, someone that doesn't question his love for them.

After all, how could he love me if I don't love myself?

"I'm sorry," I whimper. "I think it's best to end this right now before it goes any further."

I can tell my words shook him to the core.

He remains frozen.

I take that as an opportunity to flee. Despite the excruciating ache in my heart, I know it's the right thing to do.

Chapter Twenty-Three

For so long, I'd witnessed countless authors achieve the greatness I'd always strived for. The success I'd never captured. I assured myself that one day my talents will get recognition, and I would accomplish my lifelong dreams. However, I'd never considered that these talents may have never existed and that I'd been chasing the unattainable dream.

I'd been a fool, just like *Jay Gatsby*. He pursued a girl that would never love him and I pursued a dream that only existed in my sleep. One is as pathetic as the other.

I haven't left my dorm in a week. I'd been avoiding everything and everyone. *Including Campbell.* After a disastrous breakup, I've been uninterested in anything other than sulking under my covers.

Maisie had tried her best to cheer me up, but she'd started to distance herself from me. I wasn't sure if it was because she'd grown tired from my self-pitying or if it was her desperate attempt at giving me space. I couldn't bring myself to care.

Vicariously

To have the freedom to wallow in self-pity without fear of judgment is what I want.

Many had made heartbreak seem harmless, but it was the most agonizing pain I'd ever experienced, and I only have myself to blame. I'd allowed myself to be sucked into a fantasy. I'd read too many romance novels - it's given me a false sense of reality. It led me to believe that love is for everyone.

What a foolish girl I was.

I should have known that love would never come. Not for me. I'm destined to live alone. To only experience love through the words of the books. To live vicariously through the characters.

Fictional love is the truest form of love we will ever have.

How ironic.

I toss my sheets over myself as the darkness mirrors my internal sadness. Despite having a broken heart, every inch of my body aches. I yearn to travel back in time.

When Campbell Atwood was a stranger.

I regret entering that bookstore, regret conversing with him. I regret deluding myself into believing that a romance so pure would fall into my lap. I'd been a fool and I'm paying the price.

I think back to the party saga. It's been tormenting me on a constant loop. I cringe as I remember their taunting laughter. Everyone had read my most private thoughts, and it seems they found it more comedic than a tear-jerker. I could never get over the embarrassment. My lifelong dream slipped away in a matter of seconds.

How do I move on from that?

My mind bounces around between the humiliation and thoughts of Campbell.

I miss him.

Chapter Twenty-Three

He'd attempted to contact me multiple times since our breakup. He'd arrived at the dorm and insisted on speaking to me. I'd lean against the door, holding back my sobs as he pounded against it. He wouldn't stop until someone asked him to leave.

Maisie enters the room and I snuggle further into my sheets. I don't want to hear another lecture. Her footsteps become more distinct and I close my eyes, bracing myself for the covers to be yanked away.

"I know you're not sleeping." She chimes as she tosses my sheets to the ground. "It's time to get up. I want to hang out."

"No," I grumble and turn to face the battered wallpaper. "I'm going to bed."

"You just woke up."

My chest tightens because of the profound silence. In the quietude is when my darkest thoughts arise, but I allow them to torment me. It's the only time I feel something.

"I read your work," she pipes up. "Despite the embarrassing stories, I couldn't help but admire your talent."

I scoff.

"What talent?"

I can hear shuffling, but I don't look.

"Your ability to create something incredible just by using a bunch of words." My stomach clenches. "I think you're incredibly talented." She attempts to comfort me.

"That makes one person." I mumble.

"At least it's someone." She assures. "I know Campbell thinks the same."

I consider her words for a moment.

"Too bad my brain only focuses on the negative. Positivity is a momentary distraction."

Vicariously

The edge of my bed dips under her weight. My posture stiffens.

"How about we go to the bookstore?" She suggests. "It always makes you feel better."

"Not this time."

I'm taken by surprise as she grabs my arm, yanking me out of my bed with brute force. I glare at her, but she's unfazed. She places a few things in my arms.

"Go get ready. We're leaving in ten minutes."

I'd never seen Maisie so demanding before. It's terrifying. Instead of arguing, I follow orders and make myself as presentable as possible, yet it doesn't help with my internal disarray.

I return to my dorm only to find it vacant.

"Maisie?" I call, as if she's going to surprise me from under the bed.

No response.

A yellow *post-it* on my bed catches my attention. Underneath it is a copy of *The History of Love*.

Curiously, I glance at the note as I recognize Campbell's messy handwriting.

My love for you is as eternal as the words in these books.

My stomach flutters. With shaking hands, I reach for the book, opening it up at the marked page. *He'd annotated the page.* I glance at the highlighted paragraph.

"Once upon a time there was a boy who loved a girl, and her laughter was a question he wanted to spend his whole life answering."

My eyes brim with tears. There is a scrawl in the bottom right-hand corner.

I'm not good at words. I'm unsure how to express my love for

Chapter Twenty-Three

you, so I thought I could find quotes that remind me of how much I'm in love with you.

Look outside your door.

I drop the book and yank the door off its hinges. There's no one in the hallway. I step forward and feel something under my shoe.

Another book.

I reach for the copy of *Great Expectations*.

I could watch you read for hours. The *post-it* reads. I grinned as I flipped through the book until I reached the allocated page.

"I loved her against reason, against promise, against peace, against hope, against happiness, against all discouragement that could be."

My heart swells at the thought that someone had taken the time to find quotes that reminded them of me. He'd flipped through pages in search of the perfect quotes and annotated each book.

Meet you downstairs. He'd scribbled in the top corner.

With a newfound cheerfulness, I rush downstairs, hoping to be greeted by his adoring face. No such luck. My eyes flicker around the dorm entrance as I spot two more books on a table. My legs move before my brain can order them. The first book is *Hamlet* and alongside it is one of my all-time favorites - *The Great Gatsby*. I reach for the copy of Hamlet and skim through the pages.

"Doubt thou the stars are fire;
Doubt that the sun doth move;
Doubt truth to be a liar;
But never doubt I love."

I giggle as I read his comment.

Vicariously

I had to Google what it meant because it sounded pretty romantic, but the moment I knew the meaning - it was as if Shakespeare wrote it for us. As if someone destined us to find it. Find each other.

I had to not squeal in delight as I flipped through the pages of *The Great Gatsby*.

"There I was, way off my ambitions, getting deeper in love every minute."

A tiny note falls out of the book and flutters on the ground. I bend to pick it up.

It's as if all these authors knew we'd meet and fall in love. It's as if they'd written it about us.

Meet me at the cafe.

I clutch the books against my chest as I charge toward the cafe, eager to kiss him. It's crowded and I glance at every table in search of Campbell.

"Hazel Ellis." A girl I recognize from my *English Lit* class beckons me over from behind the counter.

I furrow my brows as I approach. She beams at me as she reaches under the counter before sliding a book over to me.

"Campbell asked that I give this to you."

My stomach is tied into knots as I reach for the book. She seems as excited as me.

My Sister's keeper.

I shuffle through the pages until I find the highlighted section.

"You don't love someone because they're perfect, you love them in spite of the fact that they're not."

He draws an arrow leading to the top left corner.

You're flawed, Hazel Ellis. I am too. Yet we're perfectly flawed together.

Another arrow leads to the bottom right corner.

Chapter Twenty-Three

Up for a game of hockey?

I grin at the barista before rushing towards the rink. He promised he would teach me to play hockey. I guess today is the day.

The stadium is deserted and I rush toward the locker room expecting him to be waiting for me - but the hallways are uninhabited. I bite my lip.

My ears strain at the sound of approaching footsteps. My heart leaps as a shadow rounds the corner.

It's one of Campbell's teammates.

"Hey," the stranger replies before reaching behind his back. "I believe this is for you."

I thank him, waiting for him to enter the locker room before opening the book.

"There is never a time or place for love. It happens accidentally, in a heartbeat, a single flashing, throbbing moment."

I'm in awe as I read the words.

Meet me where it all began.

He'd written on the page. I take deep breaths to compose myself.

The bookstore.

I sprint as fast as possible with the weighted books in my arms. I must have garnered a few strange looks, but for the first time in my life, I didn't care what others thought of me. My only thought is Campbell. Being able to see him. Hold him. Cherish him and promise to never let him go again. I'd been so foolish to let him slip through my fingers.

The bookstore is as forsaken as the day we'd met. I could easily spot Campbell if he were inside. I groan as he's nowhere to be seen.

"Excuse me," the elderly lady behind the counter greets. "I

believe your boyfriend left you something on that table over there."

She points toward the oak furniture. I rushed toward it and chuckled as he placed a copy of *Wuthering Heights* underneath a pink *post-it*.

This was the moment my entire life fell into place. The second I looked into your eyes, I knew we were destined to be together.

"That's my mom's favorite book." His alluring voice speaks and I can't help but chuckle at the familiar words.

I whip around to find him standing with his hands tucked in his front pockets. His tense face softens as our eyes lock.

"Hello, Hazel Ellis." He greets me with a cheesy grin.

"I can't believe you did all of this."

"It was the best way I could tell you how much I love you. How much I need you in my life."

He steps forward as if gauging my reaction to being near him. When I do not stop him, he leaps forward and smothers me with his firm embrace. I wrap my arms around his neck. He exhales as he leans his chin against my shoulder.

"I missed you so much, Ellie." He pulls his head back. "It's outrageous to think that I'd spent my entire life not knowing you, and now I cannot live a second without you."

A hot tear escapes my clutches, and he wipes it away.

"Kiss me." I plead, needing to feel his lips against mine.

A week had never felt so endless.

He doesn't hesitate. I shudder at the familiarity, savoring everything about him. I've fallen in love with every inch of him, and each kiss takes my breath away.

He's my oxygen.

His dazzling eyes are a showstopper. I can't tear my gaze away. His forehead leans against mine as we catch our breath.

Chapter Twenty-Three

"I have one more thing to show you." He whispers as his long lashes brush his cheek.

"What is it?"

His face cracks.

"Patience, Hazel Ellis." His thumb brushes against my lips.

He runs his hands down my waist until our fingers interlock. I giggle as he drags me out of the bookstore and to his truck. He opens the door for me, but he grabs my waist before I step in. His lips cover mine.

"Now we're ready to go."

It feels as if a lightning bolt has jump-started my heart as he drives along a familiar path. My lips parted in an uncontrollable smile.

"Our spot." I cheer as he halts in the parking lot.

"Our spot."

The evening sun casts long shadows underneath us as the sloping rays give a mellow orange tinge to the sky. I gaze in awe as Campbell wraps his arms around my waist. I place my head against his chest as we focus on the beauty before us. We don't move or speak until the blanket of stars appears, stretching to infinity. The bright moon rises through the darkness, commanding attention.

"There's nothing I love more than gazing up at the stars with my favorite girl in my arms." He purrs.

I shiver.

He pecks the back of my head as he sways us from side to side. His natural warmth shields me from the vengeful cold. I felt a stirring in my chest as he placed his head beside mine as we admired the galactic beauty.

"You're the most precious thing in my life and I'd give up everything to have more moments like this with you." He inhales the frosty air. "I never thought about my future, but now it's all I can think about - and every single version has you in it."

My eyes flared with excitement as I turned my head to look at him. The warmth of his gaze seems to penetrate my skin.

"I can't help but picture us graduating, moving in together." He litters my neck with kisses as I snicker. I attempt to escape, but his grip is too firm. "Kids, a few dogs."

I hide my blush as I picture what our future could be like.

I'd never been someone that thought much of the future. I never pictured myself falling in love or having a family, but that might have been because I'd never pictured someone could love me enough to want to.

I place my hands over his, caressing it with my thumb.

"I can't picture my life without you in it, either."

"You're the one I've been waiting my entire life for, Hazel Ellis." His lips linger against the back of my head. "I just never knew it."

I turn in his hold and wrap my arms around his neck. I press our lips together to convey as much love as possible. He bites my bottom lip, making my entire body tremble. I knotted my fists in his shirt, pulling him harder against me. He groans as his arms circle around my thighs, hauling me up as my legs wrap around his waist. We never break the kiss. Not even as he lures us to the back of his truck. My back meets the familiar mattress and I shimmy further up the makeshift bed.

His lips connect with my neck as I trail my hands up his back, down to the hem of his shirt. I pull the material with me, showing him to remove it. He obliges. I trail my nails down his chest and stomach. He takes a sharp intake of breath.

Our eyes connect as we savor this moment of pure, crushing

Chapter Twenty-Three

happiness. I'm overthrown with a wave of emotions as his fingers glide along my exposed skin. He dips his head lower as he tries to level our eyes.

"Every moment I look at you, I'm in awe of your beauty." He brushes his hands through my hair, brushing his nose against mine. "I cannot believe I get to call you mine."

His words made my heart flutter. His fingertips graze my skin as he slides my shirt up my torso before tossing it to the side. I place my hands in his hair, feeling his silky locks between my fingers. He trails a line of kisses down my abdomen as I arch my back to encourage his kisses further.

Our bare bodies brush against each other as we share our warmth. Every touch feels like static electricity. I pull him closer as I wrap my legs around his waist, pleading for him to connect us once more. I grip the sheets as his fingers brush between my legs. He gazes down at me before uniting us as one. Our simultaneous groans fill the truck as he interlocks our fingers together.

He takes his time, as neither of us is in a rush. We want to savor every moment. Every sense of pleasure. I place my hand on his cheek. My thumb grazes the soft contour of his mouth. He smiles before placing a peck against the palm of my hand.

"I want forever with you." He breathes in between thrusts. "Infinite happiness."

I'm overcome by a ripple of euphoria as a lone tear glides down my cheek. My toes curl as he declares his love for me at every opportunity. I become dizzy with pleasure and love as we enjoy every aspect of each other.

Campbell Atwood is mine forever. My infinite. My lighthouse.

I have loved no one until him and I will love no one after. How could I ever fall in love with someone else if I have the man of my dreams already?

He's perfectly imperfect. The sun to my moon. The light to my darkness.

I fear how dearly I crave him. How he consumes my every thought. He's my first and last.

I could live a dozen more lifetimes and I would find no one like him. We would find each other in every universe. I can no longer live a life without him. Our souls are forever connected.

Epilogue

I'd spent my entire life feeling like an outcast, living in the shadows of others. I'd used writing to escape - to live the life I could never experience in reality.

I'd always doubted my ability to let the world see the true me, and to experience new things.

I'd spent my entire life lost and alone, feeling as if something were missing. I never understood why a part of myself always felt insubstantial - it was because I'd been waiting for *him*. I'd been waiting for the perfect person to complete the puzzle. My life made sense the moment he forced himself into it.

I find it hard to believe that the arrogant, annoying, yet charming, guy I met in the bookstore had become the most important person in my life. I never thought that something as simple as a conversation about a book could have drastically altered my life.

I'd lost inspiration for writing. For living. He'd reignited my desire and passion to showcase my inner thoughts and feelings through my words.

My life has been nothing but empty promises and brutal rejections. I'd never felt as if I were worthy. As if I were important, but he'd shown me that life is full of adventure - if you're with the right person.

Campbell Atwood is the epitome of the perfect man. He's everything you could ever want. He always knew the right thing to say or do - he never failed to make me feel like the most precious thing to grace the Earth. He'd given me love beyond comprehension. I never imagined finding someone that could express their love for me in such an eccentric manner. To find someone that would take their time to love me through actions and not only words.

Which is why it shouldn't come as a shock that he was never real.

Campbell Atwood was nothing more than a figment of my imagination. My inner desire. The protagonist of my fantasies.

Every word, every touch, every declaration of love was nothing but a fallacy.

He'd only existed in my mind. In the pages of my book. Every letter, every word, every sentence - immortalized with every line.

I'd conjured up the guy of my dreams. One that could love me more than I could ever love myself. Someone to ignite confidence in me. Someone to help me ease the burden of college. He was a random hockey player I noticed on the ice during a campus visit with Nevaeh. He never noticed me, but I noticed him.

How could I not?

Our fictitious story may have come to an unexpected end, but Campbell Atwood will forever live in my heart. I will

Epilogue

always be thankful to him. For giving me the strength to keep writing. For being my muse. I will always be thankful to him for allowing me to live vicariously through him.

***

As I finish my story, I gaze around the deserted bookstore that ignited my inspiration.

I shut my laptop and gather my things, eagerly expecting to meet my new roommate.

I wave at the kind lady behind the counter and shove through the door, only to collide with a hardened figure.

"Ouch!" I exclaim and rub my shoulder.

"I am so sorry!" He exclaims.

He leans down to retrieve my tattered copy of Wuthering Heights.

I could notice that messy mop of hair from a mile away. His ocean eyes lock with mine as he extends the book out to me.

"Seems we're in the same *English Lit* class." He grins.

I clutch the copy against my chest.

It's him.

He clears his throat.

"I'm Campbell Atwood."

He extends his hand and I reach for it.

"Hazel Ellis." I muster the courage to speak.

He smiles that dashing smile that took my breath away all those months ago.

I'd never believed in fate, but how could I deny it when he's standing right in front of me?

He's gazing at me in the way I'd always imagined. My chest

tightened as his crystal eyes made my heart soar.

He's even more beautiful than I remember. After months of pining over a mysterious hockey boy, I bump into him just like I'd written.

"Pleasure meeting you, Hazel Ellis." He says, as his eyes sparkle like the brightest stars in the sky. "It seems we'll be seeing a lot more of each other."

Printed in Great Britain
by Amazon